THE CHAINS OF WAR

BOOKS BY DEAN F. WILSON

᪸

THE CHILDREN OF TELM

Book One: The Call of Agon
Book Two: The Road to Rebirth
Book Three: The Chains of War

THE
CHAINS OF WAR

BOOK THREE OF THE CHILDREN OF TELM

DEAN F. WILSON

Cover illustration by Soheil Toosi

First Edition 2014

ISBN 978-1-909356-06-1

Published by Dioscuri Press
Dublin, Ireland

www.dioscuripress.com
enquiries@dioscuripress.com

Dedicated to

FAMILY AND FRIENDS

CONTENTS

❧

SOUTH-EAST IRALDAS

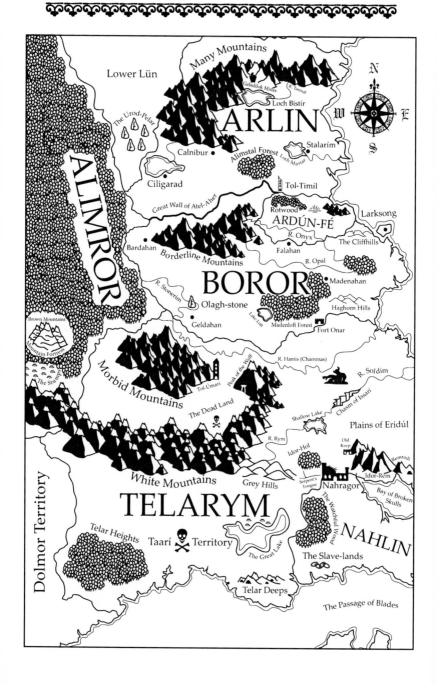

I

THE RATTLE OF THE CHAINS

The sound of celebration poured down from the Mountain Fortress like a landslide. Few slept that night, or for those that followed, and even the people that dozed uneasily heard the horns and drums in their dreams, and their slumbering lips joined in the joyful and boisterous songs that were so different to a bedtime lullaby.

Yet few were angry at the noise, for it was a welcome one in place of the dreary silence that had come before, when all was full of apprehension, when the quiet itself seemed to dread what might come next. And so the people rejoiced and celebrated as loudly as they could, and they were so deafening in their merriment that none of them noticed that there was another sound—a dark rumbling in a faraway place, a dull quake that suggested it might one day not be so far away.

Ifferon sat by the eastern windows of the Fortress, staring out at the gigantic figure of Corrias as he slowly and carefully moved about the mountain. He shimmered as he moved, and at times it seemed to Ifferon that he almost faded into the surroundings. He wondered if this was a repercussion of his decision to incarnate in Iraldas, if it meant that he was not truly there. That might be so, but still he trod carefully, unwilling to step upon anyone that might have been one of his followers.

"He is a sight to behold," Délin said, stepping up beside Ifferon with Théos in his arms. He looked younger and less dishevelled than before, for he had shaved his beard and trimmed his hair, and now his armour sparkled after a vigorous polishing.

"Yes," Ifferon said, the best he could manage. No words were good enough to describe the immensity and majesty of Corrias. Yet part of Ifferon felt concerned, for great though the father god was, there was a monstrosity out there that seemed greater still.

The knight pointed out to where Corrias drifted, and Théos pointed at the god in turn.

"That was you," Délin said.

Théos looked at him blankly. Then he shook his head. "Éala," he said.

"Does he remember anything?" Ifferon asked.

"I am not sure," Délin replied. "He remembers me, it seems, but I am not sure it is even possible to remember sharing a body with a god. Perhaps that is a good thing."

Ifferon nodded. "Yes, perhaps." At times he wished that he did not remember that he shared the blood of a god, even if it had diluted over many generations, and felt weak within his veins.

"We did good," Délin stated firmly. "Much evil has been undone."

"I cannot help but feel that the worst is yet to come."

Délin looked at him with grim determination.

"Whatever comes, we will face it."

"Do you think Corrias can defeat Agon?" Ifferon asked.

Délin sighed. "No," he said, and the word almost fell from his mouth like a leaden weight. Its echo was like the strike of metal upon the ground. "Corrias is many things that I admire and stand for, but if the stories of old are true, and I have no reason to doubt them, then he is not truly a warrior. It was Telm, and Telm alone, who defeated Agon, and so perhaps we still depend upon him."

Ifferon feigned a chuckle. "What a job he has, even in the grave."

Geldirana trained with Affon, teaching her how to ward blows, to parry, and to strike with ferocity. They both employed real blades, and both of them came away with real cuts and slashes as a result. Whenever the girl would falter, she would receive another grazing wound, and Geldirana told her, "You will not err that way again. Let the pain be your promise and the blood be your oath."

Délin and Ifferon watched this for a time until Théos ran off and returned with a wooden toy sword in his hand. He looked up with eager eyes, glanced at the Garigút woman and girl fighting, and looked back to the knight with that same pleading gaze. There was a hint of happiness in his eyes, but also a hint of sadness, as if he expected that Délin would refuse.

But the knight felt he could not disappoint the boy now, and so he called to one of the guards, who brought him a wooden toy sword of his own. He took it and was surprised at how light it was, and how small it was, and how harmless it was. He was too used to his broadsword and two-handed sword, and it had been over forty years since he had last held a training sword. Even that was heavier than the toy sword he held now.

Délin pointed the sword towards the boy, who smiled broadly, as if the gesture was an expression of praise. The knight gently tapped the child's sword, and Théos struck back softly, and he laughed and giggled. His attacks were weak, his posture was wrong, and his force was lacking, and yet he was doing everything right for what they were really doing: playing. Each strike was followed by a chorus of laughs, and Délin wished that every sword fight was filled with so much glee.

So they "battled" for a time, with Théos hopping to and fro, trying out new moves, and trying desperately to copy the moves that Affon was making across the way. He made what he must have thought were frightening noises, and Délin feigned fear and offered his surrender.

"Quite the little knight," Ifferon said as Délin and the boy retired from exhaustion. Though Théos could not quite understand Ifferon's words, he still smiled, as if he understood the intent behind them. He sat down beside Délin, clapping the toy swords together as if the battle still raged on.

"He has much potential," Délin said, and he nodded to Théos as he might to one of his brothers or sisters in the Knights of Issarí. Théos nodded back. "Your daughter has much potential also," the knight added.

Ifferon looked back to Affon, who was clearly wearied, but refused to give up as she battled Geldirana in what to some might have looked like a real battle. Ifferon knew well that for the Garigút such training often was.

"I would rather she played than fought," Ifferon said. "She is not much older than Théos."

"Perhaps that is something to discuss with Geldirana," Délin suggested.

"I am not sure I have the right."

"You earned the right when you became a father."

"And I gave it up when I abandoned both of them."

"You cannot give it up if you did not abandon them in your heart," the knight said.

Ifferon shrugged, as if he was not altogether sure what his heart felt. Perhaps it was back at Larksong, still hiding within those monastery walls.

Théos stood up, leaving the swords behind, and he stretched up to the window, barely tall enough to peer over, and he placed his chin upon the stony sill. From there the wind trickled in and ruffled his grassy hair.

"He never had a family," Délin told Ifferon quietly, despite Théos knowing very little of their tongue. "His one true family are all the other Children of Telm."

"And you," Ifferon said.

Délin smiled. "And me."

"Will he ever live a normal life?"

"I do not know, Ifferon. I cannot imagine it is

possible to share a body with a god and not be in some way changed by that. Nor, indeed, is it possible to come back from death entirely unscathed. But I hope he can live a life with love and joy, and so not be weighed down by the worries you and I are left with."

"I wish that was a life I could live," Ifferon said.

"If we defeat Agon, it is a life we all can live," Délin said. "But sometimes we must give up a little of our own that another may have more of it. We never truly lose out, however, for there is much joy to be found in the joy of others."

Ifferon nodded and smiled. The merriment of others since Corrias' resurrection had certainly lifted his spirits, even though a part of him still felt overwhelmed by the role he was supposed to play, and the forces he was up against.

"I had not quite considered what I was really fighting for," Ifferon said, but he looked to Geldirana and Affon at the western side of the courtyard, where they were feasting and talking, and smiling and laughing. It had been so long since he had seen Geldirana rejoicing, and now he realised that though she might no longer have love for him, she still had an abundance of love for their daughter.

"So I guess the old fight for the young," Ifferon said.

"Yes, but the young also fight for the old."

"I wonder how Elithéa feels," Ifferon said. "We were almost at the point of ruin."

"Almost," the knight replied. "But it is when we are on the edge that we show who we really are, and whether or not we are honourable. She chose not to mar Théos' acorn, and so we are indebted to that choice, even if there should have never been a choice to make."

"I wonder if things can be repaired with her."

"That will be up to her, another choice for her to make. Yet we all have choices. Today we have victory, but tomorrow is less certain, and all we can do is hope that what we sow this day we can harvest on the morrow. There are so few of the Children of Telm left, and yet every one of you counts beyond measure, and will count much more if Agon ever looks upon the sky once again."

"The problem is that Telm never killed Agon," Ifferon said. "The best he could do was imprison him in Halés, and to do that he had to give up his own life. That does not bode well for the rest of us."

"Perhaps not, but we have not yet faced Agon in battle. Hopefully we never will, but if that day does come, then we will find out how strong Telm's blood really is, and how strong the blood of your friends and allies are."

Théos backed away suddenly from the window, as if he had seen some horror outside. He turned sharply and ran to Délin, pawing at his arm. "*Daramath*," he cried.

"What is it?" the knight asked, but Théos only repeated the Ferian word.

"I wish I knew more of their tongue," Ifferon said as he stepped back from the window. "There does not appear to be anything amiss. Corrias still walks the land."

Délin calmed the boy down, holding him close

until he stopped shaking. He had hoped these kinds of terrors were over, that the new life for the child would mean he did not see the darkness that others appeared not to see.

"I will find out what he means," the knight said, and though he did not speak his fears aloud, it was clear that he dreaded that meaning.

Elithéa was back in her cell, though this time her arms and legs were bound as well. She was not gagged, but she had little energy left to shout abuse at passing guards. This did not altogether stop her from trying, and every so often they were treated to another barrage of derisive words.

Délin approached, and she perked up, as if she were readying herself for an attack. She led the offensive with her eyes.

"Have you come to mock me?" she asked, and her tone almost mocked him in return.

"No," the knight replied coldly. "There is no honour in striking the wounded."

"So you mock me all the same," she said. "It is easy to strike others with your so-called honour, when you think they have done dishonourable things."

"I can control how I act," Délin said. "I cannot control how you choose to react."

"Why have you come to me?" she asked. "Do you wish to look down on me one last time before I am put to death?"

"I would not have you die," the knight replied. "I prayed that I would not have to kill you, and I do not see any merit in you dying anyway. Elithéa, I understand why you did what you did, and it seems, from your decision not to go through with it, that you understand why I did what I did also, and why it was important that we try to bring them back."

"Then why are you here?" she probed again.

"To forgive you."

She scoffed and turned away. "I do not need your forgiveness."

"Perhaps not," the knight said. "But I warrant that you need freedom, that you of all people cannot bear the bonds for long. Perhaps then you will need the forgiveness of some."

With that, Délin stepped aside, and there behind him stood Théos, who looked even smaller in frame beside the large figure of the knight. He looked up curiously at Elithéa, who glowered down, as if he too had come to mock her.

"Why bring him to me?" she asked.

Délin knelt down beside Théos and nudged him closer to the cage. He clambered up and stood behind the boy, resting his gauntleted hands upon the child's shoulders.

"This is the life we saved," he told her. "He is more than a tree could ever be."

Elithéa shook her head. "He does not yet know what he is missing."

Théos reached out to Elithéa and placed his hand in her hand, in the red marking where she had been scalded by the bars that Thalla had set alight. She looked at him curiously, and he looked at her with inquisitive eyes, as if he was recognising the similarity of their races.

"*Desh i carsa'ath abutha?*" the boy asked, turning his inquisitive eyes to Délin.

"Why is she in the cage?" Elithéa translated, with a hint of satisfaction.

"Is it he or you that asks this question?" Délin wondered.

"Maybe it is both," she replied. "*Abim chasadel,*" she told the child.

He did not seem to understand, and neither did Délin. "What did you tell him?" the knight asked her.

"I am an animal."

"So a lie then," Délin said.

"Not to the cager."

Délin knelt down again and tapped Bark, the stuffed toy tree, on the shoulder. Théos turned the tree around as if it had a mind of its own. It bore its eternal smile.

"How do I tell him to play with the other children at the bunkers?" Délin asked Elithéa.

"*Pelah truas ith mishanath.*"

Délin repeated the words to Théos, and both he and Bark nodded emphatically before trotting off.

"So you need me still," Elithéa said when the child was out of sight, "as a translator."

"I think we both know that you are more than that. Perhaps the Matriarchate will not let you don the title of Éalgarth when your acorn is sullied, but you can still be an Éalgarth at heart, if the role is to guard Éala, who still needs us as much as we need him."

"In a prison I can only be a prisoner," she replied. "Agon would know that."

Délin did not like the comparison, for he felt

Agon deserved not even a fraction of the mercy he felt for Elithéa.

"The Beast is—" But he stopped suddenly when Elithéa looked away, as if her attention had been seized by something.

"What was that?" she asked.

Délin looked at her curiously. "What do you mean?"

"That noise."

"What noise?"

"Never mind," she said. "It was like a tiny tremor."

"The rustle of the wind?"

"Maybe. Maybe something more."

Though it was not cold, Délin felt a shiver down his spine, and a shiver in his mind, as if a distant quake had sent everything shaking and shivering. It passed just as quickly as it had come, but something seemed amiss, as if the world had been slightly tilted—not enough to notice, but enough to change things.

An Al-Ferian guard passed by and halted, as if he too felt unease. "Is this woman bothering you?" he asked, targeting the only source of that unease he could think of. Délin knew the unsettling feeling did not come from her, but from somewhere else, somewhere deeper.

"No," the knight replied. "But the bonds are bothering her."

"They could be loosened, but Thúalim insists they be tight."

"Where is he?"

"At the main bunker."

Délin strode off without a word. Twenty minutes

passed before he returned with Thúalim, who cast his eyes across Elithéa as if she were the lifeless body of a Nahamon.

"So this knight begs clemency for you."

"And I beg nothing," she stated.

"It is well that you have such an active mouth," Thúalim said, "for it is all you will get to use if you spend your life in bonds. And yet for the evil you sought to do there might be another answer, for we could relieve you of the bonds of life."

"No," Délin said. "If I need beg again, then I shall beg, for there is no dishonour in bowing before another, that one life might be saved. She will not ask it of you, for pride controls her tongue, but I will ask it for her: be merciful and let her live, and live free."

"No," Thúalim said in turn. "If you were the prisoner, then I would have granted this freedom, but until she asks for mercy with her own lips, there will be no cutting of her own bonds."

"Then let me rot!" Elithéa barked. "And have mercy on my ears!"

Délin shook his head. "You are not making this easy."

"I am not making it easy or difficult. I am refusing to participate."

"And so your protest will seal your doom," Délin said. He knelt down, like he had done for Théos, and he rested his hand upon the cold metal cage. "Please, Elithéa. Put aside your pride. You might think it low to ask forgiveness, but it is lower still to deny that you have done aught that needs forgiving. Why give up when this is not the end? You can atone for your old actions with new ones. And maybe mercy for you will help us be unmerciful with the real evil out there, that which we call Agon."

It took many moments before Elithéa would talk, and it seemed to Délin that she would blurt out some sharp riposte, and in a single word or phrase condemn both him and Thúalim—and so condemn her to her fate. Yet she surprised them both, for she sighed and said, "Free me, please." It was not quite the entreating for leniency that Délin would have given, but from Elithéa's lips it sounded like the epitome of contrition and humility. Even Thúalim recognised this.

"I will consider your request," he said. "Thank Éala that one of his knights sees in you something that the rest of us cannot. For one who might have lost so much because of you, he has already shown you the greatest mercy."

Hours passed for Elithéa, until it seemed that the prospect of freedom was just a lie, a punishment of its own for what they deemed as her wrongdoing. During these lonely moments, when even Délin did not greet her, she held up her tarnished acorn to the light, and pondered what tree she might have been, and wondered why it had all been taken away from her, why Éala had been so cruel.

Then Thúalim came back with Délin and two Al-Ferian guards.

"Four men for one woman," she said with a smile. "Maybe you should bring four more."

"Everyone in the Mountain Fortress could be talking," Thúalim said, "and you would sound the loudest."

"Those who have something worth saying will be listened to," she said bluntly.

"And do you still say *free me, please*?"

Elithéa furrowed her brow and shifted posture in the cage, like an animal that had been mauled by its captor. "I say nothing I do not mean," she stated.

"Free her," Thúalim said to the guards. As they approached the cage and reached for the lock, he stopped them. "This time make your life worthy of an afterlife as a tree," he said, and he strode off as the guards continued to release her. They backed away quickly after the rope around her wrists was loosened.

She stood up and stretched her legs and arms. For a moment it almost looked like she were a tree, arching in the wind. What grace she lacked in word, she made up for in form.

"So the wild things are in the world tonight," she said.

Délin did not respond.

Elithéa tutted. "Aralus would have had a retort for that."

"And a blade for your back," the knight said. "You should be less eager for war, even a war of words."

"Maybe you should be less afraid of it."

"I do not fear war," Délin said, "only what might happen to the world if we lose it."

"Then maybe you are still wearing your cage," she said. "Do you ever remove your armour?"

Délin gave a slight smile. "Most of us never remove our armour."

"*Idil garthran fíulel abu*," the Ferian said, stressing

each word as if it were a curse.

"What good is a Common Tongue if it is not common among us all?" Délin asked.

"Language can conceal like armour."

"But can it protect us like armour?"

"Telm's dying words have protected all of us till now," she said. "But what I said in my tongue was," and she almost hissed the words that followed, "some armour is a weakness."

"I suppose it is," Délin acknowledged. "But that reminds me. What does the word *daramath* mean?"

Elithéa furrowed her brow, as if the question were a riddle. "Where did you hear it?"

"Never you mind," he replied. "What does it mean?"

Just as Elithéa opened her mouth to speak, there was a loud rumbling in the distance, which sent tremors into the mountain. The noise was like a thunder in the earth.

"I think you have your answer," she said. "It means *the sound.*"

And so it came again, even louder than before, until even those who had previously dismissed it perked their ears and gulped their fear. Worried faces looked to and fro, and their expressions grew even grimmer when they looked out to Corrias, who now stood still like a ghostly tower upon the mountain— and he bore the most worried expression of them all.

II

THE RENDING OF TELARYM

Deep in the heart of Telarym, the noise was thunderous, for it was there, under the dreary darkness of the melancholy sky, that the ground rolled and rumbled, as if the earth had eaten something it should not have. And so within the belly of the earth lay the Beast, and he thrashed and kicked, like an angry child wanting to be free of the womb.

The ground shuddered, as it often did when he fought against his chains, until his anger ate up all his energy and he could no longer fight for freedom. And so he rested until the rage grew once more inside him, eating away at his body and his mind, devouring him and replacing little bits of him with an even greater anger, an even fiercer rage.

Seven chains held him in place. Two grasped his ankles, biting him with their metal maws. One ate into his waist, extending around to his lashing tail. Four gnawed at his wrists, for he had four monstrous arms, long and thick, ending in fingers that ended in barbed nails, which dug into him as much as they dug into anything he could get his hands on. The chains were more than physical, for as much as Agon was alive, they were also. Every time he pulled against them, they would pull back. Every time he resisted his bonds, the bonds grew tighter. And so the pain continued for a thousand years, until Agon grew to loathe Teron's dying words, and wished he could kill him once again.

But this time the thrashing and kicking was different. His upper right arm pulled on the chain, and it did not pull back. It did not tighten, but grew looser, until the very jaws of the metal ring no longer had any bite. And so with another angry strike he broke the chain, and he held up his freed arm like a trophy, and he banged his fist upon the stone roof above in victory.

All in Halés heard, and all in Iraldas heard.

The Call of Agon had been answered.

Melgalés fell to the ground as the tremors continued around him, and each fall hurt more than the last, and reminded him that though he was dead, there was a type of pain that even the dead could feel. He struggled to his feet and ran to the steps that led into the Halls, but he was pushed back by a powerful gust of wind.

"It is not your time," the Gatekeeper said.

"But something's happening," the Magus replied. "We need to get to safety."

"There is a rumour of something coming," the Gatekeeper said. "And perhaps it is Agon—and perhaps he is already here."

The Felokar wolves began to howl. Each time the earth shuddered, they howled louder. Some ran around the caverns, and some pawed and scratched the walls. Amidst the rumbling and the roaring, the great watcher Echarin seemed asleep.

And then the ground broke away in the darker parts of Halés, and those lost souls that stood like shadows there fell deep into the pit. Few knew that they existed, and few heard their lonesome cries as they descended and were consumed, until nothing was left but the gaping mouth of Agon, and his reaching arm and clutching hand.

And so he stretched up, and the remaining six chains struggled against his unwavering will, for this freedom for a part of him had given him new strength, and he found within him a well of resolve that could match his overflowing pain and anger.

The arm reached up like a tower of triumph. The wolves saw it as nothing but a threat, and so many of them charged towards it, and many barked and howled at it, and a few even leapt at it and clawed and snapped, but they were flicked away like flies, and the fire in them vanished, snuffed out like a frail candle.

"So he is free," Melgalés whispered, fearful that his own words might give Agon power, might further unleash the terror that had been caged for a thousand years.

"Not fully," the Gatekeeper said, though his voice offered little reassurance. "Six of his seven chains yet hold."

"For how long?" the Magus asked.

"The answer to that question is outside my jurisdiction," the Gatekeeper said. "But rest assured … it will not be long enough."

* * *

Ifferon clung to the ground, even as the ground tried to get away from him, for it shook and shuddered, and each time he found a grip, he lost it once again. Amidst the rumble there were screams and shouts, and Ifferon tried to look up, but dust sprang into his eyes as if it too were looking for something to cling on to.

In time the quake subsided, but few dared stand up until they were certain it was over, and even then they feared it would come again, and might come more fiercely than before. When finally there was silence in the world around, and a loud ringing in their ears, Ifferon stumbled to his feet and helped pull others to theirs.

"What's happening?" Thalla asked as he dragged her up.

"I do not know," Ifferon said. "But I can guess."

Thúalim raced past them in a flurry, charging down the path of the mountain to where Corrias still stood silently, gazing south-east towards Telarym, towards where the sound and the shaking had originated from.

Délin came up to them, carrying Théos in his arms. Elithéa strolled behind him.

"I presume you heard it," the knight said.

"And felt it," Ifferon replied.

"Do we let everyone out of their cages now?" Thalla asked, looking harshly at Elithéa.

"I left it vacant for you," the Ferian responded.

"The only cage we should be worrying about is Agon's," Délin berated.

"And we have a reason to worry," Thúalim said

as he rejoined them. "The first of Agon's chains has broken. It is now only a matter of time before he is free."

III

THE RALLYING OF ARLIN

"Then we have no time to lose," Délin said, turning towards the door of the Mountain Fortress with Théos still in his arms.

"Where are you going?" Thúalim asked.

"We need to act," the knight said.

"There is little we can do," the Al-Ferian replied.

"That is what I thought on the most evil days of my life at the Old Temple, when I cast aside my Sigil of Corrias. If today is to be the most evil day for Iraldas, then there is still something we can do."

"And what is that?" Thúalim inquired.

"We go to war."

So Délin began to head for the door again, until Thúalim shouted after him: "Where are you bringing the boy? He is our race, not yours."

Délin halted with a clang and turned slowly to them with a stern glare. "When your people stopped treating him as a child, that is when he stopped being one of you and became just a weapon. In the coming days I will show you that it is children like him that we are fighting for, that it is for children like him that we take up weapons and march to war."

"The Children of Telm must stay here," Thúalim said. "You cannot take him."

"You can try to stop me," Délin said. "But you should be trying to stop Agon."

And so he marched off, and Théos smiled and waved at them, as if he knew he was leaving behind the battered prison of the Mountain Fortress, which served both as his tomb and his birthing place. Ifferon did not know where the knight was bringing the child, but he hoped it would be safer than all these castles and strongholds, which never seemed strong enough.

Thúalim looked as though he did not know what to do, his usually serene expression broken by anxiety, and he became even more frustrated when Elithéa strolled after the knight, turning slightly at the doorway to blow him a kiss. "The animals are out tonight," she said.

"Do we follow?" Ifferon asked.

"I am tired of following," Thalla said.

"Then what can we do?"

Thúalim shook his head, as if in disbelief of what had just happened, and to show that there were few options available to them. He was silent now not because he was calm and centred, but because he could not find fitting words to speak.

"What of Corrias?" Ifferon questioned. "Has he given guidance?"

"No," Thúalim said, and he looked as though he clearly needed it. He lacked the experience of Rúathar, and many of the Al-Ferian were evidently unhappy about this. There was already talk of his replacement.

"Then we must ask him," Ifferon said.

"It is too late. He is already gone."

"Gone?"

"To Telarym. He is going to hold Agon down, to act as the chain that has broken."

"And then?"

"Then he will do battle with the Beast."

Délin carried Théos until he and Elithéa reached the bottom of the Mountain Fortress, where the mossy rock gave way to mossy grass, and where their murky minds gave way to fairer ones. It was difficult to feel downtrodden under the golden canopy of Alimror, where the trees rustled gently and the grass swayed slightly. The knight placed Théos down, and the boy ran ahead, and he placed his hands on every tree that he passed, and he sat down to stroke the many-coloured flowers, and he got back up again as Délin and Elithéa approached, so that he could run ahead of them again. Here and there beneath his feet a tiny flower sprang, and though it was nothing like the *waylays* he left in Telarym, if each sprouting plant was gathered up together, they would have made a most splendid garden. All the while he smiled and laughed, and the smile was like sunshine, and the laugh was like music. It was a far cry from his sombre withdrawn state when Corrias resided in him, but it was a welcome change, like the shift of seasons from winter to spring, with the promise of summer.

"He is full of joy," Elithéa said as they walked.

"Yes," Délin replied, and smiled. "Just as it should be."

Elithéa grumbled, and though she tried to hide it, Délin heard it plainly. "Not what should be," she said.

"Look at the joy he gets from the trees. He could have given much joy to others."

"He already does," Délin said, "and will, for as long as he lives. And may that life be long and joyful."

Elithéa grazed her hand across the bark of an alder tree as she passed it. "It could have been the life of a tree."

"Yes, yes, and what could or might have been is over," the knight said sternly. "What is left is what is, and what can or might be still. This is why we go to war."

"I will fight with you," the Ferian said, "even though I fought against you. I cannot say I am happy that I lost our fight, and I am not accustomed to losing, which makes it hurt all the more, but I think I lost the greater fight with Aralus, who took more from me than I from him."

"You took his life," Délin pointed out.

"He took more than mine," she said.

They continued on, but soon their enjoyment of Alimror was interrupted by a stark reminder of the battle at the Mountain Fortress, for lining the path ahead were many Nahamon bodies, beginning the slow and disturbing process of decay and putre-faction. These dotted the area almost as frequently as the trees, but Théos did not skit from one to another to place his hands upon them, and his sunshine smile and his musical laugh were turned into a troubled expression and an unhappy silence.

They slowed as they passed through this forest mausoleum, as if fearful that they might somehow wake the dead. Théos still walked ahead, but much more slowly, and it appeared at several times like he was ready to bolt back to Délin.

The knight sighed as he looked around. "Many artists paint the battleground, but few paint the graveyard it becomes. Even though I will march to war, as I have done time and time before, it brings me no joy to know that this is what becomes of my enemies."

"They fought for the wrong side," Elithéa said. "They got what they deserved."

"No one deserves death," Délin replied.

"Aralus did," she said, and she looked to him with her glimmering green eyes. "Teron did."

Délin did not respond. Though suddenly he felt a flare of anger at hearing Teron's name, and though it brought to mind that the head-cleric did indeed deserve to die, he knew that there were others in the world who thought the same of Théos, and if he could not abide one, he felt he could not abide the other.

"When evil is done to evil, it does not become good," the knight said, feeding his anger into the words until it was transmuted into a steadfastness of will, until he felt as certain as ever that all acts must be made with honour.

Suddenly an arm reached up, as if of its own accord, and it seized Théos by the leg. The boy screamed, and Délin immediately reacted, charging at the Nahamon that seemed to have returned from death. In moments he unleashed his two-handed sword and struck down on the clutching arm, but just as it severed the limb, the remainder of the Dark Man rose up and swelled, and he looked more demonic now than he had done in life.

Délin advanced once more, but now the Nahamon was stronger, parrying the knight's blade as if his remaining arm were a shield and his bulging body were a suit of armour. It seemed to Délin that this being had a strength like that of the Sentinels of the Old Temple, and the knight was still tired from the battle at the Mountain Fortress.

But Délin was not alone. As the Nahamon lurched forward, reaching out with his one remaining hand, Elithéa snuck behind it and began to beat it viciously with her staff. Though the strikes did not slay the creature, they drew its attention, and it turned to Elithéa and stared darkly into her eyes. It heaved up, as if to attack, but it slumped down swiftly again, for Délin swung once and cleaved the head from the fiend, ending its life, if it could be called that, once and for all.

"So some serve Agon from beyond the grave," Délin said with a pant. "Who knew that there were some who would fight and die twice for the same evil master?"

A rumble echoed in the distance, and though it was faint, they were certain they heard something that was not the songs of birds, nor the whistle of the wind, nor the rustle of the trees. They strained their ears, and they thought they heard the rattle of a chain and the rending of a manacle.

"Were it any other time, I would think little of that sound," Elithéa said. "Yet now I hope that I make of it too much."

"Let us hope," Délin said, but he was not hopeful.

They left the unmarked graveyard and travelled swiftly to the very edge of the forest, where they could rest safely. Délin sat with his back to a tree, and Théos sat beside him, clutching Bark tightly and leaning his head against Délin's armoured shoulder. The knight wondered if the cold steel provided some comfort to the boy like it did for him.

Elithéa was restless, marching to and fro across the clearing, turning sharply so that her ponytail sometimes struck against one of the trees. She impaled her staff into the ground as she walked, and Délin wondered how she could be so violent to the earth, but he knew that she had less regard for the soil of Alimror. She seemed deep in thought, sometimes raising her hand as if to seize upon an idea, and then bashing her fist upon her thigh whenever it seemed that the idea had escaped her grasp. In time she stopped and turned to her companions with a knowing look.

"Perhaps the Al-Ferian err to leave the Nahamoni dead above the ground," she said, "where they can, from whatever evil magic is upon them, return to life again. Perhaps it would have been better if they had been buried beneath the earth, and so the earth, which is to us our freedom, may be to them their prison."

Délin nodded, but only to half of what she said. "If for nothing else, everyone deserves the honour of a proper burial. We spit on life itself if we do not afford this to our enemies also."

"Were it not for our more pressing need," Elithéa

said, "I might have buried them myself." Her anger then changed to sadness, and with it her aggressive stride changed to a slow saunter, until finally she stopped in a clearing devoid of the remains of the Nahamoni.

"Now it is time for me to bury my own dead," she said, and she knelt down and dug a small hole in the ground with her hands. Into this she placed her black acorn, with its black markings. Into it she could not place the blackness she felt in her heart of the evil that had been done to her. She covered it up, and she chose not to leave a marker, for she did not want any to know where she had buried her shame.

"So that chapter of my life is over," she said. "And whatever chapter it might have been … will never be."

"But another chapter lays before you," Délin said, placing his hand upon her shoulder. On the other side of her stood Théos, and he looked up at her, matching her sad eyes with his own. As the knight held her shoulder, the boy held her hand, and though she did not feel joy, she felt less her sorrow.

Délin thought that it might have been him doing this act, burying the acorn of Théos, and burying his body, and not knowing which was worse, and knowing with certainty that he could never bury the memories.

Délin felt that something more needed to be said, that something must fill the silence, and that it should not be sorrow, but the recognition that nothing truly dies. He scoured his memory for any tale to tell, and he found one that spoke of Man and nature.

If Man had caused the earth to crack and break,
Or caused the violence of the winter storm,
Or spoke with venom like the rattlesnake,
Or stung with needles like the scathing swarm,
Then Man would seem to all a vicious race,
Too proud to grow, unable to reform,
And the righteous would judge us a disgrace,
Yet none would judge the flood, nor chide the quake,
Nor think the hail of having made mistake.

If Man caused drought, or drowned the tender soil,
Or caused the autumn leaves to wilt and die,
Or forced the flowers to fail, and fruit to spoil,
Or threw volcano ash into the sky,
Then we would think Man full to brim of hate,
Too evil to forgive, a race awry,
And gods would think we earned an evil fate,
Yet none would damn the cold, nor blame the broil,
Nor think the sun a demon for our toil.

If Man caused typhoons, or tornadoes blew,
Or set the beasts at war just to survive,
Or wielded weather as the gods now do,
Or made some dwindle, and some others thrive,
Then Man would seem most cruel of all, not kind,
Yet from Nature these traits we all derive,
For in it we were born, from it designed.
What fair Nature birthed, foul Nature slew—
So Man can create life, and take it too.

"And what of Ferian?" Elithéa asked. "Or does Man think he alone is of Nature? He destroys it well enough, so does he destroy himself?"

"Some do," Délin said, "but Man is more than one person, and we are as diverse, and divided, as Nature herself."

Instead of travelling back east into Telarym, where danger thrived, or north-east into Boror, where danger festered, they continued mostly north through the thick and sometimes bewildering forest of Alimror. They knew that to the Al-Ferian it was many woods, and they knew it like Men know their cities, with all their various streets, but to the company it seemed endless, with no natural divisions, and certainly no artificial ones, for the Al-Ferian lived among the trees as if they never lived there at all. And yet Délin knew that some of those very trees were likely the ancestors of Al-Ferian now living in the Mountain Fortress and other less conspicuous settlements. While the sight of trees grew tiresome, and the maze of forest paths grew baffling, the canopy was their helm and the branches were their shield, and so they walked through protected and mostly unseen on their journey to Arlin.

Théos was at home in Alimror, Délin could plainly see. The boy raced about with a freedom he had never seen, and he was saddened that their journey led not deeper into the boughs and branches, but out into the wet and cold land of Arlin, where Délin felt at home. Yet the knight knew that this forest, beautiful and peaceful as it was now, was no haven, and that the trees that offered little protection around the Mountain Fortress would offer even less in the emptier parts of the forest.

They stopped to rest, and Délin gave his helm to Théos to play with, like he had done many times before, when the boy was but a shadow of himself, and not filled with the joy of one unburdened by the weight of gods.

Théos banged the side of the helmet with his hand. He was so small in frame that the noise it made was minuscule compared to the usual clangs and clatters it made in the heat of battle.

He looked expectantly at Délin, as if he wanted him to explain the noise.

"Metal," Délin said.

"Metal," Théos repeated slowly. He looked as though he was repeating the word in his head many times, internalising it and attempting to understand it.

Then he pointed to his head, placing his finger on his right temple, and said: "*Roth.*"

"Head," Elithéa translated.

Théos nodded, though it was clear he did not understand the word from the Common Tongue.

"*Metal roth,*" he said and pointed to Délin.

Elithéa laughed. "Metal head. I guess you have a new name."

Délin smiled, and then Théos smiled in response. That was a language they both understood.

By the third day they came to the end of Alimror, where it fed into Arlin. Délin had often wondered how the borders of maps were drawn, for they seemed almost arbitrary, and so they were to the cartographers of the war-mongers of old, who drew the maps like they drew blood, and redrew them again, as if in the very blood of their victims. Yet here it was clear where Alimror ended, for the trees suddenly stopped, as if they themselves knew not to invade Arlin. Délin had rarely seen such an obvious boundary, bar perhaps the Wall of Atel-Aher, which he could see now in the distance, or the eerie crossing of the Issar Chammas, which he hoped never to see again.

They stepped onto the soggy ground of the Motherland, where a fresh rain fell as often as day turned to night. There was a light wind, with a gentle coolness, not enough to shiver, but just enough to wake the soul from slumber, and bring alertness to the eyes. Délin felt it very reassuring, but it was clear that neither Elithéa nor Théos cared much for the cold. They shivered, and Elithéa tried to hide it, and Théos could not hide it at all. Délin wrapped his cloak around the boy, and as he did so, the child looked up to the dimming sky and was transfixed by the sight.

"*Elas tra súa íotath el agath,*" Théos said, and the wonder in his eyes matched the wonder in his voice.

"Look at all the little dots in the sky," Elithéa translated.

"Stars," Délin said with a smile.

"Stars," the boy repeated, as if he had learned a magic word, and perhaps he had, for it caused an even greater transformation in his face, from wonder to joy.

"Let us hope we live to see them for many nights to come," Elithéa said, and it seemed that she was talking about the threat of the cold night air as much as the threat of the Beast.

It did not take long before they came to Ciligarad, for Délin knew these lands like he knew his armour, or like he knew the tales of old. The proximity of his home town gave his legs new fuel, and his heart new life. Though Théos did not like the cold, he never seemed to lose his energy, racing to and fro and splashing himself, and them, in puddles.

Ciligarad greeted them with a flurry of lights. It was known as the City of a Thousand Guards, and though its watch had dwindled over the years, the Knights of Issarí still kept it well protected. Three knights on horseback charged out from the city to halt them, but they halted themselves instead, shocked to see their leader returned from Telarym.

"Trueblade!" Brégest called from atop his steed. He dismounted immediately with a crash of steel and a splash of water from the rain-clogged ground. "You have returned!"

"*Lamar í Lamon. Hómadés dú!*" the other knights cheered in unison, as if it were Corrias or Issarí who stood before them now.

"For Lady and Lord," Délin said. "But there is little time to rejoice."

Brégest nodded. "We have heard the rumours—and the rumbles. Has he arrived?"

"So it seems. Corrias has gone to Telarym to stop or slow him."

"Then we are saved," Brégest said. "We heard that Corrias had returned, and just in time."

"Yes, yes, but we are not yet saved, and I fear

Corrias may not be strong enough to stop Agon."

Brégest's eyes grew dim. "To some that would sound like blasphemy."

Délin thought his own eyes might be grimmer. "Perhaps, and I would rather be a blasphemer than a soothsayer, but my mind tells me that Corrias was not strong enough a thousand years ago to defeat Agon, and my heart tells me he is not strong enough to defeat him today."

"So what can we do?" Brégest asked.

"We must rally to him. We must offer him whatever aid we can, and so fulfil our oaths to our god, to our land, and to our people."

"And so we shall," Brégest said. "But first, you must rest one last night and take one last feast here in Ciligarad ere we ride to war."

Délin did not say anything, but he knew his eyes said enough to his fellow knight, his brother in arms. One last night and one last feast—because it might be one last battle, and one last draw of breath. This was the threat and promise of war, and one it rarely failed to deliver.

Brégest did not remount, but led his horse by the reins back into the city, letting Délin walk ahead slightly, holding Théos by the hand. Elithéa strolled behind, flanked by the two mounted knights. She looked about with scorn, and perhaps she thought: *so much water to feed new life, and not a tree in sight.*

The city was bustling as they entered, and it became even busier as soon as word got out that Trueblade had come home. Many came out to greet him, and some threw ribbons into the air, and some others began to play music, and none seemed to mind the never-ending rain.

The mead hall was opened, as it was for special occasions, and the company gathered inside and dried themselves off. Délin had to stop one of the knights from reefing what looked like straw from Théos' head, which was instead part of his unruly mop of hair, like a little garden of its own.

"Is that the child I have heard rumours of?" Brégest asked Délin, and he glanced anxiously at the boy, like many of Délin's companions had done when they first encountered him.

"Assuming I know the rumours, yes."

"What will become of him?" Brégest asked.

Délin sighed. "He has been in too much danger already. I would that I could find a safe haven for him, but even Ciligarad does not seem safe enough. I would offer my sword, and my life, to protect him, but I am sworn also to protect Corrias and all good people in Iraldas. So I am torn. But I can best serve both Corrias and Théos on the battlefield, while there are still battles to be fought."

Délin's heart panged, and he was reminded of that sorrowful day when he sent Théos away with Adon of the Garigút to avoid an even more painful parting. And he was reminded of that even more painful day when Théos fell to Teron's traps in the Old Temple, and Délin's faith crumbled. He knew that Théos would be safer at home, and yet a large part of him hoped and prayed that he would not rue his decision to leave the child behind, without the protection of his armoured knight.

No decisions were made there in the mead hall beyond how many draughts to pour. The knights drank heartily, and some told of Herr'Don's visit, and Délin was greatly comforted to know that the prince had not given up, and that he was still doing some good in the world.

Délin did not drink much that night, leaving behind many pints of ale, for he knew that the battles ahead would take much of him, while for some that night the ale alone would do the job. Elithéa drank more than most, and it seemed to affect her little, bar perhaps eliciting from her a smile here and there in place of a frown.

While Délin was not looking, Théos tried to take a sip from his mug, but he was caught in time, and the boy complained in the Ferian tongue. The knights laughed, and one joked about trying the wine instead.

"I thought you only drink water," Délin said to the boy, but Théos did not respond.

"Perhaps you are a bad influence," Elithéa said as she stacked her seventh mug upon the last.

"Aren't we all?" Brégest said. "He'll fit in just fine here."

Some drank into the small hours of the night, when the owls set up watch in the rafters, but many of the fighting knights retired to bed, some under orders from their commanders. Those who remained would not march to battle, but would keep the fires in Ciligarad burning, even as their comrades hoped to keep all kingdoms from the flames.

Théos fell asleep in the mead hall, and Délin

carried him to his room. He watched him for a time, where the moonlight shone upon him like a warding light, and then when the knight's eyes grew heavier than his hurts and worries, he retired to bed and dreamed that he might one day be able to retire from battle.

Théos rose with dawn, and he urged Délin from his slumber. They broke their fast and regrouped with Elithéa, whom Délin called to help with his parting words. He removed his helmet and gave it to Théos, as he had done many times before, but now he would not take it back.

"A gift," he said.

"*Tóthel*," Elithéa translated.

Théos smiled broadly, the kind of smile that Délin would always remember, even in the Halls of Halés if he should fall in battle. The child clutched the helm like he held his stuffed toy, and though it was clear that he struggled with its weight, he refused to place it down.

"*Dóshel*," Théos whispered, half to the helmet and half to the knight. "Metal *roth*."

"A treasure," the Ferian explained. "I think you know the rest."

Délin smiled and ruffled the boy's hair.

"I have to go now," he said. "I might not come back."

"*Lathim—*"

"No," the knight interrupted. "Do not translate. I do not want him to know. Tell him I will be back soon."

"*Úlsé arba garmil abu*," she said.

Théos nodded, and he placed the helmet down just long enough to hug the knight, before taking it up again and struggling once more. Délin ruffled his hair a final time and turned to leave. As he reached the door he looked back, and he thought he saw a mixture of emotions in the child, a glimmer of joy in one eye, and a gleam of sorrow in the other.

"Goodbye," he said, and this was a time he was glad Théos could not understand him.

Délin returned alone to his chambers, where he stood for a time by the open doors that led out to the lake. The presence of Issarí had faded, and he knew clearly that she meant it when she said they would never hear her counsel again. He hoped that even if she passed on, the knights that bore her name would remain. He hoped that even if he joined her, the knights would still go on.

He spent another moment before the mirror in his room, where the candle obscured his view, that he might never think himself greater than the true flames of the world. Yet the light illuminated his face, showing all the crags and cracks, the scars of age, and the even greater toils of war. The greatest was yet to come, and he would be lucky to come away with only scars—or to come away at all.

He set aside his swords. Though everyone knew him as Trueblade, and knew his motto, he never revealed the names of his weapons, which were to him his most prized secrets. He had inherited an old superstition from his father that an enemy that knew the name of a blade could never be felled by it. Though many enemies knew the feel of Délin's swords, they never knew the names.

He removed his armour, the first time he had done so in many weeks. It was difficult to remove, just as it was difficult to put on, and so the squires used to jest that the greater the difficulty, the greater the defence. This had proved true for Délin, and he did not like the feel of the cool wind upon his under-clothes when his breastplate lay beside him on the ground.

When finally he had removed his greaves, and he felt naked to all, he turned again to the lake and knelt, and prayed a silent prayer. Then he began to hum, and then he began a gentle song:

The battlefield is our bastille, the bodies walls,
The swords our prison bars, the lives our lock and key.
We are the jailer and the jailed, consumed by brawls
Till war in turn consumes, leaves none among us free.

We are divided by our lands, bound to our creeds,
United only in the clash of sword and shield,
A short accord that lasts till one of us concedes,
And yet the victor to the gods of war will yield.

We fight for freedom, and for all that we avow.
We take up arms, march out, and battle to the last.
We fight for the future, and for the here and now,
And because we still wear the shackles of the past.

Conflict is the rope to bind our hands, strife our noose,
And, seeing blood, madness would have us seek out more.
It will not end till in our hearts we call a truce,
Not break the bonds of peace and don the chains of war.

He went over to his bed and reached beneath it. He pulled out a large wooden chest, plain in form. He unlocked it and looked inside, and nodded firmly. He took out an ornate helmet, which carried an intricate interlace, between which was a field of blue. It was crowned with three small swords, like something a king might wear to war.

He held it before him and bowed his head. "I honour you, father. You fought and won in this, and you fought and died in it. Let our name continue on, and be forever true. De'Marius."

Some did not recognise Délin when he emerged, but some others knew immediately what this new attire meant. Horses were made ready, weapons were sharpened, and rations were packed. Flags and banners were unfurled, and trumpets were sounded.

Before Délin went to the stables, he headed for the library, wherein he had spent much of his free time in both his younger and older days. It was as much a home to him as his own chambers, and often he was found asleep there, with a book or scroll his pillow.

Talaramit, head scholar of the Knights of Issarí, greeted him. He was young for such a role, but only in body, for his mind was old, wrinkled from the work of many tireless nights of study. He was also a knight, but he wore his armour mostly for ceremony now, for he rarely left the walls of the library, where books were bricks, and Talaramit was their labourer.

"The boy Théos is in your charge now," Délin told him. "Teach him the good things of this world, the words and numbers, the tales and songs. I go now to teach the evil things a different lesson."

IV

THE SWORD THAT WAS SHEATHED

Yavün heard and felt the quake more than most in Iraldas, for he was in Telarym, where the Beast had emerged from his prison, where Agon was held back by bonds that all knew could not hold him for long. The Great Lake shuddered, sending ripples to all edges, as if the very water was trying to escape to land. Yet it was from land that Agon came; in land and under land, and yet all the creatures of the sea and air felt him too.

Elilod was in a frenzy. The fear he felt was palpable, and this made Yavün even more afraid than he thought he could be. He knew the stories and the rumours of Agon, and they were unsettling, but Elilod was Elyr the Issaron, the River Man, the spouse of Issarí. He knew Agon, and from the look on his liquid face, that knowledge was terrifying.

"If ever I lament being incarcerated here in Iraldas, it is now, for in Althar time passes much more slowly, so much so that we barely notice it," Elilod said. "Yet here it seems I cannot blink my eyes and days have passed. Agon has arrived much sooner than I expected, and far sooner than I had hoped. Little fish, there is no more time to study the sea, no more time to learn to swim. We are all in the deep now, and the shark has smelled our blood."

In time Narylal calmed her leader, bringing him back from those endless wars a thousand years before, where the empire of the Céalari crumbled to the Beast. Though Elilod said little of those dreadful times, Yavün could see in his eyes the cutting of the roots of the Great Tree that bridged Althar to Iraldas, and the dousing of the Lamps that put an end to the immortality of the gods that were now trapped inside the mortal world. He also saw in those eyes the fear that those dreadful times had come again.

When Elilod had calmed sufficiently, he began to tell Yavün of the Sword of Telm, called Daradag, the Hammer of Adag, for as much as it pierced, it struck, and as much as it sliced, it beat. "Adag was the greatest craftsman of the Céalari," Elilod said, "and he crafted himself into a new blade for Telm to bear, gave up his very life that the sword might take Agon's."

Elilod went into great detail about the life of Adag, and how he lived on inside his own creation, as many of the gods did. Yavün was so moved by the tale that his mind immediately began to form a ballad to honour the god.

The greatest of the smiths, Adag his name,
Excellence his hammer, perfection his swing.
Across Althar went tales of his acclaim,
And in the forges he made the metal sing.
He held a vice of frost and tongs of flame,
And for a fitting title, he held "Craft-king."

By furnace fathered, cast and wrought inside;
By fire mothered, from the hottest air he nursed.

An anvil for a cot, upon it plied.
Gold nuggets for food, liquid tin for his thirst.
Born clutching every ore, the baby cried,
And from that small cry, to life the bellows burst.

He made many of the gods' finest things,
From great swords and shields to boots of lightning speed,
Copper brooches, and shining silver rings,
And more still, as metal from the earth he freed,
To make sceptres for gods, and crowns for kings.
Accomplishment was his drive, success his steed.

When Agon appeared, and all weapons failed,
Telm came to Adag to seek new tools of war.
In this great quest the god at last prevailed,
And he made himself into the blade Telm bore.
Agon was vanquished, and in Halés jailed.
Adag paid a price—he was a god no more.

Yavün had barely finished his poem when Elilod turned to the Great Lake as if Adag, or even Agon, had appeared there. The manner in which he did this, with the grace of gods, brought Yavün's eyes upon the body of water that stood before them like the wash basin of the Elad Éni.

Then Yavün beheld a wonder of wonders which made many of his past adventures seem insignificant. From the Great Lake, which imitated a sea, rose a colossal sword held horizontal, a sword that could only have been held by a colossal hand, and could only have been designed to fell a colossal enemy. Its blade was silver and its hilt was gold, and embedded within it were many gems of every colour imaginable, and many colours Yavün previously had not the imagination to muster.

Yavün was so awestruck that he initially failed to notice the hundreds of Taarí who held the sword up from the waters. Even after he saw them he could not help but think that they were the frothy waves that had brought this relic of the gods to the surface.

"This," Elilod said, his voice an ocean of its own crashing at Yavün's ears, "is Daradag, the sword that Adag crafted, the sword that he himself became, and the sword that Telm brought to battle—the sword that struck the Beast."

Yavün did not deny the words he heard, for his eyes still denied the sight he saw before him. If any weapon had been held by Telm, by the Olagh the stableboy had prayed to in his youth, then this could only be it. He could imagine all manner of things, possible and impossible, but he could not imagine any sword greater than the one before him.

"This," Elilod said, his voice returning like the tide, "is now your sword."

For a moment Yavün did not register these words, and even after they filtered into his mind he found he did not register their meaning. "Mine?" he asked, the word tumbling out of his mouth as if it had fainted from the shock.

"Yes, yours, little fish."

Yavün remained dumbfounded, and he showed it with silence. Narylal laughed and placed her hand upon his shoulder. The cool touch was a distraction from the wonder before him.

"I think it's a little big," he managed after a time.

"I think I'd need larger hands to hold it."

"Or a smaller sword," Elilod said. "Look at me. I am Elyr Issaron, the River Man. You saw Issarí, my spouse, and she is greater in size than I now appear, for this is not my true size, but a guise I wear that I might walk this world unnoticed. The rivers may be long and thin, or short and broad, and some may wind, and some may flow straight. They are all made of water, little fish, so size can be altered."

With these final words, Elilod held his right arm aloft, and the wonder of wonders that Yavün beheld became even more wonderful, for the gigantic sword rose into the air, and the Taarí that held it up fell from it like drops of water. As it rose it began to shift upright, and it started drifting towards where they stood on the shoreline. Yavün watched in amazement, for as the sword came closer, it grew smaller, the opposite of how his eyes should have worked, and as he blinked in silence, he found that the sword was in Elilod's hand, no larger than any Yavün had seen used by Herr'Don or Délin.

"Telm fought the Beast for many years, holding him back with this sword, and he inflicted many wounds upon Agon, scars that he still bears in Halés, but when Agon finally slew Telm, the force of Telm's dying breath sent Agon into the Underworld, and Daradag into the Great Lake. Here in the depths it lay for a thousand years, and though we knew of it for many centuries, we kept its location secret, so that Agon's forces could not steal it from us, so that we could wait until a rightful heir came along."

"Why doesn't Ifferon have this?" Yavün asked. "Is

he not more a rightful heir than me?"

"Telm's bloodline spread wide and far, so his potency is found in many, not in one. Thus his legacy, and his heirlooms, belong to several, not to one. Ifferon has the Scroll. You have the Sword. Both of you have the Blood, and either of you can bear the heirloom of the other."

Elilod handed him the sword, which he took awkwardly, not because of his little experience with weapons, but more because he feared he would drop or damage it. Initially it felt extremely heavy, as if it was many times the weight of what it appeared to be, as if, indeed, it still held some of the weight of the colossal form he saw in the lake only moments before. In time, however, the weight adjusted, so that he felt he was holding it naturally, as if it had become a part of him, an extension of his being.

"So this is why I'm here," he said.

"Yes, little fish. You fell into the Chasm of Issarí, and perhaps you thought it was the evil Taarí that pulled you under, that separated you from your companions, but that was not so. It was us, us who dragged you down, and us who pulled you up. And the bridge fell because Issarí, who still holds some sway upon that passage, willed it, that you might be swept down to us, where you might take on your true role, that you might fulfil your true duty."

Yavün felt overwhelmed by all of this, and though part of him felt immensely special and privileged, another part felt like he was a puppet being pulled to and fro, and that any movement he seemingly made of his own was willed by another. It was a very unsettling feeling, and it made him wonder if he was being used or lied to.

His thoughts were jarred by a strange sensation from the sword, a dull vibration that sent tiny shudders into his body, and in these shudders he thought he could recognise a pattern, as if it were a language of some kind. He then began to suddenly become aware of a powerful mind within the sword, a force beyond anything he had ever felt before.

"What you are feeling is the mind of Adag," Elilod said. "For he is made into the very metal, beat into the blade, hewn into the hilt. The sword is known by many names, but one of these is the Old Arlinaic title of *Délrachúgorin*, the Sword that Lives."

That night was one of the oddest in Yavün's life, in a life filled with many odd moments. He slept by the Great Lake, with the Sword of Telm beside him like a sleeping lover. He kept his hand upon the blade while he slumbered, and so at times it thrummed, and so at times his dreams took on new meaning, as if Adag were speaking to him in sleep.

When day came, and he found he was less rested than before, Narylal came to him to tell him that Elilod had another gift to give. Her voice and eyes betrayed that she was jealous that this token should go to him instead of her.

"There is one other trinket I would have you wear," Elilod said, and he produced a strange ring from his vestments. It was an odd type of silver, with two bands that interlocked with one another, so that it could be worn upon two fingers instead of one. It looked almost like a tool of bondage, a manacle for a finger instead of wrist.

"What is this?" Yavün asked when he felt its cool touch upon his hands.

"This is the ring Issarí gave to me many ages ago," he said. "It means more to me than any other thing in Iraldas, and yet means nothing in comparison to her, to her love, and to my love for her."

Narylal looked coolly upon Yavün, as if in the eyes of a father she was no longer the favoured child.

"It is called in the Taarí tongue *Ada Pysaa*, Two Fishes, and it has spent most of its time beneath the sea, where for a long time all that it has united is metal and water, giving birth to rust. Yet even though its sheen has faded, it is still dear to me."

"Then why are you giving it to me?" Yavün asked.

"Some in this world are gifted with the clearsight," Elilod said, "but there is another type of sight that the Céalari have, and it is a kind of foresight, showing us what shall come to pass. In this way we are fated to a certain end like any other, and we do not need to look within the waters of the Issar Chammas to see what doom lies before us. And so I know that my time here is waning, and clutching to a trinket would not make that time pass more slowly, nor save me from my fate. I do not know how it all will end, only that the end is fast approaching, and I would that this small symbol of love live on beyond me, and perhaps bring some love to others."

"But I am alone," Yavün said, and he felt it more than ever now, and resented that he was reminded of it, as if lovers must mock the lonely to better enjoy their love.

"Then make of it a promise, little fish," Elilod said, closing Yavün's fingers until they tightly clutched the ring. "The sword must find its sheath in the heart of another. It is the promise it made to the smith who crafted it. This ring must be worn by two in whom each is the part of their heart that is missing. It is the promise it made to the jeweller who made it, and she made naught that did not live up to its promise. So then, find another little fish to share the *Ada Pysaa*."

Yavün accepted the ring, though he did not know what to think of pledges and promises, so easily broken. In his short life he had been promised many things, few of which ever transpired. Now he had been given several gifts, gifts he could feel and hold and touch, when life had previously given him the gift of disappointment and defeat. He did not like promises any more, and yet he knew that even in his blood there was a promise, and facing Agon was its fulfilment.

V

THE KILLING OF THE CROW

The Al-Ferian began to arm for war, with Athanda taking charge now that Mathal had passed on. She was less wiry than her sister, though still she hunched her back and bent her limbs, as if she were a maple tree. She began to issue orders in direct opposition to those that Thúalim had given, but he did not fight her, knowing that she would win.

"We cannot afford to send an army of many," Athanda said, "and leave our home unguarded. What good is victory if there are none to celebrate it, and what good is marching to war if there is no home to march to when it is won?"

"Assuming it is won," Thalla said.

"Let's not assume, but make it so," Athanda replied.

"How many can we spare?" Thúalim asked.

"At best, a hundred."

"That will not be enough."

"It will have to do," Athanda said. "Let's hope that knight has a larger army."

"I am not sure they do," Ifferon said. "But if they are all like Trueblade, we will not need so many."

"Throw a thousand Trueblades at the Beast and it may not be enough," Athanda said.

"The enemy only needs one soldier, and that is Agon," Geldirana said. "Our victory will not come through numbers, but how we play the numbers that we have. Against a god, only a god will do." She looked at Ifferon.

"Let's hope Éala will do," Athanda said, and though she was Al-Ferian, she looked as though she had much more faith in her own sword than in the strength of the Céalari.

Before the army was assembled, scouts returned from the forest with news that a giant crow had been spotted, heading for the Black Eyrie with what appeared to be a scroll in its beak. Ifferon perked his ears at this news.

"That nest should be black from the soot of flames," Athanda said. "If we did not march to Agon, I would have us march there instead to teach the fowl what it means to break their oaths."

"Agon will have to wait," Geldirana said. "If that crow has the Scroll of Mestalarin, then we must hunt it down, like the Garigút hunt the crows of Boror."

"Yes," Ifferon said. "It may be the only real weapon that we have." Though a part of him still wished that someone else was there to wield it, he felt more and more that if another claimant came, he would deny them the heirloom.

"Do as you will," Athanda said. "I will take my people to where Agon is, that Éala might not stand alone."

Geldirana urged the remainder of the Garigút to go with Athanda, and though they seemed reluctant to follow another leader, there was no reluctance in them to engage in a new battle, even if the battlefield had just one enemy upon it.

As the army was readied, a much smaller force comprised of Ifferon, Thalla, Thúalim, Geldirana and Affon assembled. Ifferon initially objected to Affon joining them, but this only raised the ire of Geldirana, which came at him as if it were another member of the company. As they argued, Thalla brought Affon aside.

"You have no right to tell me how to raise my daughter," Geldirana scolded Ifferon.

"I only want to see her safe," Ifferon said.

"And will she be safe here?" Geldirana asked. "Here where there are barely enough guards to stand by the many open doors? It is a mountain, that is true, but it is no longer a fortress. I sent Affon here to be safe. I sent her here because Oelinor urged me to, as you now do, and he had more of a right than you to tell me what to do. But now she will be safer with me."

"Battle is no place for a child," Thúalim said, voicing what Ifferon thought, but dare not say.

"Battle is the place of all who are at war," Geldirana replied. "No one is exempt from the battlefield, which we call Iraldas. When Agon hunts down the Children of Telm, he does not stop when he is faced with an actual child. Théos is proof of that."

Ifferon shook his head. "All the more reason to—"

"No," Geldirana interrupted. "If there is one who is not invited to the battlefield, it is reason, and if he were, he would be slain there ere he could do any good. In this war, Agon will not be reasonable, and so we should not be either.

"Besides, Affon has been cooped up in this castle for too long, caged like a hen, when the Garigút need to roam. If she is to one day lead my people, she must know the freedom of the open battlefield, which is as much to us a home as Boror itself."

"If all of Iraldas is the battlefield, let her fight from a safer part," Thúalim said.

"Here I end my argument with words," Geldirana said, and she placed her hand upon the handle of her mace. Thúalim glanced at Ifferon and shook his head.

They grudgingly accepted Geldirana's decision, knowing that she would not back down, and knowing that they needed her, and perhaps needed Affon too, in the thick of battle, where every sword, even one held by a child, affected the outcome.

They set out from the Mountain Fortress, down its many winding paths, through the blood-stained and body-filled valley beneath it, and under the boughs of the seemingly endless forest of Alimror.

"It seems like our mission is a trifle," Ifferon said, "compared to that of others around us who march to war."

"We also march to war," Geldirana replied. "We are just marching at a slower pace. Ere we hasten to the Beast, we must find the Scroll of Mestalarin or we may never stand a chance."

"Can you track the bird?" Ifferon asked Thúalim.

The Al-Ferian took a while to respond. He seemed distracted, watching every fallen leaf, every scrap of tree, and every tuft of grass. "Yes," he said in time, but he seemed like he was tracking something else.

"You're not exactly one for words, are you?" Thalla noted.

Another long pause. "No," he said.

Suddenly he stopped, and the others stopped in turn, as if their feet were chained to his.

"What is it?" Geldirana asked, and she looked around, as if preparing for an advancing enemy.

"This is where he died," Thúalim said, and he spoke as if the very forest had been cut or burned down.

They ventured a little further in, and they found the resting place of Rúathar—though he did not look restful. He had clearly been trampled and beaten, and though he was tall and broad, and stronger than many others of his race, the life had been sucked out of him by the shadow, leaving just a shadow of his former self, a broken shell abandoned by its soul.

Thalla closed her eyes and shook her head. Ifferon could not help but think of Melgalés and how Yavün had found him. Geldirana bowed her head. While Thalla perhaps could not help but think of the Magus laying dead on the ground, Ifferon's thoughts were with Geldirana, who could have so easily joined her fellow Ardúnari—and who might still.

"I am but a glimmer," Thúalim said. "He was the light."

He knelt down and closed Rúathar's eyes. All were glad to no longer see his endless gaze, and the moment of horror captured therein. Now he looked more peaceful, while all others prepared for war.

Affon was unusually quiet. It was difficult to be

brash in the face of death.

Thúalim noted the fallen Ilokrán, mere inches from Rúathar's broken fingers. "A shield that was not strong enough," he said. He took it up and handed it to Ifferon, who reluctantly accepted it. He already felt guilty for losing the one Melgalés had given him, and for holding the second Shadowstone that Rúathar had, which might have combined with the first for a stronger defence. He did not feel he should hoard these all to himself, and he looked to his silent daughter, who still did not know he was her father, and he realised what his first act as a parent could be. He handed her the Ilokrán, and hoped it would do her more good than it did for Rúathar. As the girl took the stone, he thought he saw a gleam of a smile from Geldirana, just a hint of something veiled by her solemnity.

Thúalim then took the pouch from Rúathar's waist and stood up. He emptied the acorn into his hand. It looked so plain and simple, dull and brown, small and round. It was no Ilokrán or Beldarian. It did not glint, and it had no markings. To anyone else it was just an acorn. To the company then present, it was Rúathar's life.

The group gathered around as Thúalim planted the acorn in the ground close to where his leader had fallen. He scooped out some dirt, delving deep into the earth that was everything to the Ferian and Al-Ferian. To some this was an act of a gardener; to others it was the act of a grave-digger. He planted the acorn, and covered it up. So it was that his people came to bury their dead.

Ifferon was surprised to find that nothing was done with Rúathar's body. He remembered Elithéa's words in the Amreni Elé, when she tried to convince them that the body was but a shell, that the true life of a Ferian was to be lived as a tree.

They stood for a time around the tiny mound under which the acorn lay, and upon which a tiny sapling might one day grow, if the world was not destroyed by Agon. Ifferon was reminded of the Amrenan Adelis, the Mound of Mourning, where they had buried Belnavar in what almost felt like another age. He looked to his new companions—and he hoped he would not have to bury them too.

They left behind the body of Rúathar and the promise of a new oak tree, and they left behind their sadness and their sorrow, spurred on by their anger and their determination to reclaim the Scroll of Mestalarin, and put the Last Words to their final use.

As they delved deeper into the forest, following a series of markings that Thúalim identified as that of the evil birds, they found that it grew darker, and that the trees grew closer together, as if they huddled tightly in fear of something.

Suddenly that something came into view.

In the growing blackness between the twisted boughs, red eyes lit up like lanterns, and instead of illuminating the land, they seemed to cast it into an even greater darkness. As one set of eyes sparked alight, another set joined them, as if the fire was spreading from lantern to lantern. Ifferon thought of the Felokar wolves, but he knew that they were too far from the entrance to Halés to be attacked by those beasts. These were not the yellow eyes of those neutral hounds, who served neither the Céalari nor the Beast, but the red eyes of creatures that bowed down and knew Agon as their master.

Ifferon drew his sword and Geldirana waved her mace. The others raised their weapons.

"Come forth if you dare!" Geldirana cried.

And so the eyes came forward, and the company saw what they belonged to: many black stags, larger than any of their kin, and more evil. Their antlers twisted and curled around in more extreme forms than Ifferon had ever seen, and some looked even more tangled than the branches of the trees around them. Their fur was black as soot, accentuating the evil glower of their eyes.

And so they attacked. In a sudden flurry the stags charged forward, and they rammed and reared, and they bit and bucked. All the while the company staggered about, striking the animals and warding blows, and sometimes being knocked to the ground from the force of the stampeding herd.

Ifferon narrowly dodged a charging stag, which thundered past and struck a tree. The oak quaked, and the stag's antlers were stuck deep inside the bark. It pulled and kicked, and it squealed and hollered, as if somehow the tree were attacking it. Ifferon stabbed it with his sword, and so it squealed much louder, but did not squeal for long.

Around him Geldirana moved like lightning, dodging and striking. Thalla and Thúalim had climbed into the trees, from where they both sent down arrows, real ones from Thalla's bow, and arrows of light from a spectral bow that Thúalim summoned, and they felt no less real to the stags below.

Suddenly Ifferon realised that he did not see Affon in the frenzy, and he called her name, and he heard her call his in return. She was lying several metres away, struggling against a wounded stag, which thrashed its head at her. She clung to its antlers, and she was cast this way and that like a rag doll. And though she was wounded, she did not scream. And though the stag did everything in its power to kill her, she did not call for help.

Yet help came without her call, for Ifferon charged at the animal as if he had antlers of his own. Thus the stag felt his blade, and it bucked no more. Affon still clung to the beast's horns as its head slumped down, and Ifferon had to pry her fingers off, and hold her quivering hand as he led her away from the battle, where Geldirana laid waste to the remainder of the possessed brutes.

But the battle was not yet over, for the stags had another master, and it was a larger creature of a similar make, but with horns of brilliant white. If the others looked strange, this one looked stranger, as if it had been cobbled together by several different makers. An aura of unease surrounded it, and even Geldirana backed away.

"Go back to your crypt!" she said, and she waved the mace before her, as if she were striking that unsettling aura.

The creature stood there, unmoving and un-blinking, its red eyes like eternal fires. Then it prepared to charge, kicking up the dust into an aura of its own.

And suddenly the dust became so blinding that none of them could see the white-horned stag—until it was upon them. Thúalim gave a cry as he was knocked down by the beast, and then Geldirana gave an answering cry as she smashed through one of the stag's glistening horns with her mace. The creature roared and bucked, but Thalla fired several arrows into it, Ifferon stabbed it in the stomach, and Geldirana struck it in the head until it fell dead before them upon the bodies of its kin, until those fiery eyes no longer burned.

Before they even had time to catch their breath, the ground rumbled around them, as if another great stag was still kicking and bucking upon it.

The company regrouped, and Thúalim shook his head as he looked upon the remains around them. "So much waste," he said, clutching his chest. "I hope Rúathar did not see these things ere his death." Ifferon knew there was little hope of that.

"You are hurt," Thalla said to Thúalim, and she helped him up.

"My Beldarian is safe," Thúalim said.

"You are also hurt," Thalla said to Affon, who tried to hide the bruises on her arms.

"The medals of battle," Geldirana said. "We pin them to the flesh."

Thalla looked at her as though she could not believe her ears. She clearly had little experience with the Garigút. Though it had been many long years, all of this was very familiar to Ifferon. Yet now it seemed a little crueller, perhaps because he had grown older, but perhaps because it was his daughter that she now spoke of.

"I am fine," Affon said gruffly, and she tried to fold her arms, but bit her lip from the pain.

"This is no place for a child," Thúalim said.

"There are worse places," Geldirana replied. "I have been to some, even as a child. So they shaped me, and so I moulded them in turn. She will go where she pleases."

"You weren't of the same mind when it came to Théos," Thalla said.

"He was different," the Way-thane replied, and Ifferon noted the dissatisfaction in her tone at being challenged by Thalla.

"He was still a child."

"And look what became of that. He was where he should not have been, and so he died."

"And now he is alive again, with Corrias too. Perhaps he was meant to die," Thalla said.

"Perhaps we all are," Geldirana replied, and there was the subtle suggestion in her voice that she had the power to make it so.

"These creatures are new to me," Ifferon said. "Even the evil birds seemed tame compared to them."

"The Alar Molokrán of this moon has an affinity with nature," Geldirana said. "But I have never before seen anything quite like this. Too many beings will bend their ear to the shadow. Thankfully we are in the final week of this month, and so the Molokrán have retreated once more for the Passing of the High. We can be sure, however, that they will be out in force again when we are on the battlefield with Agon."

"And what is the power of the next Alar Molokrán?" Ifferon asked.

"Weather," the Way-thane replied. "He can control the winds and the rains, and so we will have many enemies in our war."

So they continued on, until the trees parted like retiring sentries, revealing a large rocky knoll that marked the border of Alimror with Telarym, and the western terminal of the Morbid Mountains, which looked more morbid than ever now that Agon had arisen.

The knoll reached up like a crooked finger, a broken digit of some ancient relative of the Moln. Its grey rock was even greyer than the faded land of Telarym, and perhaps it stood out so much because it sat against the black mountains of the Morbid range.

Upon this knobbly piece of rock, many metres high above the company, was the Black Eyrie, in which nested all manner of foul birds. Their intermingling species might have been commended as a show of brotherly acceptance were it not for the unbrotherly actions they so often enjoyed, against both each other and any other creature upon the earth. They lived on outcrops, where straw and twig was knitted together to cushion their young, and each outcrop gave way to the next like a series of awkward steps, leading up to the pinnacle, upon which the oversized black and red-feathered crows not only lived, but thrived and reigned supreme.

"So this is where they are," Thúalim said with

scorn.

"Defilers and deceivers," Geldirana said, and she matched his contempt.

Ifferon peered up to see if he could spot the Scroll dangling over the edge of one of the outcroppings, or nestled like an egg with some confused chicks. Had he not experienced the attack on the Mountain Fortress, where the birds bit and clawed, he might have felt some concern or compassion for them, but that was now replaced by a mounting rage, which compelled him to reclaim the relic they had stolen from him.

"So we climb," he said, and he began the ascent without awaiting their approval. He hauled himself up the wall, which had many round knobs, perhaps for future nests, but now for foot and hand. Affon quickly joined him and soon passed by him, nimbly scaling the rocky ladder. The others joined, Thúalim and Thalla straying to the rear, and Geldirana keeping alongside Ifferon. He was curious that she did not race ahead, as she might have done in her younger days, but stayed with him, as if to protect him as he went.

The climb was tiring, and Thalla complained of vertigo, but soon they all approached the summit and peeked over the first of the massive nests, which might house a hundred birds. This one was empty but for many broken eggs, some of which looked as though they had been forcibly torn apart long before the young inside were ready to face the world.

The wind whistled by, highlighting the uncanny lack of other noises. There were no flaps of wings, nor taps of beaks. There were no caws or screeches, nor cries or songs. Just the taunting wind and its unnerving whistle. It almost threatened to blow them off, almost asked them if they had wings.

Affon hoisted herself into the nest before Ifferon could pull her back, but there was no movement or noise in response, and so the others joined her there, from which vantage point they could see the next nest a metre or so up from the current one. It too looked abandoned. The wind whistled again.

"I thought you could track them," Ifferon whispered to Thúalim, and though he noticed a hint of disdain in his voice, he did not feel apologetic for it, for his desire to reclaim the Scroll of Mestalarin topped his thoughts and erased his emotions.

"I can, and I did," the Al-Ferian said. He seemed more confused than the others for the lack of activity in the Black Eyrie. They all knew well that many of the evil birds had survived the assault on the Mountain Fortress, and that this was their perfect resting place, a mountain fortress of their own. And the wind whistled.

Geldirana rummaged through the broken eggs for clues, and she found a dead chick amongst them, which looked as though it had been half eaten. From her estimates, it had been dead for days. Apart from that, and the feathers and droppings of other birds, there was little sign that this nest had been used.

Geldirana stood up, dropping broken egg fragments from her hand. "I do not like the feeling this gives me," she said. "Something is not quite right here."

None of the company answered her, for there was little to say, and their own fear was as much a gag to their mouths as a vice to their hearts. Yet the wind answered, and it whistled once more.

They climbed up further into the next nest, carefully edging around the grey tor to where the rock began to blacken, to the very part of the abode that earned it its name. The climb grew steeper here, and they wished they had wings, not merely to make the ascent, but for fear of the sheer and terrifying descent that was possible on a slight miscalculation of foot. They kept close to the central spike of rock, both for balance and support, and to hide behind as they peered around to see the third, equally abandoned, nest.

"So do we climb to find nothing at the top?" Thalla whispered, and she clung to the rock more than the others, and she dared not look down, not even in her imagination, in which the drop was even greater than it was in reality.

"I worry about what we might find," Thúalim said, voicing the opinion of them all.

"Yet still we have to look," Ifferon said, speaking another view they all reluctantly shared.

And so they continued up, climbing and clambering, and sometimes jumping across the growing gaps between each nest. In time they passed through a dozen more nests, all as deserted as the others, and came to the pinnacle, where the gigantic nest was filled with bones that stood out palely on the soot-coloured ground. There were many bones of all shapes and sizes, but no birds to gnaw them. Just the uneasy presence of the all-pervading wind.

Just as it seemed that naught would come of the company's climb, Affon spied a hidden crevice within one of the many oddly-shaped obsidian rocks that lined the place like tombstones. In this she found several unhatched eggs, and further in was the rolled up Scroll of Mestalarin, hiding its power like an egg hides the vulnerable young inside.

"It's here!" Affon cried, and her voice was so loud that many knew immediately that no good could come of it. The wind caught her voice and carried it high, and instead of its usual whistle, it gave a different response this time: the screech of a crow as it came in for the kill.

As Affon stretched her thin arm into the crevice, the huge black and red-feathered crow, which seemed even larger now than it did when it stole away with the Scroll from the open rooftop of the Mountain Fortress, swooped in and snatched her before she could snatch the parchment. She yelped as the talons caged her, and she screamed as they hauled her into the sky. Geldirana and Ifferon gave another cry, both in unison, the kind of cry the crow made when it saw the girl's mauling hand reach in towards its young. And then their voices were stolen, for the crow released its grip, and Affon slipped out and down, plummeting towards the edge of the Black Eyrie, and the edge where all who looked upon the scene knew she could not grasp, but would fall down to her death in the bleakness down below.

Ifferon's horror, which was like the endless lash of a thousand whips, stayed his mind, but his instinct spurred his feet. He raced to the edge, as if he might somehow extend the arm of Telm the Lighthand, and reach out further than the arm of a Man could reach, and grasp Affon's hand with the strength of a god. But he reached for nothing, and held nothing, and saw nothing. Even the girl's voice had faded out as she fell, stolen by the taunting wind with its mocking whistle.

A new horror nested in Ifferon's heart, and perhaps it nested also in the hearts of the others, but all he could think of was Affon falling, and his heart falling, as if leaping to save her. Suddenly he thought of Théos and that harrowing moment when all turned to madness, and that haunting moment when he saw Délin's will break, and those hounding moments when he thought the knight could never be whole again. And even more suddenly he felt all those emotions he had felt in empathy, but now he felt them truly, and felt that none could truly empathise.

But the hunter leaves no time for grief, and in those brief moments that felt endless to the company upon the Black Eyrie, the crow circled around and came back in again, like a black cloud streaked with the angry red of the vengeful gods of the sky. Its eyes were little comets of their own, burning with an intensity that seared all they looked upon. But Ifferon turned to it, and his eyes burned back. He stepped forth, and the sound of his foot striking the ground was like the foot of Telm upon the earth. He continued on, and the armour of that god began to form around him. As he passed the crevice, he reached inside and seized the Scroll as if it were the handle of the sword called Daradag.

All who looked upon the god emerging, and the crow descending, were stunned into silence, frozen to the spot as if they could do naught in the battle ahead. The crow crashed down just as Ifferon's Telm-armour formed fully around him, and the strike was like lightning, and the sound was like a thousand thunders. Feathers flew into the air like arrows, and light sparked violently from the impact. Ifferon was knocked back, and the crow came down upon him, but the force of the conflict sent both of them over the ravine, down to where Affon had fallen, as if the very Land of the Dead lay in that direction.

Geldirana raced to the edge, and just as she peered over, she was caught off guard, for the monstrous crow came back up, clawing and scratching. She unleashed her mace, and she swung at the feathered beast. Her blows would have crushed skulls and broken limbs, but they did little to harm or hinder the crow, which struck back with a crushing of its own. Geldirana was thrown back into a bed of shell shards, and she cried out as her back struck the ground, reminding her of her old wound.

All the while Thúalim was summoning a force of his own, and Thalla armed her bow, firing shot after shot, and discovering one disappointment after another, for the arrows bounced off the bird as if it were wearing armour. And so it was, in its own way, for its form had grown huge over these last few days since the attack on the Mountain Fortress, its body bulging beyond any natural mass, and once Thúalim called down a single bolt of lightning upon its head they discovered just how it had grown so large. The bolt forced a cry from the crow, and when it opened its beak some could see the bits of bones of other birds stuck in its mouth, and then they could see parts of its belly bulge as if some of its victims were still alive inside.

But there was no freedom to be had, for the crow reared up and flapped its wings violently, and the force caused a whirlwind there and then upon the Black Eyrie, sending both Thúalim and Thalla over the edge. They fell, despite clawing for a grip or hold, and they landed several metres down upon one of the many nest ledges around the monolith. As they struck the nest, sending twigs and egg fragments into the air around them, they saw Ifferon, still shimmering in the armour of Telm, and he leapt across from one nest to another with an agility they had never seen from him before. They struggled up, but he was already out of sight, returning to the arena where Geldirana now faced the crow alone.

Geldirana had barely struggled to her feet before the crow was upon her again. It snapped and pecked at her, and she narrowly dodged the sharp beak, but she never dodged the evil look of its eyes, which fixated upon her as if there was nothing else in the world. She swung her mace at it again, but it bounced off the feathers as if its body were a pillow, and Geldirana thought suddenly of the futility of this fight, and that she might die not to the Molokrán, but to this creature of the air that all the laws of Iraldas suggested should never be able to exist. But it existed, and it reminded her constantly of just how real it was, and that just as it had in some way been made, she could be unmade.

It stretched its wings out wide, knocking the mace from her hands, and the gust of air that came through sent her back to the familiar ground. The bird loomed tall above her, stepping forth, and in those moments she could see that between its feathers there were many bulbous sores, as if it were afflicted by some great and terrible disease. It looked at her and stepped forth, and there was menace in the step, and murder in the glare.

But before the crow could finish her, Ifferon leapt onto the pinnacle with a murderous glare of his own. "*Dehilasü baeos*," he shouted, and there was anger in his voice. "*Dehilasü baeos*," he cried again, and there was anger in his stride. The crow backed away, its looming presence diminished by the greater presence of Telm in the shimmering armour that surrounded Ifferon, and the glow of light that surrounded the Scroll.

He advanced upon the beast, and it retreated, but before it could take flight he seized it by the wings, and the touch was as Telm the Lighthand, and the crow cried out like Geldirana had cried, and like Affon had cried. It jumped up, trying to get airborne, but Ifferon pulled it down with a strength that was not his own, and yet one that formed the very essence of his blood. The crow snapped and bit and pecked and clawed, but just as Geldirana's mace struck at nothing, the bird's attacks were blocked by the glimmering armour of Telm. The light around the Scroll grew larger, shifting shape and form, until it seemed to Geldirana's eyes that it became a sword. Ifferon stabbed the creature with this, and it gave a terrible cry, and then its terror was no more.

Yet Ifferon continued to strike the beast even as it lay limp upon the ground. He tore feathers from its coat, and he bashed it with his fist and with the sword of light, until the armour around him collapsed and dissipated like water, and he found he was still bashing the bird with the rolled-up scroll, still striking it even as the ground beneath him quaked. He continued this for a time, shouting that same Telm-cry in the Aelora tongue, as if it were the most terrible of curses, until Geldirana came up behind him and grabbed him and held him, and they collapsed together, and he wept.

"It is dead," she told him, repeating what his eyes said. "It is gone."

Ifferon sobbed, for though this was a victory, the Scroll had been reclaimed at a price. "She is dead," he whimpered. "Just as I learn I have a daughter, she is taken from me."

Geldirana did not weep, even though a part of her heart tried to mock her with that weakness. She locked it away, imprisoned it, so that it could not imprison her. She knew well what grief could do, and she had seen what it had done to Délin, whom she tried to protect from a fate that was beyond all of them.

"There might be a time for sorrow," she said, "but not while Agon still threatens this world. You have an armour that none of us can match, but I would not have told you that Affon was your child if I had known it would become a weakness in you."

Ifferon shrugged off her embrace, for it felt at odds with her words. "Do you not feel?" he asked.

"I feel everything," she said. "More than you know. It is not courage to not know fear, but rather it is courage to know fear and face it anyway. It is not strength or resolve to not know the pain of parting, but rather to know that pain like a partner, and not let it destroy you."

"How can we go on when there is so much pain?"

"Because not going on is no absolution from that pain," she said. "It might feel like a prison to escape from, but letting it control you and hold you back is the real prison." She embraced him again, and he did not resist. "Ifferon," she said, more harshly than before. "I may die in the coming battles. In fact, it is likely I will die. Perhaps even you will die. Perhaps we all will. I have come to terms with that, because this is greater than all of us individually and all of us combined. We are not just battling evil—we are fighting for the very survival of good. Sometimes that means a sacrifice has to be made."

They sat together, shoulder to shoulder, for what felt like a lifetime, and it reminded them of the time they had spent together, a decade ago in what almost felt like another life. The threat of Agon was always there, but it was a distant one, and the dwindling bloodline of Telm had less meaning then than it did now. There was just Ifferon and Geldirana, and the happiness between them. There was no child, no daughter, no Affon. And as they sat together again these ten years on, with sadness between them— there was no child, no daughter, no Affon.

The tears fell from the ledges of Ifferon's eyes, to the ground where they could not be saved. Though he tried to stop them, they continued to fall, and though he could see little through the glisten, he could see that Geldirana's ears were not altogether dry.

"What kind of world is this?" Ifferon bellowed to the sky, as if beseeching what few gods still lived there, as powerless as the people of Iraldas. No answer came; more tears came instead.

"Tears are for cowards," a voice came suddenly, and they all turned in amazement to see that it was Affon. "Blood is for warriors. Blood for the Garigút!" She held up the remains of a large crow, whose neck had been slit. The blood left a trail behind it, from where she limped.

Ifferon and Geldirana jumped up and ran to the girl. The three of them hugged, though it was an awkward hug, made all the more awkward by Affon refusing to drop the dead bird.

"Hugs are for the weak," she said, shaking them off her.

"Some are for the strong," Geldirana said.

"He's not strong," Affon said, gesturing to Ifferon.

"Affon," Geldirana said. "He is your father."

Ifferon held his breath, waiting for some rebellion, some dismissal. He almost did not want to hear her response, did not want to be reminded of how much he had missed, of all the years he was never there.

"I know," Affon replied, and she smiled.

* * *

The Black Eyrie became their home that night, and all of them felt like Garigút, taking whatever dwelling they came across, feeling that little bit more barbaric in this bastion of blood. No birds returned there while they rested, warded off by the remains of their kin.

"We might not have vanquished Agon," Ifferon said, "but we have dealt him a grievous blow." He held up the Scroll of Mestalarin. "He will rue this moment when we reclaimed this relic."

The group cheered, in as much as they had energy for cheer, for many of them were more content with their survival than any possible damage they had done to Agon's mission. They rested briefly, and from that vantage point they looked at the jagged ridge of the Morbid Mountains, and further south-east into the heart of Telarym, where they could almost sense Agon struggling to get free.

Ifferon and Geldirana had the clearsight, but their vision did not stretch far enough, and so they could only ponder how things had gone for those who marched towards the Beast—and for the very Beast himself and his eternal struggle.

Deep in Telarym, where the sky was a new colour darker than black, and where the ground could no longer be seen in the bleak oppression of the night, there was a constant sound of battle and a constant wail of pain. Deep in Telarym, where Agon thrashed and flailed, as if the very air around him was an enemy, there was the sound of straining steel. Deep in Telarym, another chain broke.

VI

THE MARCH OF MANY

❧

Ifferon and his companions led the long march into the heart of Telarym, towards where the periodic quakes emanated from, towards where the air seemed to grow tight and tense, as if it could not bear to be breathed in and out by the ireful lungs of the Beast.

They followed the winding path of the Issar Chammas, which crossed from west Telarym before dropping into the sea in the east. The river was a constant companion to their left, and they never crossed it, and they never strayed too close to its deceptive edge, and yet at times it seemed that it strayed close to them, and at times it seemed that the path it led was changing, if ever so subtly.

A more reliable guide was their companions to their right: the Morbid Mountains. For all of the Issar Chammas' guile, like a skilful painter, this sentinel ridge was always blunt and obvious, carving its black silhouette into the canvas of the sky, with no grace or tact, and no deception. It almost seemed like a chasm into nothing, where the spectrum simply ended, and beyond which there were only the unseen colours of the dead. Behind those black tors were the snowy peaks of the White Mountains, and between them lay the Dead Land of Feloklin, a land of eternal grey. From there the grey seeped into every part of Telarym, sapping it of any colour, stealing it of any splendour.

The hours passed, until what little there was of day was lost in darkness, when the sky and the silhouette of the mountains became a unified mass. They continued to travel for a time, until even the stars went to sleep, and then they rested as best they could, knowing that two great barriers lay on either side of them, a ruin lay behind them, and death lay before them.

The next day brought less light than the one before, and the company blamed this on the ominous shadow of Tol-Úmari, which they fell under once again. It was here that they stumbled upon a pile of Al-Ferian bodies, upon which rested a lonely unlit lamp.

"Is this the army we just sent forth?" Thalla asked, disturbed by the sight.

"No," Thúalim said, though he was no less horrified.

Ifferon found markings in the ground not far from the bodies, where he theorised the acorns of the fallen Al-Ferian had been buried.

"This was one of the search parties we sent to find Théos," Thúalim said. "We sent out many. Few returned."

"I imagine the army that went ahead of us buried their acorns," Ifferon said.

"But what about their bodies?" Thalla asked.

"They do not honour their dead," Geldirana said.

Thúalim glared at her. "We honour them by

planting their acorns."

"In Telarym soil, there can be no such honour," the Way-thane said.

"Your Garigút did not bury them either," Thúalim said.

"It is not my people's responsibility to look after your dead."

"Let us hope you do not have to bury your own then," Thúalim replied, "for you shall toil alone."

"Not alone," Ifferon said.

Ifferon offered to bury the fallen, but Thúalim would not have them waste time on shells. "When the snail leaves behind his shell, he does not worry if it should crack or break."

"But would he worry that it might become the home of another?" Geldirana asked. "The Dead Land is near. There are many souls that lust for a new body."

They passed by Tol-Úmari, and day seemed a little fairer for a time, until the shadow of that tower was replaced by the shadow of the Peak of the Wolf, where the ethereal door to the Underworld stood open, and from which wafted a humid air, as if from the pyre of dead souls burning. They began to feel more than ever the presence of Agon, and they began to dread more than ever that they might look upon that door to Halés, but look upon it from the other side.

Though night was fast approaching, they did not tarry near the Peak, where Ifferon and Thalla remembered well the Felokar Wolves, and where Geldirana knew enough about the dead to not want to know that much more. So they continued to follow the Issar Chammas until the oppressive atmosphere of the Peak felt less intense. It was there that they camped for rest, in the open plains, where the eyes of all who might be watching was less a risk than the eyes of those few whom they knew to bear an evil glare.

They did not sleep soundly, however, for during Ifferon's watch he saw a glimmer on the horizon to the north, a line of shimmering light in the darkness. Initially he started from fright, where his mind jumped to the worst possible scenario, for often the reality he faced nowadays was even grimmer than in his imagination. But logic trumped fear, helped by the fact that it was a mass of light that was advancing towards them, not a mass of darkness.

"An ally, I hope," Thalla said, rubbing her eyes.

"More than one, I hope," Ifferon replied.

"Maybe it's more Garigút," Affon suggested. Ifferon looked to Geldirana, whose eyes told him clearly that there were too few Garigút left in the world.

They sat in the open for over an hour, staring into the distance, their minds racing as fast as the light raced towards them. In time it became clear that this was not some strange effect of the heavens, like the colourful lights in the snow-covered land of Caelün. It was an army advancing, and by the sound of the stampede, they were on horseback, and they were numerous.

Ifferon almost dozed off by the time they arrived, but the noise became so tumultuous as they pounded over the final ridge that he was dragged back awake, his eyes wide and alert. Then he saw a sight that warmed his heart: at least a hundred Knights of Issarí, led by Délin De'Marius, all on horseback, all in armour, and all bearing weapons and banners in their hands—and a grim determination on their faces. Though they had just crossed the Issar Chammas, all of them looked untroubled, for they had all ridden out knowing that death might be their destination.

The army drew to a halt just before Ifferon and Thalla, sending a spray of dust into the air where the hooves stopped suddenly in the dirt. The horses neighed and whinnied, and some reared and bucked, and many bore the same look of determination as their riders.

Délin rode at the front, tall and broad, and he looked like he did when Ifferon first encountered him in Alimstal Forest, when he knew him only as Trueblade, and when the most immediate threat was the wild Bull-men, not the emergence of Agon and the advancement of his armies.

"The skirmishes are over," Délin said, his voice muffled by his helmet. "Now it is time for war."

Délin dismounted and greeted his companions. He seemed more expeditious and serious than ever, with little time for pleasantries. He appeared ready at any moment to face battle, and often he cut their conversations short to consult with Brégest or another of the knights' tacticians.

Yet despite this abruptness, which set Ifferon on edge, Délin called him aside and placed both his gauntleted hands upon the cleric's shoulders. He had removed his helmet, and he seemed for a moment less daunting.

"I have brought a gift," Délin said. He stepped aside, revealing a wooden crate that had been unloaded from the horses. The lid had been loosened, but its contents were still shrouded.

"Open it," Brégest said, and all the knights looked eagerly to Ifferon as he approached the box. He pushed the lid aside, and from the darkness came a sheen and sparkle. Before him lay a suit of silver armour, more beautiful than any he had ever seen. He held up the breastplate, which carried the emblem of a quill in the centre, like the one he wore on his sash in the Order of Olagh. He almost wept as the moonlight shone upon it, revealing its careful craftwork.

"War is no place for a cleric," Délin said, smiling. "But it is the place for a warrior, a soldier."

Ifferon could not muster any words of response. It seemed to him through the glisten of his eyes that the armour had even been inscribed with the Last Words about the waist, neck, and arms, and that there were many emblems of the gods, many crests and sigils, and many symbols he did not even recognise, but could not help but find beautiful and moving.

"It was worn by another knight, many years ago," Délin said, "though we have added some … embellishments. It looked to me your size, though we have few knights as tall and thin as you, and had not the time to set the smithy working."

"It is perfect," Ifferon said.

Délin placed his gauntleted hand upon Ifferon's shoulder. "So then, friend, is it time to arm for war? The heavier the burden, the heavier the armour."

He looked at Geldirana, who was studying him with her eyes. He remembered her words. *I could not fathom how this man I once loved, who was strong and full of adventure, had tamed so much, and given up his armour for a frock.* Now it was time to give up his frock, and to don his armour once again.

The knights unpacked many of their things and set up several pavilions. This would be their new base of operations, their new home away from the Motherland of Arlin. They did not bring much, for their horses were already weighed down by armoured knights, but they brought enough to remind them of their homes and their families—and what they were fighting for.

The largest pavilion was set up for Délin, but before he would enter he invited Ifferon to try out his new attire, the sight of which the knight said was worth more than shelter in these lands. So Ifferon went behind the curtained door, and two squires helped him with the many pieces of his armour, and he realised then why Délin never removed his armour, for it was almost like a puzzle to put together, and so perhaps, he hoped, it would be a puzzle to any searching blades hoping to find an opening to his vulnerable flesh beneath.

When Ifferon emerged from the tent, few recognised him. The thin, tall man with the shaved head and sour face, had become a sentinel of steel, an armoured knight who could have blended in with any of those around him. The metal plates made him seem broader, and while he lacked the mass and strength of knights like Délin, he looked to some quite formidable.

"Who goes there?" Délin jested. "And what have you done with our dear cleric?"

The knights laughed and cheered. "For Issarí! For Corrias!"

Ifferon pushed up the visor of his helmet. "Hopefully Agon does not recognise me."

Délin smiled. "I think he is in for a surprise."

Ifferon was as surprised as many others when Elithéa appeared from one of the pavilions, attired in the finest armour of a knight. Though it was beautiful upon her, she walked awkwardly, losing almost all of the grace that she normally had. She stumbled over to them and grunted from inside the visor of her helmet.

"It doesn't suit you," Thalla said.

Elithéa pushed up the visor aggressively. "Perhaps it would suit you more," she said. "It is, after all, as much a cage as a costume, and perhaps it fits some better than others."

"Yet you're the one wearing it," Thalla responded.

"Perhaps the knights care more about my survival than yours," the Ferian said. "Ack! I can barely move," she added, and she seemed to be struggling within the suit of armour. "How can you stand this?"

"Comfort is our last concern," Délin said. "Yet the sword is less comfortable when embedded in you."

"So then dodge the sword instead of parrying it with your body," Elithéa said.

"Not all of us have your reflexes," Délin replied.

Elithéa shifted again, until it seemed that she

was actually fighting with the garb she wore, where she could not dodge its icy touch or awkward edges. Finally she stopped still and looked to the others with frustration in her eyes.

"No, this will not do," she said. "I will never understand Man and why he tries to suffocate his form with these metal housings. This is not the garb for me."

She began to walk off, and her words were echoed in her floundering stride.

"Don't let the clothes defeat you," Thalla called to her.

Elithéa glared at her as she retreated back to the pavilion, bashing the curtain open.

"You have been hanging around Elithéa too long," Ifferon said.

Thalla smiled. "I guess I have."

When the Ferian returned, she was not only back in her familiar attire, which looked lighter than ever, but she carried several wooden staves and a large knife. "It is time for a new *thalgarth*," she said, and she began carving immediately, refusing rest or refreshment. She toiled even into the small hours of the night, when many turned to their makeshift beds and their uneasy dreams.

Ifferon awoke suddenly in the dead of night, and he must have given a cry, for the eyes of several guards were upon him. He turned to find Délin was sitting up, his helmet placed down beside him.

"Did I wake you?" Ifferon asked.

"Yes," Délin said. "You still talk in your sleep."

"Maybe I am just the party's rooster," Ifferon said. "We all need a morning call."

Délin smiled. "There are many hours left until morning. How is it that the days most in need of rest are always preceded by the nights most restless?"

"Some ancient law, perhaps," Ifferon said. "I do not think I was having much of a good sleep either. Sometimes it is better to stay awake than toss and turn in dream."

"Are you ready for what will come?" Délin asked him.

"Honestly, I do not know," Ifferon said. "We are so close to Agon now that I can almost feel him, can almost remember Telm's battles with him as if they were my own. But it is easier to study the tales of ancient wars than to fight in new ones. The page bleeds with ink, not blood."

"Few bleed with the blood of Telm," Délin said.

"I am not sure it will do much good if I am bleeding," Ifferon replied.

Délin looked as though he was brooding upon a troubling thought, and he took his time to reveal it to Ifferon. "If it comes to it ... will you die like Telm did?"

"I think that is more in Agon's hands than my own," Ifferon said. "I do not like to think of it, and I am not sure if I could ever be a willing sacrifice. Maybe I am still a coward at heart."

"A coward would not be here, having uneasy dreams on the eve of battle," Délin said. "A coward would be sleeping sound in a land far away, like so many kings and queens, so many lords and ladies. Yet we fight the real nightmares of the world, that others might sleep safely. So we are always making small sacrifices in the name of good."

Their conversation died down, leaving behind the stillness of the dark, where the only sound was the flickering of a few failing fires and the whittling of wood as Elithéa continued to craft into the deepest stretches of the night.

Day did not dawn before all were roused by the watchmen, who spied the advance of the enemy from the south. Some glanced with sleep-clogged eyes to see if they could judge the numbers, while others like Délin began to issue a rapid series of orders, like arrows from a bow.

Ifferon looked to the south, and he saw a darkness approaching, a darkness dappled with a flicker of many lights, as if the night sky had fallen to the earth and was now rolling towards them. Yet Ifferon wished it was the darkness of the night, for this, he knew, was worse. From the north an army of knights had emerged, but from the south came a different army, with a different purpose.

When finally the dark mass drew close enough that it no longer blended into a single unit, Ifferon could hardly believe his eyes, for the Dark Men must have numbered in their thousands, swarming the land like a black river that had broken its banks. Further still in the distance Ifferon thought he could see more black shapes, and he wondered if they were just the trees or the mountains, or if they were more Nahamoni—or if they were something else, something worse.

Délin was already on horseback, as were many of the other knights. His horse now bore a blue caparison with white frills and small white sword emblems dotted throughout. It also bore a large metal champron to protect its head, with a ridged crest adorned with three miniature swords, like the crown of a king. Ifferon was so entranced by the design that he barely noticed that Trueblade also wore this same design on his helmet, which was more ornate than the one he had worn before. His cloak also matched the caparison, and it blew in sympathy with the many banners the Standard-bearers held.

Though many of the knights wore helmets that hid their faces, Ifferon could almost see their stern eyes peering through the steel. He could certainly see the looks upon the horses' faces, as if the Nahamoni were the Gormoloks or their kin, and their glares were stern enough for both horse and rider.

Brégest pulled up close with a second horse in tow, covered in elaborate barding and a white caparison. "This is no time for hiking," he said, handing the reins to Ifferon. "You do know how to ride, I presume."

Ifferon nodded, but he was not so sure. It had been many years since he had ridden a horse of his own, and though he thought he might never forget, there was always the thick of battle to challenge his memory. He tried to climb up on his horse, but he struggled, for his new armour was heavy, and he had barely grown accustomed to standing still in it, let alone riding a horse into battle.

Thalla drew up on horseback, and she looked

like a natural. Ifferon could almost imagine her and Yavün riding through the fields on a summer's day. Yet he knew it was likely Herr'Don who had given her these lessons, and regretted giving her anything at all.

Geldirana and Affon rode upon the same horse, but Elithéa refused to force any animal to bear her weight, and she made sure to deride all of those who did, especially the knights with their heavy armour. Thúalim joined her on foot, though he said nothing to explain his decision.

"Leave the fight to us," Délin said, which did not go down well with many. "Protect Ifferon and you will be doing a greater service than our swords and lances will."

"I'll protect him by killing the enemy," Affon said.

"Why bring her here?" Délin asked Geldirana.

She almost slew him with her eyes. "I seem to recall that you brought an even younger child to my battlefield at Nahragor. Here now, I return the favour on your front line, and she has earned her right to be here more than most, and will slay more tonight than your boy will slay in his entire life."

Délin glowered back, but said nothing. He turned back to his knights and signalled for them to line up in formation. In moments they were assembled into a wedge. There they waited, like the tip of an arrow drawn tight inside a bow.

In time the Nahamoni drew close enough that their grizzled features became clear, and Ifferon almost wished for them to become a single mass of shapeless darkness once again to avoid seeing their scarred faces, and to avoid being scarred by their evil glares. They shouted and taunted, and they waved their weapons madly in the air, as if the sky were their enemy.

At the head of the regiments of Nahamoni marched two giant men, twice the height of the others, twice the width, and from the looks of them, many times the ferocity. One was completely covered in ink markings, and he was bald. The other bore no markings, but instead had many scars on his pale body. Otherwise they were of similar build and appearance, and to some they might have even seemed like twins. These were the Nahamoni leaders, their generals, and they were here to lead their armies to war.

Délin raised his sword, and the flags were waved and the horns were sounded. And so the knights began to trot out towards the advancing army, gaining speed with every step.

"For Corrias! For Issarí!" the knights cried in chorus.

Despite Ifferon's pleas, Geldirana and Affon led their horse out to flank the enemy, with a volume of weapons to match a number of knights.

"Blood for the Garigút!" Affon cried alone.

The battle was a bloodbath, and though it started with the colours of many banners, it ended with the colour red. The knights did not wait for the enemy to make its move, but began their charge from horseback, drowning out the beats of their horses' hooves with a chorus of horn cries that rent the earns of all who heard them. Lances were thrust forth, blades were swung low, and the armies clashed like a clap of thunder from the angry sky.

The initial force of the knights' charge crushed the first ranks of the enemy, and those who ran towards the stampeding horses went down quicker than those who dug in deep with spears, which snapped like the bones of their bearers. Chaos rode a horse of its own, and it was called Panic, and he drove down those who were not killed by the knights.

Geldirana and Affon were espied here and there, mowing down small battalions as if they were solitary soldiers. Only two sat upon that one horse, and yet it seemed that there were the hands of many, waving with flail, striking with mace, and slicing with sword.

Though Ifferon hung back with many of the others, he could not escape the battle, for arrows began to fly in all directions, many into the sky, as if aimed at Althar, and many towards the pavilions, where no doubt the enemy deemed the knights were housing their generals and other important officers. Yet this was not the case, for Délin led the charge, and he bore down upon those archers more than others, greeting their dishonour with his sword.

But the mass of the enemy was too much, and even as the knights wheeled around to give themselves new speed, the Nahamoni numbers swelled, until it seemed that none of them had fallen at all. The knights charged again, but this time the horns were fewer, and this signalled to the ears and hearts of all more than the sight of their dwindling numbers could. So the ranks of the knights grew thin, while the Nahamoni replaced all of their dead with a steady stream of reinforcements.

Ifferon and his companions were about to dive into the fray when Délin led the remainder of the knights back to the pavilions, exhausted and defeated. Less than two dozen remained, while at least a thousand of the enemy still stood, emboldened by the blood of their comrades.

Délin dismounted harshly and cast off his helmet. "They are too many," he said, and he took a gulp of water from his flask. "All of Nahlin must be emptied to make such a host. Would that I had the numbers that Boror has to fight them."

"Can we retreat?" Ifferon asked, and even as he spoke Geldirana and Affon returned, for they were almost toppled from their horse. "Can we retreat?" Ifferon repeated.

"No," Brégest said. "We have been surrounded, and we have too few horses left to break their ranks, or bear away our forces."

"Can we at least get Ifferon out?" Délin quizzed.

"Not without heavy losses."

"We may need to make that sacrifice," Délin said, "to stave off greater losses."

But the opportunity to flee was slain like a charging knight, for the enemy drew in closer, and the knights could see that their ranks were too many to pierce, even if they threw all of their might against one point.

"So favour flees instead of us," Délin said. "We cannot meet this force with strength."

"I will not surrender," Elithéa said. "I would rather die."

"They might be most obliging," Thalla said.

"I can blind some with a spell," Thúalim said, "but not all of them, and not enough to change our fortune."

"Then we must buy time," Délin said. "We must pay with our pride."

Brégest must have known what this meant more than the others, for he immediately protested against it. "We cannot do that, Trueblade. Honour demands we fight until the end."

"And now is not the end," Délin said. "Let us save the fight until then."

"Even if we wave the white flag, how do we know they will stop waving the red one?" Ifferon asked.

"All now is a gamble," Délin said. "And we bet our lives."

So the Chief Standard-bearer Ergrid conducted his most humiliating duty: replacing the flag of Arlin and the banner of the Knights of Issarí with the white rag of acquiescence, the cloth of capitulation. In all the long history of the Knights, they were rarely forced to raise this flag in place of their own, and those few who still lived felt a devastation beyond death.

"Our prides can take this hurt," Délin said, "if it will give us time to defeat Agon."

"How can we fight the Beast when we too are in bonds?" Brégest pleaded.

"Some will come," Trueblade said.

"What if they do not?"

"Have faith, friend, if not in them, then in me."

Nervous glances were exchanged, and Ifferon

could see in their eyes that they had never before questioned Délin like they did now. Even Ifferon could not see how any would march to their rescue, when so few had marched to war.

An answering flag was waved by the Nahamoni, but this one was black, and it did not mean surrender, but instead was a summons to discuss their terms. Délin and Brégest rode out to meet the two giant generals, who stood gloating in their victory.

"Don't say the knights don't have wisdom," the pale giant said. "You know when you've been beat."

"Our terms—" Délin began, but he was cut short.

"You ain't got no terms," the dark giant interrupted. "Surrender or die are your options."

"You must abide by the laws of war," Délin said.

"And whose laws are those?" the giant asked.

"They belong to all of us."

"And who's gonna enforce 'em?"

"There are places worse than Halés," the knight replied, "for those who break the codes of battle. There is space with the Elad Éni in the Void."

The Nahamoni were a superstitious people, and the mention of the Elad Éni had a clear effect upon the giants, for they looked nervously to one another, before returning their hardened gazes to the knight.

"We're the most obligin' hosts," the pale giant said with a grin, and he extended his arm as if inviting them into his parlour.

"We'll treat you just right," the dark giant said, and his grin was more menacing.

"Our surrender is on the condition that none of our people are killed," Délin said.

"If you don't surrender, all of 'em will be killed," the dark giant said, and it seemed that he almost hoped the knights would lower their white flag.

"Perhaps we are of more use alive than dead," Délin said.

The giants looked to one another and mumbled something about the Slave-lands and a "slave bounty," which seemed to capture the greed in their hearts, which revealed its nature in their glimmering eyes.

"Right then," the pale giant said. "Let's have your wrists."

Délin held his arms up. "When you shackle me, it will seal our contract, and both our fates."

This unnerved the pale giant more than the other, for he turned the manacles over to his twin, who glowered at Délin before fastening them about his wrists. Brégest followed, and he looked at Délin and shook his head. Délin could almost feel the shaking heads of the others further behind him, and it felt worse than the steel around his wrists.

VII

PRISONERS OF WAR

❧

It did not take long to round up the survivors and put them in chains, but not all of them went willingly. Elithéa fought off her assailants fiercely, perhaps because she did not want to be so soon returned to a cage, and she battered many of them with the staves of her newly-crafted *thalgarth*. It took several dozen to eventually restrain her.

Geldirana might have done even more damage, but she gave up willingly, and Ifferon could see in her eyes that it took great restraint on her part to let her hands and feet be bound. Affon had no such restraint, for she bit the hands of any who grabbed her, and she only quietened when Geldirana gave her an admonishing glare.

Thúalim caused an even greater stir, for every time they manacled his wrists, he would appear moments later in total freedom, with no sign that he had ever been shackled. So they began to fasten his ankles also, but this only made the insult more wounding than before. Délin tried to urge the Al-Ferian to simply give in and save his tricks for later, but the memory of the loss of Rúathar and so many of his people at the Mountain Fortress made Thúalim defiant. So he taunted his jailers with his freedom, until finally the dark giant seized him.

"Escape this," he said, and he plunged a dagger into the Magus' chest. Thúalim collapsed upon the ground, where his blood mingled with the blood of others, and where suddenly all eyes could see the many shackles he had previously escaped from.

The knights cried out, and some of them began to kick their jailers in protest. They stopped only when the Nahamoni began to issue lashes from their whips.

"You have no honour!" Délin shouted. "May the Void have you!"

"That conjuror conjured his own end," the pale giant said. "Do as we say and you'll live long enough to die in Nahlin."

Thalla managed to escape in the commotion, hiding amidst the many large boulders and dead bodies that were strewn across the plains. The stench was horrific, and it seemed to forever linger in the prison of her nostrils, but Thalla felt that anything was better than being locked inside a cage.

I have to do something, Thalla thought. She peered out from behind the large rock she hid behind in the flurry. Her breathing had barely returned to normal from when the battle begun, and though part of her wanted to race out and confront the enemy, another part wanted to stay where she was and avoid joining those knights who had been captured—or those knights who had been killed.

She saw Délin, bruised and beaten, but she could not see Ifferon amidst the rows of armoured bodies. She could barely tell who was alive, who was unconscious, or who was a difficult meal for the carrion circling high above.

She ducked behind the boulder again, her back against the rock. She began to wonder what kind of spells she might cast, and she began to consider the possibility of lighting every candle in her mind, and sending a blaze of fire into the armies around them, even though she knew that she would die in the process. At least she would go out fighting. At least she would take many Nahamoni with her when the fires went out.

She peeped out again, and just as she was about to race out to the armies, and to her doom, she caught a glimpse of something flickering on the ground several metres to her left. She thought it was a shard of steel from a weapon cast aside in battle, but her gaze was drawn by it like a fish is drawn in from a lake. There, almost in arm's reach, was a Beldarian. There, almost within her grasp, was the Soul Pendant of Thúalim, whose body lay mangled a few feet further on.

She hid behind the rock again and began to ponder. The Beldarian was clearly still intact, and so she knew that Thúalim could not yet go to his final rest. So she should destroy it, to free him from his prison. And yet it was the key to her own prison, dangled before her while the jailer turned his back. The warden was called fortune, and when it turned its smile away from someone else, it turned its smile upon her.

I do this for them, for my friends and comrades, she thought, but she knew it was not wholly true, and she wondered why she felt the need to lie to herself, when her conscience could not be silenced. Yet it could be shackled; it could be held back long enough that the voice of doubt might be replaced by a voice of regret.

So she reached out her arm from behind the rock, like a fishing rod of her own, and she fished in the dirt as the Nahamoni continued their interrogations only metres away. But her arm could not reach, and so she was forced to stretch out further, her chest pushed flat against the ground, until she almost felt the scouting eyes of the Dark Men around her. She extended her hand again, and this time her fingers grazed the chain, but they did not grasp it. She breathed in dust, and she felt she needed to cough to clear her lungs, but she fought the urge as she felt the wandering eyes draw closer to her. Then she caught the chain with her index finger and dragged it slowly towards her as she pulled herself back behind the rock. She pulled it out of view just in time, for a guard walked past and peered into the distance, as if he had noticed something.

Thalla looked at the Beldarian. It was beautiful, even if it was not her own. And it was powerful, even if its master was dead. This was the last hurdle for her conscience, for it was always possible to break the *beldar* gem or throw it back, to save Thúalim the pain of waiting, knowing he already had the pain of living, and the pain of death. But the fire in her yearned for release, and she felt she could not restrain it for much longer. So she placed the chain around her neck and felt the cool touch of the Beldarian upon her chest.

The cold tempered her flame, and in moments she felt a part of her merge with the pendant, where it became shielded from the danger of magic.

So it was too late for Thúalim. And it was just beginning for Thalla De'Hataramon, who felt as though she could set the world alight—and live to feel the embers.

Thúalim awoke in Halés, where he lay upon the steps that led up into the Halls. He groaned as he turned around, and he saw the boots and robe of someone he thought he recognised.

"Not much luck for the Ardúnari, it seems, no," Melgalés said. "Not much luck at all."

Melgalés extended his hand and pulled Thúalim to his feet, and Thúalim felt an odd sensation, as if instead of him moving, the world around him moved. When his head settled enough that he could look around him, noting that he was alone with Melgalés, he said: "Maybe it is just us Magi that are so unfortunate."

"If you mean because we are dead, then no. I have seen some other Magi pass through here. For me, there is a reason I sit on the doorstep."

Thúalim nodded his head. "Then that is why I am here also."

"But who is the thief this time?" a haunting voice said.

"The Gatekeeper," Melgalés commented. "The voice, I mean, not the thief."

"And of the thief?" the Gatekeeper asked.

"A girl," Thúalim said. "I do not know her."

"I do," Melgalés said. "She was my apprentice."

"You always were the odd one," Thúalim said.

"I'll take that as a compliment," Melgalés replied. "Yes, *quite a compliment.*"

Thúalim sat down with a sigh. "I have failed my people. Rúathar was a better leader than I."

"He died too," Melgalés said. "Death is not failure."

"He led the Molokrán away. He achieved something with his death. I have not."

"Who knows what you have achieved," Melgalés said, "or what you have set in motion." He toyed with the beads in his hair, and his mouth moved as he did so, as if he were counting them. Thúalim knew this was not a tool of augury used by the Magi, but something unique to Melgalés.

"So we wait," Thúalim said. "I wish we could do something. They will rot in the cells of Nahlin."

Melgalés stood up. "No," he said sternly. "There is something I can do." He whistled, and the sound echoed out like the cries of many lost souls. Then from the shadows emerged many Felokar wolves. Thúalim flinched, but Melgalés placed his hand upon his back. "These are allies," he said. "Yes, new allies."

"Your pets?" Thúalim asked.

"Of sorts, yes."

And so the Magus spoke to the wolves in their tongue, using again their names to order them to do his will. And he willed them out into the wild, out past Echarin the Unsleeping, out through the door of Halés, out into the Dead Land, and out into Telarym, where an army of Nahamoni rested and feasted—

where an army was about to become a feast.

In the pavilion field, which was now their prison camp, the knights continued to endure interrogation. The Nahamoni seemed to enjoy this more than battle, for they cheered and celebrated as a knight was dragged off, or flailed and beaten.

The dark giant barged through, knocking aside many of the smaller Nahamoni. "Now, you lags, tell us who you are," he barked, wiping the spittle from his mouth.

Délin looked defiantly at the man. "I might have told the jailer," he said sternly, "but not the murderer."

The giant raised his monstrous fist to the knight. "We've a saying. *The brash get a bash.*"

"A bit of a motto," the pale giant said, drawing close to flick his tongue at Délin.

"You are the master and we are the guests," Délin said in his most feigned dignified voice. "It is customary to introduce yourself first."

"Is it now?" the pale giant said, sitting down. "Whose customs is that?"

"Everyone's," the knight replied. "Even yours."

"Right then," the pale giant said, licking his lips. "Mustn't forget me manners. I had a proper name once, but now I'm known as Shackles."

Délin held up his bonds and rattled the chains. "I wonder why," he said.

"He's a funny one," Shackles replied.

The other giant pounded over, stooping down to glare directly into Délin's eyes. His stare was almost demonic, and almost entrancing. "I've no time for funny ones," he hissed.

"And who might you be?" Délin asked.

"He's Irons," Shackles said.

"Fed up with you knights is who I am," Irons said in that same low hiss, as if his tongue were a snake.

"Kill us and be done with it!" Elithéa shouted.

"Not quite what I had in mind," Délin said.

"Don't worry, love," Shackles said, and his voice was sickeningly sweet. "We'll kill you all in time. For now, you're our prisoners."

"Tell us who you are," Irons shouted, and he raised a red hot poker to their faces. "Or tell this."

"Surely our banners say enough," Délin said. "Why carry flags if they do not announce us?"

"We know you well enough, *Trueblade*," Shackles said, "even if you're wearing your father's armour."

"Then why wonder who we are?"

"Because last we heard, you were with a certain cleric. The kind of cleric who carries around a certain Scroll."

Ifferon grew suddenly more nervous than he was before, and he was glad to be wearing a helmet to hide the sweat upon his brow, and disguise his worry. He was also glad that instead of hiding the Scroll in the pocket of his habit, it was firmly hidden behind his right greave. He was thankful for his fortune, and yet he feared that fate might balance such kindness with some other cruelty.

"Do we look like clerics?" Elithéa barked.

"You look like a Ferian woman," Shackles said.

"We've allowed women into our ranks before," Délin said. "For one who professes to know so much about us, you are ignorant of many things."

"Are we now?"

"That is … Anrin," Délin said, nodding towards Elithéa. "She has served us well."

"I bet she has," Shackles said, and he sniggered and drooled.

"And this one," Irons said, pointing to Affon. "Is she another of your whores?"

Ifferon bit his lip to curb his retort, and he could see that Geldirana was doing the same. Affon snapped at Irons' finger as he pointed to her, and he looked as though at any moment he would seize and crush her.

Délin was clearly struggling to find an explanation for her presence. "She's a—"

"I'm a warrior," Affon interrupted. "Cut my ropes and give me a fair fight. I'll cut your neck!"

The Nahamoni laughed derisively. "A big mouth for such a little thing," Irons said.

Affon began to respond, but Geldirana elbowed her harshly. The girl scowled at her mother before turning the scowl upon the giants.

"There's little here to find," Délin said.

"I'll be the judge of that," Irons replied. He thundered through, eyeing each of them in turn, stopping here and there to prod one of the knights. He passed Ifferon by completely, but his interrogation of the others offered the cleric little relief. For a moment Ifferon felt like uttering his name, that his companions might be spared, but Délin gave him a stern look, and he knew that it would be folly.

In time the dark giant made a full circle of all in chains, returning to Délin, where Shackles stood guard. The knight had repositioned himself, laying on his side, and this brought suspicion into the eyes of his jailers.

"Why are you lying like that?" Shackles asked.

"It is an injury," Délin said, but it did not look like they were falling for it.

Irons turned him over, exposing an ornate satchel.

"What's this?" Irons said, snatching the satchel from Délin's waist. Délin sighed as the giant emptied the contents onto the ground and backed away. There before them lay the Perasalon fragments of the broken Ferhassan used in the ritual to bring back Corrias and Théos, and it was clear that neither Shackles nor Irons liked the look of them.

"You," Shackles said to the nearest of his forces. "Get those out of here."

"It was a gift," Délin said as they took them away. "A gift for Agon."

He regretted the comment, for Irons smacked him across the face with his boulder-like hand, knocking a splatter of blood from his nose.

"Maybe Agon will get a different gift," Irons said. "You'll do nicely."

Few of the prisoners slept that night, even though exhaustion came upon them like the lashes of their jailers. They heard the Nahamoni talk of splitting into three forces, one to bring the prisoners to the Slavelands, one to attack Boror, and one to guard Agon as he toiled against his chains. The pavilions were taken over, housing the giants and other generals of the

Dark Men, who seemed to grow more awake as the night drew on.

Ifferon tossed and turned in his uneasy sleep, made all the more uneasy by the bonds that bit into his wrists and ankles. He dreamed evil dreams, where he was chained in place of Agon in the Underworld, and he felt the pain and torment of the Beast, and he felt an anger and a deep desire to end it all, that he might be free of the torment.

But it did not end, and instead of freedom he found that the chains grew tighter, and the more he struggled, the less he could move, until it even felt as though he could not speak. He tried to cry aloud, but his tongue was curbed, his voice entrapped.

Something evil slithered into his thoughts, forming in the darkness where he struggled. He could not see it, but he could feel its overpowering presence, and it held him in place more than any manacle could.

"Tell me your name," it said, and he felt his voice suddenly free to speak, and he cried the answer aloud, as high as he could, as if his very name might free him from his confines. And so it did, for he awoke.

But he was not free from his bonds. Lumbering over him were Shackles and Irons, and both bore smiles that unnerved him, and told him that he had betrayed himself, that he had spoken aloud his name in his sleep.

"Ifferon," they said together, and their smiles widened, and their hands seized him.

VIII

THE VISAGE

Ifferon was snatched by the Nahamoni giants like a child might seize a rag doll, and though he now wore armour, their clutch was tight, crushing him within the metal suit. He considered invoking the armour of Telm and fighting his captors, but he thought better of it, for that would confirm to them what they could never be entirely certain of: that he was Ifferon, that he was a Child of Telm.

There was a clamour all around him as he was dragged away, for many of the knights were awake, and it seemed that Délin had not given in to sleep at all. They shouted and struggled in their bonds, and some kicked at Shackles and Irons as they passed, and others called out in hopes that a distraction might provide some opportunity for rescue. But no one came, and nothing came of their efforts except exhaustion.

Ifferon was hauled into a ragged tent, where he was thrown down before the feet of another Naha-mon. This one was unlike all the others, for though he was grim, there was an elegance about him that made him seem much higher up the chain, and much more dangerous. He wore a mix of metal and robes, and they were oddly positioned, for the cloth hung in the more vulnerable parts, while the metal seemed merely ornamental. Even the metal mask he wore seemed more for show than for protection, but it was effective, for its iron glare was almost hypnotic, and very frightening.

"This is the one," Irons said.

"We got 'im," Shackles added with a grin.

The masked man did not respond, and since Ifferon could not see any flicker in his eyes, or any twitch of his mouth, it seemed that he made no reaction at all. Even his body was still like a statue, and this was unsettling.

Despite the silence, the giants seemed to catch onto something, and they looked at one another, and they seemed suddenly on edge, as if some portent had been read. Within moments they left the tent, leaving behind their lingering foul odour, and the painful marks on Ifferon's arms through the dented armour.

Ifferon clambered to his knees and looked up at the masked man, if indeed he was a man at all and not just an ornamental suit of armour. Yet there was a presence there, the kind of oppressing feeling of sentience that Ifferon had felt in the dream that had given him away. The more he looked into the blank, expressionless eyes of the metal face, the more he felt like his mind was being probed, like a spell of sway was being cast upon him.

To break the trance, Ifferon spoke aloud: "Who are you?"

There was no response, and yet Ifferon felt as though this was the question being levelled at him, the one that no longer needed an answer.

The silence was like torture, so Ifferon spoke again: "I don't know why you think—"

"Telm is dead and his children are all dying," the masked man spoke suddenly, and the voice was muffled, but it echoed in the mask, giving it greater resonance, enhancing the distressing presence.

Ifferon did not know how to respond, and yet he was sure that he gave away many secrets with his eyes. He fought against the urge to glance towards his shin, where the Scroll lay hidden.

"What do you want?" he asked eventually.

"I am known as the Visage," the masked man said.

"So that is your name?"

"I am known as the Visage," the Nahamon repeated again, as if he did not have a name, just a title, and just a job to do.

"What do you do?" Ifferon asked.

"The Visage extracts truths from liars," he said. The brevity of the statement was like the brevity of the guillotine, and yet Ifferon got the feeling that the Visage's work was not quick, but painfully slow.

Ifferon tried to hide his fear, like he had tried at Larksong during Teron's interrogation, but just like it was not easy then, it was not easy now. Even more was at stake, not least of all his very life, and the manner in which he might pass on.

"The Visage uses many tools," the masked man said, and he began to circle Ifferon, highlighting as he went the various metal prongs and pincers, blades and other objects of butchery that lined a series of tables around him.

"I am not afraid of you," Ifferon said, but he knew the tremor in his voice betrayed him as much as his talking in his sleep did.

"The captive has some tools of his own," the Visage continued, as if he was not even aware that Ifferon had spoken at all. "The first is the mind, which allows good sense, and so the captive might use this tool to halt the use of the others. The second is the mouth, which allows the mind to speak the good sense that it has mustered, and so provide what might otherwise be extracted."

Ifferon gulped and shuddered.

"Are you willing to die?" the Visage asked.

Ifferon knew he was not, and yet he knew even deeper down that he might have to, that even if he did not die to the tools of a torturer, he might have to lay down his life like Telm had, to ensure Agon was returned to his prison. Yet Agon was now breaking free, and Ifferon was the prisoner.

"If you are willing to die, then what follows will be of little consequence," the Visage said. "Each tool will merely be a helping hand towards the Halls of Halés. If you die for a greater purpose, it gives meaning to your life, a life which up to now has had very little meaning. The Visage is willing to die at any moment, without notice and without complaint. This makes the Visage the perfect orchestrator of the death of others, especially the death of liars, wherefrom they may be reborn as speakers of truth."

He spoke all of this while passing a set of pincers between his hands, as if he were performing some act of alchemy, turning liars into truth-sayers, even as war turns the living into the dead.

As Délin and the other knights continued to struggle in their bonds, they caught sight of a flickering of lights from the north, spanning the entirety of the horizon, as if the stars of the night sky had suddenly fallen to the ground.

"An army comes," Brégest whispered to Délin.

"Thank Corrias it comes from the north," Trueblade replied.

"The army from the south is here around us," Brégest said, and they surveyed the great force that surrounded them, each soldier another brick in their prison walls.

The knights did not need to whisper, for the Nahamoni saw the lights as clearly as they. While the knights felt a sudden hope, and hoped that the Nahamoni would feel a sudden fear, both Irons and Shackles roared towards the north, mocking the advancing troops, and welcoming the coming battle.

"Send a scout out," Irons said, and one of the lightly-armed Nahamoni immediately set out towards the approaching lights, disappearing into the darkness of the plains inbetween.

"Let's see just who we're going to kill tonight," Shackles said with a hint of glee.

Thalla watched as Ifferon was taken away, and she almost leapt into view, but wisdom stayed her feet. She watched as the knights were beaten and held down, and her heart almost leapt on its own. She watched as the lanterns emerged in the north, and then she watched as a lanternless scout headed out to spy and judge the enemy, and bring back information that might help douse the flames.

She thought of killing the scout, but she knew that it would cause too much noise, or that her usual affinity with fire would light up her location as much as the army of lanterns in the distance. She thought then of the spell of confinement that she saw in one of Melgalés' books, a dangerous spell that she was glad her soul was confined to the Beldarian for.

And so, as the scout cast his eyes north, Thalla cast her net around him. An emptiness opened up beneath the man, a hole into nothingness, which sucked him in before he could even scream. Where it brought him, she did not know. Perhaps it was the Void, or perhaps it was some place better, or some place worse. She did not even know how to undo the spell, or if he would be freed with the passage of time. She had little time or energy to worry about her captive, however, for she knew that more scouts would be sent out soon, and the spell of confinement was more draining than anything else she had attempted before.

The night marched on, and with it came the army of lights, growing larger and brighter, and becoming more of a comfort to the imprisoned knights, and more of a menace to the Nahamoni. As the night grew darker, and the lights grew brighter, Irons began to pace around restlessly.

"What happened to our scout?" he asked. "At this rate we'll know who's approachin' before he does.

Send another."

And so another scout set out, this time with two accompanying guards. Thalla did not know what to do then, and she thought it would be better to catch them on the way back than cause a commotion now. Her thoughts were short-lived, however, for it seemed that as soon as they disappeared into the blackness, they emerged before her suddenly, and she was so caught off-guard that they seized her and knocked her to the ground.

Then a volley of arrows came through, and several of them pierced the scout and guards, and several more narrowly missed Thalla on the ground. Horsemen drew up close, bearing the banners of Boror, and among them was Herr'Don. Thalla almost did not recognise him, for his clothes were new and clean, and they were a better fit, and better spoke of his royal line. His new cloak was not tattered, but whole, and he no longer looked like a broken man.

It seemed that he did not recognised her, for he said, "You there! What enemies await?"

"At least ... a thousand Nahamoni," Thalla stuttered in response.

"Let's give them a little welcome gift," Herr'Don said, glancing to a man on horseback beside him, whom he called Edgaron, and then to a riderless horse on the other side, whom he did not call at all.

Thalla saw then what he meant, for behind the horsemen were many legions of infantry, and behind the infantry were the Magi of Boror, and behind them were many siege weapons, all illuminated by a myriad of lanterns. Thalla had never seen anything like it, and last she heard of such an army, the King rode with it.

"They have prisoners," she told them.

"How many?" Herr'Don asked.

"Enough. Ifferon is one of them."

Herr'Don shook his head. "This is not a rescue mission," he said. "We march to fight Agon."

"Then we better rescue our best weapon," Thalla said.

The Visage circled Ifferon once again, and his movement and words were as much a form of torture as any of the grisly tools at his disposal. Yet when he stopped and fell suddenly silent, the new fear of pain joined the old fear of everything that had come before.

The Visage lifted up a poker, which he thrust suddenly into the fire, and Ifferon flinched. His wide eyes saw the little embers that leapt out of the furnace, as if trying to escape. The masked man held the iron bar in the flames for what felt like an eternity, turning it slowly, and looking back at Ifferon with those same iron eyes, which thrust through him just as easily.

"There is nothing I can say that you do not already know," Ifferon said. "And if you want me to do something I will not already do, then your efforts are in vain."

Another turn of the weapon, and another empty stare. Its emptiness filled Ifferon with the greatest dread, and what he could not see in his enemy's eyes, he knew he revealed in his own.

"I have nothing I can give you," Ifferon said.

The Visage drew the hot poker from the fire, like a soldier draws a sword from its sheath. As he did this, Ifferon knew that he would be its new sheath, that the burning embers would be holstered in his heart.

"We all have something to give," the Visage said as he drew close, and as the hot poker drew closer. "Our lives."

The attack came like the suddenness of lightning. Horsemen rode in, followed by swordsmen and halberdiers, and they came without lanterns, while many thousands hung back to distract the enemy with their lights. They clashed with fierceness and fury, and some of the Nahamoni fled in shock and surprise. For those who stood and fought, they were pressed back and destroyed, and as some of the Bororians fell, more lanterns flickered out in the distance, and more troops charged in to join the fray.

Herr'Don dismounted and unsheathed his sword. He held it low, as if he needed no defence, and as he passed by Délin he swung the blade and cut the bonds around the knight's wrists. He pressed on as Trueblade untied his feet, and he bore down towards Shackles, returning the giant's evil glare with his own.

They clashed like the angry ocean against the stubborn shore. Herr'Don swung his sword at the giant, who parried it with his granite arms, before returning the blow with his flail. Herr'Don narrowly dodged the studded chain and swiped again at the beast before him, slicing into his belly, and then again across his thigh. Shackles roared out, but the pain only fuelled him, and he began to swing madly at the prince, until finally Herr'Don was struck back several feet. Shackles loomed tall before him, and Irons joined him.

But Herr'Don was not alone, for Délin returned from freeing his fellow knights, and he helped the prince to his feet. Then both of them stood to face their oppressors, sword in hand, with anger and honour driving their blades.

Shackles swung his flail, while Irons stabbed with his dagger and prodded with his poker, but they were large and clumsy, and Herr'Don and Délin moved between them with ease. The prince made short work of the pale giant, slicing here and there at frenzied speed, while Délin parried Irons' attacks, which hit harder than his twin, until the giant knew why they called him Trueblade.

And so in moments Shackles collapsed to the ground, and the ground gave a tremor, as if it were shuddering from the feel of the giant. Then a louder and fiercer quake followed, and another came as Délin drove his sword through Irons, freeing him from the bonds of life. The ground rolled beneath them, and they thought they heard the sound of rending steel upon the wind, but it was drowned out by the din of battle.

While the knights fought outside, Thalla freed Elithéa and Geldirana, and they raced towards the tent to which Ifferon had been dragged. They reached it just in time for Elithéa to knock aside the hot poker with her staff, eliciting an audible sigh of relief from

Ifferon.

Thalla confronted the masked man, and she cast a bolt of fire towards him, but he dispersed it with an icy touch, and she knew then that he was one of the Magi, that deep beneath his armoured chest there must lie a Beldarian. She had little time to find out however, for as she cast another fiery ball towards him, he disappeared in a shroud of darkness, and the fire continued until it engulfed the fabric of the tent.

The three women hauled Ifferon outside, avoiding the licking tongues of flame that leapt out to taste them.

"Saved from fire, by fire," Ifferon said, but the ever-present thought of Agon told him that there would be much more fire to come.

As the battle continued, many slowed their attacks or stopped completely when a large carriage rolled in, adorned with a canopy and numerous flags and banners bearing the royal seal and the colours of the royal house. It was pulled by two majestic horses, one black and one white, and inside it sat Herr'Gal the King of Boror, covered in armour and carrying a ceremonial sword.

"All hail the King!" some cried, though none of the knights repeated the words; some instead prayed to Issarí and Corrias, or looked to Délin in surprise.

"So he finally comes to the battlefield," Délin said. "Perhaps Boror still has some honour left."

"More than a little," Herr'Don said as he wiped the side of his blade across his thigh, smearing the blood over his already richly red attire.

"You fought well," Délin said with a nod.

"You managed well enough yourself," Herr'Don replied with a grin.

Délin placed his hand upon Herr'Don's shoulder as a token of fellowship.

"I would return the gesture," Herr'Don said, "but my sword is in one hand, and the other is a little preoccupied strangling ghosts in Halés."

"I am sorry for the loss of your shield arm," the knight said.

Herr'Don paused and looked to the ground before looking up again, and Délin caught a glisten in his eyes. "I am not," the prince said. "It has made the Great even greater. One arm will do, as this Nahamon knows well. Besides, I never used a shield. It was a second sword arm to me."

Ifferon could barely find the words of thanks to give to his saviours, but they did not need or want such praise.

"We couldn't let our best weapon burn," Thalla said in jest.

"I might have allowed a singe in payment for betraying Ferian secrets," Elithéa said, but her actions suggested otherwise. Ifferon knew that she was still torn between the sacred fate of her people and the reality that they had succeeded in restoring life to Théos and Corrias. "I only wish we could have sent that evil Magus to the fire instead," she added.

Geldirana said least, but her eyes said most of all. She looked at him like she had when they emerged from the Black Eyrie. Her intense stare was overpowering, and Ifferon could barely keep her gaze.

"Thalla," he said. "When did you earn your Beldarian?"

They all looked to her now, like the moon shines a focal light in the blindness of the night. Her face reddened and she looked away, but instead of keeping her eyes averted, as she often did before, she turned back to them and held their gaze.

"Thúalim fell," she explained. "I took his place."

Ifferon wondered if this was the natural order of things in the Order of the Magi, but something told him that it was not. He imagined the others were thinking similar things, for all of them were silent, and in that silence there could be heard on the edge of hearing, a faint whisper from the Halls of Halés.

In time the Nahamoni army had been destroyed or routed, and those that held the knights in bonds became prisoners of their own. The survivors stumbled from the aftershocks, and though they had won this fight, the tremors brought their attention further east, to where their strongest enemy still struggled, and still lay undefeated.

The company reunited, and many were cheerful to see Herr'Don again. Pleasantries were exchanged between the old and new, and in time they all came before the King of Boror and gave their, often very brief, acknowledgement.

"It looks like Arlin still needs Boror after all," the King said. "It's lucky Atel-Aher didn't build a wall around your prison or you'd still be prisoners."

Délin grumbled, but said nothing. A chorus of

grumbles echoed around him.

"So this is the cleric," the King said, eyeing Ifferon up and down. "Looks like another knight to me."

"Then our aim is achieved," Délin said. "Let the enemy be blind."

"Agon will see through this mask," the King said.

"Then let us blind him."

The King looked at the knight harshly. "Look around you, knight. Your army might try to blind him. *My* army will do far more than that."

"So then," Délin said. "What brings you out of your throne room? Has Herr'Don managed to convince his father to defend his people?"

"I did not come for or with him," the King said. "I cam *in spite* of him."

Délin looked to Herr'Don, whose chest heaved and whose mouth trembled just a little.

The King held his head high, as Herr'Don often did. From the darkness around him emerged a metal mask, followed swiftly by a hand around the King's face. Herr'Gal cried out, and others cried in turn, but as they charged towards him and his attacker, there was a flurry of darkness, and he was gone. His crown tumbled from his head in the assault, and it did not vanish with him, but crashed down upon the ground, where it span for a moment, and then slowed, and then stopped with a clang.

IX

LONG LIVE THE KING

There was chaos upon the plains, as if the battle had erupted anew, but this time the armies battled with their confusion, and their eyes fought with the darkness. The search for the King of Boror was frenzied, like how a mother might search for a child, but instead the massive armies of Boror searched for the one they would call "father," and the one Herr'Don would not.

The prince joined the search, not out of love, but duty. It would mend no hurt to see the King dethroned, even if that was the very chant of many of Boror's people. Instead, it would be a new hurt to Boror itself, for the insult was less to who wore the crown, but to the crown itself. It was a symbol, like the entwined serpents of the royal house, and the seizure of the King had given Agon a powerful symbolic victory.

"The night that was our ally in our march is now our enemy," Herr'Don said. "We need light if we are to make good of this evil."

And so the archers were gathered, and they shot arrows of fire high into the sky, which rained down into the empty parts of the plains. The sky brightened for a moment, and then darkened again, as if it were the eyelid of a god that had stirred momentarily from its slumber. Then the Magi joined the illumination of the heavens, sending up great sparks of lightning and fire, and some sent up orbs of light, and others sent up strange creatures and birds that glowed and glimmered. Even the foot soldiers did their part, carrying their lanterns here and there, fanning out to cover large expanses of land.

And the search was fruitless, and an hour passed, and then another, until it seemed that every fleeting minute was like a drop of blood from the veins of the King.

King Herr'Gal rummaged through his garments for something to end the torment, for a dagger to drive through his heart, or a poison to funnel through his veins. Each frantic pat met with nothing to free him, and all the while the Visage continued to prepare another series of instruments, and another round of torture.

And then, as if in answer to his fervent prayers, Herr'Gal found a vial hidden deep within his shirt. He knew instantly that it was one of Daralus' concoctions, and that it was enough to kill any man. He thought for a moment of trying to force it on the Visage, but he knew he had not the strength to fight the Magus, nor the skill to evade his spells.

So then he resigned himself to the fact that he must take his own life before his torturer did. He thought little of his kingdom then, nor of his people, nor of his son, nor even of the one whom he trained to be next in line; he thought only of his life and his desire to live, and that which conquered that desire: his aversion to pain.

The Visage continued to busy himself with his wicked weapons, and Herr'Gal knew that this delay was part of the torment, the part that played on the mind. Yet it was his moment of opportunity, and so he slipped the lid off the poison vial, and he swamped it down in one fell swoop. Immediately he felt the burn of the liquid in his throat, and then down into the pit of his stomach, and it conjured a new pain to join those the evil Magus had summoned.

And he waited.

The pain rose and fell, like all the pains he had felt so far this night in captivity.

And he waited.

The pain dissipated completely, leaving behind only his other pains, and a new pain of the mind: that the poison was not enough. It could kill any man, and he knew that he was like any other, with one key difference: his daily dose of poison, and the gradual immunity it gave him.

And so the Visage turned around, with a fresh array of devices, ones that even Herr'Gal did not recognise from those who worked for him in his own dungeons. Each of these the Visage used in turn, tearing from him his fingernails, ripping from him his tongue, and wrenching from him a constant wail, punctuated only by a series of even greater cries. And so it continued, until Herr'Gal begged for death, pleaded for poison, and found none but that which already rested in his veins.

The night was long, as if the sun could do

naught but avert its eyes. No one came for him, as if no one cared for him. He yearned for saving from this misery, and as his final moments came, and did not come soon enough, he even thought of his son Herr'Don, and wished the prince could have saved him from this fate.

The armies of Boror were too late when they found their King, and many suspected that it was not a chance discovery, but a deliberate attempt to break their morale. They stormed the lonely tent, which stood out almost too obviously in the empty plains, and they found their leader dead, bearing all manner of scars, some too terrible to behold. In place of his royal red robes, he wore a garment of blood. Even those who despised him or were highly critical of his rule could not help but pity him and shake their heads when considering his final moments.

Herr'Don could barely stand the sight, and he left the tent almost as quickly as he had entered it. He had been ready for battle—not for this. His firm grip upon the handle of his sword had almost faltered, and his firm stance upon the ground had almost toppled. Ifferon and Délin helped him stumble outside.

The horror of what had happened was on the lips of many around them, and if it was not on their lips, then it was on their minds. Herr'Don looked at Ifferon and could tell that he was lost in his own thoughts, perhaps thankful that he had escaped a similar fate. For Herr'Don, there was nothing he felt thankful for. Though the King was barely a father to him, there was nothing Herr'Gal could do in death to make amends for that, and there was nothing in the manner of his death that could repair the broken, or heal the wounded. Fresh wounds upon some do little to ease the stale wounds on others. He thought of Ilokmaden Keep, which had taken his arm. He thought of Telarym, which had taken his father whole.

"We have found the captive," Délin said, "but where is the captor?"

They looked about, but found nothing. Then, from the darkness behind Herr'Don, where their lanterns did not shine, Ifferon thought he caught a glimpse of something. And then he saw that familiar, unsettling mask.

"There!" he cried, and he pointed to the figure.

Herr'Don swung around suddenly, but before he could unleash his sword, he was thrown away into Délin and the guards. Ifferon reached for his own sword, but as he unsheathed it he suddenly felt the handle burning, and he dropped it just as quickly. Swords dropped all around him as other guards encountered the same phenomenon, and many began to back away as the figure emerged not just from the gloom, but from a nothingness beyond the gloom.

"*Dehilasü baeos!*" Ifferon cried, but the Visage appeared undaunted. He stood there with his hands raised, as if at any moment he would begin a spell.

Then just as he appeared like he was about to act, a shimmering cage closed around him, and he looked this way and that to find whoever assailed him. The tent ripped up from the ground and was cast away, and there around them all stood the Magi of Boror, dozens in number.

"Give it up," one of them called, and he looked old and grim, and very powerful.

The Visage turned to him slowly in his astral cage, and Ifferon could almost feel the masked man's eyes settling upon the Magus, like a Gorgon might cast its gaze upon its stony prey. There was a visible strain upon the Magus, and even upon those around him, and the bars of the cage began to flicker and bend.

"Resist and we will destroy you," the Magus said, but his voice was as strained as the bars.

"I do not fear death," the Visage said, and the cage fell apart around him.

What happened then was so fast that Ifferon could only make some of the details out later in the annals of his memories. Bolts of lightning, beams of fire, and swords of light were cast at the Visage, all of which were parried and tossed aside, like a tree casts dew from its leaves. Many of the Magi were cast back with returning bolts and beams, and one or two seemed to disappear entirely. There was a flurry and a chaos upon the fields, for some guards ran towards the Visage, only to be killed instantly, while others ran away from him, trying to duck and dodge the magical barrage.

The battle moved across the plains, and it seemed like a constant tug of war, for just as the Visage seemed to be beating back all opposition, the Magi would suddenly renew their attack with greater ferocity, with some of those who disappeared returning to the field, as if released from whatever prison they had been cast into. And then just as the Visage appeared to be losing, and several more cages of light formed around him, with each side appearing suddenly and snapping together to form what might be to any other an impenetrable cube, the Visage cast them off suddenly, and sometimes even fired the cage at one of his attackers. And so cage doors clanged shut, and were blown open, and this continued for a time, until it seemed that the very air was alive with magic, making each breath that little bit more intoxicating, and that little bit more dangerous.

And then Thalla joined the fray. Ifferon would have barely known it was her, for she brought down pillars of fire all around the Visage like Melgalés might have done if he were still alive.

For a moment it seemed that the Visage was caught off guard by her ferocity and skill, for his magic turned entirely defensive, and he began to form orbs of water around him, which were subsequently crushed by the pillars of fire. When he regained his composure, he began to destroy the fiery pillars by casting the orbs at them, and sometimes he lifted up the pillars with his mind, casting them back in the direction of Thalla.

But Thalla knew many of the same spells that the Visage did, for the books she stole from the shelves of Melgalés' house were ancient and arcane. As the pillars came towards her, she disappeared in a flurry of red cloaks, reappearing metres away, from where she renewed her attack.

But the Visage knew some spells that she had never studied, and he had experience that she lacked.

So in time he began to make simulacrums of himself, and though they were mere illusions, the spells they cast were just as real as the Magus himself. So the battle grew more fierce, and the Visage broke down Thalla's defences, sending bolt and beam her way. She struggled, and even when she evaded one attack, another was ready for her in the new location where she appeared.

Just as all seemed lost, and Thalla would apprentice her master in the art of death, red eyes appeared suddenly upon the battlefield, followed swiftly by the form of the Felokar wolves, who pressed forward, growling and bearing their teeth, while fiery embers flicked off from their fur to singe the skin and clothes of any left standing.

The Visage halted and turned his metal gaze towards the wolves. For a moment it looked as though he might battle them, and then he suddenly gave up, raising his hands no longer to cast spells, but to offer his surrender.

"Someone else is their master tonight," the Visage said as he looked at the growling beasts.

Ifferon could sense it too, as he was sure many others could. Though they looked the same, these wolves felt very different to those which Délin fought several moons ago.

"Why do you give in now if you do not fear death?" Thalla asked the masked man.

"I do not fear death," the Visage stated, "but I do fear the second death." He paused for a moment before adding, "You should too."

They put the Visage in chains, the kind of manacles that even the Nahamoni giants could not break out of, and yet it seemed that there was little point, for this evil Magus could easily escape the much more powerful prisons of the astral world. What kept him in place were the steady eyes of the Felokar wolves, like a reflection of the eyes of the Gatekeeper himself.

As they began to drag the masked man away, he turned and glanced towards the hills. It might have been just a curious look, but there was something in the movement that made many turn their eyes to where he stared. For most, there was nothing to see there. For Ifferon and those few who had the clearsight, there was the silhouette of a Shadowspirit.

X

THE AMASSING OF ARMIES

The Arliners and Bororians were shocked to see the Shadowspirit upon the horizon, but they were even more shocked to see that it was alone. They waited, and many grew anxious, but it did not move, and some began to doubt the reports of the clearsighted, and others began to wonder if it was some trick of the eyes, or the weather, or just an oddly-shaped tree in the distance.

Ifferon did not have any of these doubts. The Scroll of Mestalarin began its subtle alarm call, and in his heart he knew that what he saw was a Shadowspirit, and that more were on the way.

Over the next few hours, the armies began to fortify their position, digging trenches and building barricades. Some began to talk of returning home, and within their dwindled numbers thronged another army of doubt and despair.

"We have to do something about this," Edgaron said. "The morale is failing."

Herr'Don looked around at the toiling troops, at the fearful faces, at the worried expressions. Agon was so close he could almost feel the presence of the Beast, and yet there lay so many obstacles between them, not least of all the threat of the Shadowspirits, and the more impending threat of the failing spirits of those around him.

"The King is dead," Herr'Don said, standing up and embracing, and breaking, the silence. "I can never replace him. I can never be king. The crown is not for me, nor is it even for the one who will next wear it. It is for all of us, a symbol of unity. In that circlet there is the circle of people that make a nation. In the toughness of that gold there is the emblem of the resilience of our race. In its pronged tips lies a message to all our enemies. In its glisten is a reminder of the spark of light within us all."

He looked through their ranks, staring down the meek, renewing confidence in the strong. As his eyes passed from one to another, he caught sight of Belnavar, standing where others might see only an empty space. Belnavar gave him a firm salute.

"You have fought many battles when the King was never on the battlefield," Herr'Don continued. "Some of you fought with me at Larksong, and you fought not because there was royalty in the ranks, but because there was something worth fighting for. You did not come here to fight with the King, but to fight against Agon. Our king is dead, but the king of our enemy still lives."

The troops rallied, even some of those for whom fear had routed before.

Herr'Don consulted with many generals and advisers, issuing orders and making plans. At times he went off alone, and it seemed as though he were consulting himself, for he talked to the wind, conversed with the emptiness of the air.

"Who are you talking to?" Edgaron asked when he found him like this on one occasion.

"I will tell you because I trust you," Herr'Don said, "but I trust that you will not reveal this to others, and I trust that you trust me in return, and will believe in what I say."

"You have my trust," Edgaron said, "and my confidence."

Herr'Don appeared to struggle with how to share his experiences, but in time he found the words. "Belnavar fell, but he rose again without a body."

Edgaron looked around, as if to see this spectral form, but he saw nothing except Herr'Don before him.

"He's real," Herr'Don said.

"I should hope so," Belnavar remarked.

But Edgaron looked doubtful.

"I'm not crazy," Herr'Don said.

Edgaron smiled. "It wouldn't matter to me even if you were."

Ifferon sat with Geldirana, and though there were many things he wanted to say before, but could not find the courage for, the brief respites from battle proved the perfect opportunity, and perhaps the only one.

"Do you forgive me?" he asked her, and he thought he might be asking that same question for a long time, if he was given time enough to ask it.

"Ten years of faults and failings," she said, and

though her voice was soft, the words were like lashes. "Give me ten more to forgive them."

Ifferon looked to the ground, where the ants and other bugs surely felt less low. "I guess I deserve that," he said. He did not say it for pity, and he knew with certainty that she would never grant it, for she deemed it a weakness.

His eyes hugged the ground, but her eyes burned through him, like they always did, right into his very soul. He hoped she could see his sorrow, that his apology was true.

When she eventually spoke, she withdrew into the shadows, as if to make it seem like the words did not come from her. "It will take time," she said.

"If Chránán is kind, I will have much time to give," Ifferon said. "Perhaps all I can give."

"There is more," she replied, and paused. "What of love?"

"I cannot give it to those who won't receive it."

"Time may soften some hearts," Geldirana said, "while deeds may do the same for others. My clemency cannot be bought, even if it were paid for with time, for it is time itself that adds upon the hurts, that makes them fester. But what cannot be bought may perhaps be earned."

So they sat together for a time, and Ifferon knew that these brief moments, cherished though they may be, were not enough to make up for all those lengthy moments where he was absent from her life, and for his daughter's entire life. He prayed, as he might have done back in the monastery at Larksong, that there could be some absolution, that even as he willed that the evils of Agon were made good, he could correct his own evils, and truly be worthy of the blood of Telm, and the company of those he loved.

As the Bororian force continued to set up camp, Délin began to question the wisdom of digging in, when they should be setting out. All of his knights agreed with him, and it seemed that many were eager to leave this battleground, where the grey of Telarym had turned to red, even though they knew that another battlefield awaited them in the east.

"The battle is o'er yonder," Délin said, pointing east, to where glimmers of red flashed across the sky, to where the frequent rumbles of the ground emanated from. "Corrias is there now, battling the Beast, and what are we doing here but waiting?"

"That is not the only battle," Herr'Don said, and he pointed south-east, to where another army was forming. They would not have known who this new assailant was, but for the numerous banners that bore the symbol of a drop of water. "Taarí," Herr'Don growled.

"And there," Ifferon said, pointing to the south-west, where the one Shadowspirit became many. "They have grown in number, but still they wait."

"They wait for their masters," Geldirana said, and all their minds fell under the oppressing shadow of the thought of the Molokrán.

"I do not see them," Herr'Don said, "but that does not mean they are not there." He glanced at Belnavar.

"*I* see them!" Affon cried, patting Ifferon on the arm.

"These armies are a distraction," Délin said. "They have come here to stop our advance on Agon. If the Beast needs time to break free, then we are giving him that time; we are gifting him his freedom."

Herr'Don shook his head. "If we assail the Beast now, then what will happen when his armies come upon us from behind? What good will we do then?"

"The time for tactics is over," Elithéa said. "Now is the time to act."

"The time for tactics in a war is *never* over," Herr'Don said.

"If they tarry to give Agon time, then let us bring the battle to them!" Elithéa cried.

"No," Herr'Don said, and they were all surprised. He was usually the one to call for battle, or to make no call at all but that which his sword made as it left its scabbard. "We have another army on the way."

"What army is this?" Délin asked. "I thought all fighting men of Boror marched with the King?"

"They did, and Arlin has not spared us any more," Herr'Don replied, "but look north and see if you can guess who comes to fight with us."

"I see naught," Délin said, straining his eyes against the darkness.

"Look further north," Herr'Don said.

At last Ifferon knew the answer to the riddle. "The Aelora," he said.

Herr'Don nodded, and they all looked to the north with expectation.

The Men of Boror dug in deep, and they erected barriers and barricades around their siege weapons, which where brought to topple the towering figure of Agon, not the armies he sent forth to delay his assailants.

"We must protect these machines at all cost," Herr'Don said. "An army may fight an army hand to hand, but against the Beast we must use siege."

Though Délin thought little of these weapons, he still aided the soldiers in defending them, for he thought much less of Agon, and he had begun to learn that in a war with the Beast, honour was not the strongest weapon.

In time the army of the Aelora appeared on the horizon in the north, where the glimmer of their bodies outshone even the many lanterns of the Bororian force. The enemy was not blind to their advance, for lights began to appear in the Taarí army in the south-east, while only darkness thronged in the south-west.

And so before the Aelora could move into place, it seemed that the Taarí began to march, like a grey mass, and the Shadowspirits began to drift towards them, like a black fog.

"So we fight again," Délin said, and though he seemed weary, the drawing of his two-handed sword seemed to give him renewed strength.

"Let them come unto their doom," Herr'Don said, and he held up his own sword, which glinted in the darkness, and he stared at it with a kind of manic glee, as if it were called Doom.

The drums of battle began to sound, followed by horns and trumpets, and Ifferon yearned to hear instead the soft melodies of harp and violin by the fireside in a tavern in Boror. The music mounted, as if upon a steed of its own, and it travelled to every ear and invaded every heart, until everyone who stood there began to feel the imminence of the clash, like the final strike of the cymbal to mark the start of chaos and discord.

Then suddenly Ifferon's eyes were stolen by another sight. Another Shadowspirit appeared to the west upon a hill, but this one seemed somehow different. It looked the same, for those who could see it, but Ifferon could not help but feel that there was something else behind it, that someone else looked out through its eyes.

Suddenly it seemed that the Shadowspirit would dart forth, and the battle would begin, but instead it dissipated, and there, in its place, stood Yavün. Even from this distance Ifferon could recognise the youth, though he seemed less young and naïve now, holding firmly a large sword, and surrounded now by a small army of Taarí warriors.

"Has madness come upon me?" Ifferon asked. "Or do my eyes deceive me?"

"If they deceive you, then they deceive me also," Herr'Don said.

"He is back from beyond the grave," Ifferon whispered.

"Amidst the ranks of Shadowspirits and Taarí," Herr'Don said. "Back from the grave, perhaps ... but he came back on the wrong side."

XI

THE BATTLE OF WATER AND SHADE

જ⁆

Yavün stood beside Elilod, surveying the battlefield. They saw the armies that surrounded the Men of Arlin and Boror, and even though the gravest threat was the unseen swarm of the Shadowspirits, more eyes were set upon the evil Taarí further afield.

"They have shackled themselves to the shark," Elilod said, "to save themselves from being eaten. But when all the other fishes are gone, and the shark is still hungry, who then will he turn to, and who then thinks that his hunger will be abated?"

"At least the waters are not all full of sharks," Yavün said.

Elilod smiled.

"I see Ifferon," Yavün said, pointing down towards the band of knights. "He's in armour now."

"Good," Elilod said. "He will need it."

For those entrenched in the mire of Telarym, surrounded by armies on almost every side, it seemed that armour was not enough. Dawn broke over the horizon, invading their eyes, and as much as it announced a new day, it announced a new battle. The stand-off ended, and the armies charged.

Taarí splashed down with their limbs of water,

and the Shadowspirits strode forth with their limbs of shadow. The Bororians and the Knights of Issarí braced themselves, shoving halberds and spears into the heart of the angry wind.

They clashed. The strike was like a tidal wave crashing against the stubborn shore. The cries and shrieks grew high and fell, like the wall of water, until the tumult grew so loud that each cry drowned out the other, each shriek silencing the next, until the real sounds that could be heard where each soldier's own breath, each soldier's own grinding muscles and clattering bones, and each soldier's own unnerving thoughts.

Though the Taarí were made of water, they could strike like land. Their weapons were as real as any other's, and though their tendons and sinews were of another substance, they still made up a body that could hit with great ferocity. Many on both sides fell to the initial attack, and while some Men were knocked dead, some Taarí were cleaved asunder, splashing upon all around them.

The attack from the enemy was swift and unmerciful, for they too had seen the Aelora force further north, which they knew could overwhelm them if they did not destroy or rout the Bororian army. Yet they had an ally of their own in the Shadowspirits, and as much as the Aelora could blind with light, the Molokrán could blind with darkness.

For the forces of good, the reinforcements could not get there soon enough, for even as the Aelora marched towards the desperate clashes, the survivors of the Nahamoni army, which were earlier routed by the army of Boror, began to return to the battlefield, and though their numbers were much smaller now, they were more daring with the support of their allies.

So the battle continued, and those Bororian infantry who pulled back to catch a moment's breath were hunted down by the invading shadow, until that breath was a final one. The bodies of Men formed little hills upon the flatlands, and the bodies of Taarí formed little rivers between them. Chaos and cruelty fought among them all, and they seemed to every soldier to be fighting for the opposing side.

"Here come the Taarí on our flank!" Herr'Don called to his troops. "Archers at the ready!"

Ifferon grabbed Herr'Don by the wrist before he could give the order. "But Yavün—"

"He's one of *them* now," Herr'Don said. "And maybe he was all along."

"I do not believe it," Ifferon said, but he doubted his own words.

"You have the clearsight," Herr'Don said. "Look at them. See it for yourself!"

And so Ifferon looked again at the Taarí who approached from the west. They looked like any others of their race, glistening with the glint of the river, glimmering with the sheen of the sea. They marched just like those in the south-west had marched, and they carried weapons just like those who assailed them did. All that was different was the strange presence of Yavün at the front, and the standard-bearer with him, who bore the emblem of three fishes, two pointing east and one pointing west.

"They fly a different banner!" Ifferon cried.

"They can fly my own and I still will not trust them," Herr'Don said. "Fire!"

The arrows darted forth like an army of their own, crowding together here, spreading apart there, and coming down like stabbing rain. The Rebel Taarí broke apart, some falling to the arrows, others falling in their chaotic flight from the chasing darts.

"They're firing at us!" Yavün cried in disbelief, as if saying the words might somehow stop the truth, or bind the bows of his assailants. He crouched down and stumbled here and there, avoiding the onslaught, and he cowered beneath his sword, which was large enough that it was now his shield.

"When the waters are dark, every glimmer of light is seen as a shark," Elilod said. He crouched also, but he did not cower or shield himself, and no arrow fell upon him, nor near him.

"But they're friends," Yavün said, and it was more a question than a statement. He looked down at Ifferon, who seemed confused in the heart of battle. He looked at Herr'Don, and he saw the prince turn a regiment of swordsmen towards them.

"Wave the flag!" Elilod called to the standard-bearer further up the hill. The man looked less proud now that arrows came down around him, even piercing the banner he held. He waved it now from right to left, slowly and methodically, and they hoped their attackers would realise that they were not the Taarí who submitted to Agon's rule, but those who came here to fight him.

The arrows stopped, and the swordsmen below halted. Everyone breathed a sigh of relief, and Yavün and Elilod stood up.

Then suddenly a single arrow hurtled through and struck the standard-bearer, slicing through him and splashing out the other side. He collapsed forward, the banner falling on top of him, and sinking as the liquid of his being wept out to water the lands around.

Yavün stood in shock, but he was quickly knocked from his feet by Elilod as another arrow darted by, a bolt that would have sent him to join Melgalés in Halés.

"Retreat!" Elilod called, but many of his forces had already begun racing back up the hill, like the tide returning to the safety of the sea. Elilod dragged Yavün to his feet, and they raced back to where they had come from, hounded now not by arrows, but by the cheers and jeers of the soldiers far below.

When they were out of range of the Bororian archers, they stopped and rested, and Yavün had time to nurse his tired legs and his wounded heart. He could not believe that his friends would attack him, and he thought that Ifferon or Thalla, at least, could have stayed Herr'Don's hand.

"They do not fire at you," Elilod said, noticing his puzzled expression. "They fire at what crawled out of the grave to drag them into it."

Yavün stared blankly at him.

"They think you are dead, little fish," Elilod explained, "and that we are the enemy. There is not much we can do to make them realise the truth. We cannot get close to them without being killed."

Then Yavün perked up, and he saw in Elilod's eyes the wonder that was reflected in his own. "There is a way," he said, and the tide rose once again.

The evil Taarí that crashed down on Herr'Don's armies were fierce beyond measure, and though they were crafted of water, it seemed to some that they were made of fire. Many drowned beneath the wave of attackers, but Herr'Don worked himself into a frenzy that showed them what real fire was like. He slashed his way through the waters, attacking everything in sight, and many of his own soldiers cleared the way as he approached, for he seemed like he would strike out at anything or anyone in sight. He was pushed to and fro, like a man bobbing amidst the waves, but this only propelled him from one dead foe to another for whom death was imminent.

And so Geldirana joined him on the field of battle, but where Herr'Don stumbled to and fro, cleaving and cutting, Geldirana's movements were like a dance. She waded through the foes, turning this way and that, striking and continuing forth as if there were no obstacles before her, just the choreography of battle.

Elithéa too entered the battlefield, and though she did not have the grace of Geldirana, she had something of the ferocity, and her enemies were not thankful that she carried a staff instead of a mace, for it struck them dead just the same.

Thalla joined the other Magi with attacks made from range, trapping and killing reinforcements that flooded down to join their comrades.

But Ifferon and Délin left the Taarí to their companions, for an even bigger threat was soon upon them. The knights braced themselves as the darkness they could not see flooded down towards them, and Ifferon waited for that brief moment before he could say that they were here. And then it came.

The shadows seemed all of one type, mingled together so that bits of one seemed to merge into another, and what seemed like a wisp that blew from one became a smaller thing of darkness that moved on its own. Some of these were Spectres, and they hounded all around them with the flails of fear and the daggers of dread, while others were Meddlers, and they hunted all around them with very different weapons: claws made of shadow, which struck like sickles.

Yet the knights did not fall like their Bororian brethren might have, for their armour was thick, and their training was another shield. They swung and struck at the darkness they felt around them, and Délin cut his way through the assailants, showing them the feel of the sickle-edge of his two-handed sword.

Ifferon stabbed at a few shadows that formed around him, and they wailed like the cries of the dying, and the more haunting cries of the dead in the bitter watches of the night. He began to feel things crawling around him and upon him, and even when he turned to them, ready to fight, he found nothing there to greet him, and he began to feel the same kind of fear he knew the knights without the clearsight must feel. This grew to the edge of terror when the things that rubbed against him seemed to crawl inside him, and the fear almost drove him over the edge when those things began to give birth to thoughts inside his mind that he knew were not his own.

And so Ifferon abandoned his sword and took out a weapon better suited to this foe. He unfurled the Scroll of Mestalarin, which immediately banished the evil thoughts and the eerie feelings, planting firmly in their place a sense of strength and courage.

"*Dehilasü baeos!*" he cried, and it was a sound that drowned out the cries around him, and silenced the tumult of the dead.

The shadow was swept back, and the knights found for a moment that they were fighting nothing. Then it came back in, and Ifferon repeated the words, forcing it back once more. The ebb and flow continued, a tug of war between light and shade, the land around darkening and brightening as each of them pushed and pulled against each other.

Then suddenly a shadow drew up beside Ifferon, and he cried out. The Last Words had no effect upon this one, and already Ifferon was beginning to feel the strain of his contest with the Shadow Kingdom.

The deathly voice of the shadow spoke, and its words were like hammers. "Ifferon," it said. "I am not as I appear to be. This is Yavün."

Ifferon almost stumbled from the shock, and it gave the shadow he fought to hold back an advantage in their tug of war.

"I survived the Chasm of Issarí," the spirit continued. "I was found by the Rebel Taarí, led by Issarí's spouse, the River Man."

Ifferon could barely believe these words, and yet he recognised in them a hint of the youth he had met back in Larksong, of the boy who yearned to be a man, and of the man who could not escape his own boyish ways. Yet now the naivety was supplanted by knowledge, the innocence replaced with experience, and for every part of him that he knew, there was another he could not recognise.

"Yavün," Ifferon said, half to acknowledge who stood in this body of shade before him, and half to test the spirit with that name, as if it might send an illuding force away.

"The shadow could control me," it said. "Now I can control the shadow."

This statement came like dawn in the bleakest night, and it brought light into his mind, and illuminated his soul. He felt a weight had lifted, and the clouds seemed suddenly less oppressing, and the wall of shadow that stood before him seemed less daunting.

But as much as there is relief in dawn for the creatures of the day, there is relief in dusk for the creatures of the night. The weight returned, and it was heavier than ever, for in it was the weight of all nations, of all peoples, and all his predecessors, and the weight of history itself. The clouds returned, and in their gloomy glare was the reminder of the shackles of shadow, of the rule of darkness from its lofty throne. Inside Ifferon there formed a new wall of darkness, cutting off his mind from his heart, and cutting off his courage from his hope.

The darkness before him changed shape, like the shifting figures upon the land as the sun rises and falls. The pawns of the Shadow Kingdom gave way, and the kings appeared. The Molokrán came forth, and a new Alar Molokrán took the crown.

Ifferon could barely take in this new sight before they were upon him, and he was thrown back, and the Scroll fell from his hands. Délin and his knights charged forth, but they too were thrown, and they found that stabbing blindly in the dark was less effective when they were faced with the masters of darkness itself.

Then the spirit that Yavün controlled leapt upon the Alar Molokrán, and the Lichelord struggled with it for a moment, before casting it aside and turning to it with confusion. He raised his arms towards it, and it seemed that he was attempting to cast some spell upon it, to return it to his dominion, but instead it leapt upon him again. This time he seized it and swallowed it, until his own darkness swelled and grew.

The distraction gave Ifferon enough time to reclaim the Scroll, and so he unleashed it and the Ilokrán, and he cried aloud the dying words of Telm, and that god's shimmering armour formed around him, like a halo to the silver armour he wore beneath.

"*Al-iav im-iavün im-samün im-samadas, dehilasü baeos!*" he cried, and it felt more forceful than ever, so much so that a gust of violent wind was blown forth with those words. The knights stopped for a moment to look at him, like they did when they saw Issarí, and like they would have if they had been there for

Corrias' resurrection.

And so the Lichelord also stopped to look upon him, but there was no awe in the darkness where his eyes might be, and no shock in the blackness where his mouth might be. Instead he seemed amused.

"Your *little fire* colludes with the darkness now," he said, "and it will not be long before that candle is put out."

Ifferon did not have the time to decipher these words, for the Molokrán attacked again. The Scroll, which mimicked now the Sword of Telm, did little to threaten them, and the Shadowstone, which mirrored the Shield of Telm, did little to ward them off, or protect against their crushing blows.

And then Geldirana returned to the field, with the memory of the Molokrán as much in her muscles as it was in her mind. She held her mace to the sky, and a bolt of lightning struck it, and then she struck the shadow as if she were lightning too.

"Blood for the Garigút!" she cried, and the look in her eyes showed that she was willing to give of her own blood as much as she was willing to take it from her enemies. But the shadow had no blood to give.

Affon also charged into the fray, waving the Ilokrán that Ifferon had given her in one hand, while waving a small mace in the other. She worked her way to where Geldirana toiled, but she was driven back, at times by the shadow, at times by her mother, and at times by her own fear, which she had never known so closely before.

In the flurry of the battle Ifferon could not tell which of the Molokrán he was attacking, or which of them was attacking him. They combined into a singular darkness, and even when at times they spread out and seemed to form distinct shapes of their own, they were merely doppelgangers of each other, and doppelgangers of the fears in the hearts and minds of every man and woman, and those forgotten fears that plagued the hearts and minds of every child.

And so they toiled in this new tug of war, where the Last Words clashed against the threat of the final words of everyone still living, and everyone who still had a last breath to give.

Yavün was still in shock from his conflict with the Lichelord, and though it was a body of shade that was absorbed into that dark master, he felt a strain in his own body, and an even greater strain in his mind. He managed to get out just in time, and he knew with great certainty that had he not abandoned that shadow body, he might have been lost in the darkness—his own light might have been blotted out, and he might have become part of the Molokrán.

Yet he could not abandon the battle, and leave Ifferon to whatever evil fate might await him. He caught sight of another Shadowspirit, and he cast his mind across to it, seizing it suddenly and taking control. He was tired, but he knew that the time of rest for the Molokrán had come and gone, and that the only rest they would grant to their enemies was the final rest in Halés.

He crept around the battlefield, watching carefully as the Molokrán advanced and fell back, like a hammer struck against an anvil, and pulled back not to rest or recover, but to add more force to another strike. Just like the anvil, the armour of Ifferon, Geldirana and Délin was battered each time, and Yavün wondered just how much they could take under the hammer of the shadow.

Then suddenly he heard a sizzling and a crackling, and he felt a great heat well inside him, as if the shadow he possessed were on fire. He began to make out whispers, and then the voice of fire he had heard so many times before. He looked down to see the Beldarian, but all he could see was the shadow, with not a hint of flame.

"The shadow will destroy them," the voice of fire said, though there was something strange about it now, as though the fire had been lit in a different place.

"Let me in," it said. He felt himself agreeing almost against his will.

Suddenly Yavün felt as though he were losing his grip. For a moment he was reminded of his fall at the Chasm of Issarí, and the pain of the rock slicing into his arm as he lost his hold and tumbled down into the ravaging waters below.

Even more suddenly, like that moment when he felt himself losing consciousness beneath the waters, he felt himself locked out of his own body, pushed and held down, suppressed and supplanted. He looked across the plains with his eyes of shadow, and he saw his body slump. He tried to raise his arms, but all that moved were the arms of the Shadowspirit. He was exiled from his own body, and it sat there like a shell, waiting to be occupied.

Before he could do anything, before he could run to it, or cry out, or even think of what his options were, he saw the Alar Molokrán disperse like dust in the wind, and before he could think of what this meant, and act upon it, he watched as his body stood up of its own accord and turned to Elilod, who stood there unaware. Before he could warn him, or do anything that might save him, he watched as his own hand drew his own sword, and plunged it with his own force into the belly of the River Man.

XII

DUSK

༚

Elilod collapsed upon the ground, with the Sword of Telm still lodged inside him. Had it been any other sword, a blade made by mortals, the River Man may have survived its embrace. Had it been held by the Lichelord instead of Yavün, then he might have seen it in time, and dodged the blow. All the things that might have been passed before his eyes, and he tried to catch them, but they slipped from his grasp, and they swam away.

He looked at Yavün, and though he saw that familiar young face, and those familiar curious eyes, and that familiar mouth full of questions, he did not recognise him.

"Little fish," he said, and said no more.

The Rebel Taarí backed away from their fallen leader, but Narylal ran to Elilod and crouched down beside him, holding him in her arms. There was water in her eyes that was not part of her fluid form, and even from across the plains Yavün could see the glisten, and it wounded him like his own hands had wounded Elilod.

Narylal wailed as she held her leader, her god, in her arms. If there was a god of sorrow, a Céalar who dealt with tragedy, then she would have prayed to him. But there was no one in Althar who could answer such prayers, nor answer the difficult question of why these evil deeds were allowed to happen, in a world which even the gods could not control.

Yavün struggled with all his might to regain control of his own body, but he failed, and so he swept across the battlefield in his shadow form and leapt upon whatever it was that made his flesh its home. As soon as he did this, he began to see a little out of his own eyes, but then it went dark again, and his sight returned to the eyes of the Shadowspirit.

His anger gave him momentum, and so he lunged again, and his real eyes saw a little more. He repeated this until eventually he knocked the Lichelord from the shell of his body, and he leapt inside and turned to the Alar Molokrán with the Sword of Telm held high.

"We smote the River Man before Issarí," the Lichelord said, "and now finally he rests upon the river bed."

Yavün stabbed the air before the Lichelord, as if it had made those offending words, and the Lichelord flinched and grimaced, and then turned its dark mouth to laughter.

"So the River Man found something on the river bed," he said. "Another token, another relic, another heirloom from a dead god and a dead legacy. Has Ifferon finally given up his claim and made you the heir instead?"

Then Ifferon stepped forward, and the Lichelord flinched once more, as if he had caught sight of something great and terrible, and then he stood resolute, as if he realised how small and trivial this power before him was.

"And who is this," the Lichelord mocked, "but another relic?"

Ifferon stood unblinking, and Yavün had never seen him look so strong. His armour glimmered like stars, and the Shadowstone pulsed like a little lightning, and the Scroll thrummed like a tiny thunder.

"I know a little weather of my own," the Lichelord said.

Suddenly the clouds in the skies began to change, spinning and bobbing, and in those undulating clouds could be seen a mirror of a stormy sea. From the tempest of the sky a torrent fell, and those who had not been felled by sword or arrow were now struck by the battering of the breeze and the flailing of the flood.

Just as it seemed like night would set in, that the clouds would act as curtains, and the sun would be snuffed out as if it were but a tiny candle flame, the Aelora arrived on the battlefield, and the very light that emanated from deep within them was enough to stay the darkness, to halt the advancing gloom. The armies of allies and enemies both looked at the lights, and some were forced to turn their gaze aside, for here and there a spark would turn brightest white, and it was blinding.

But the Aelora did not let their inner lights do all the work, for bright though they were, the bleak blanket that stretched above them all sent a darkness past all eyes and into the very souls of everyone beneath. The weather was a weapon that day, but it was one that more than the Molokrán could use.

Oelinor appeared at the front of his force, and he began to cast a magic of his own into the sky. The other Aelora followed, and soon there were streams of white light flooding the heavens. In time the clouds were driven back across the battlefield, and the sun arose, and it was day again.

But just as the previous Lichelord had an uncanny power over nature, and the one before it had an unearthly power over stone, the newest Alar Molokrán made the weather his slave, driving it forth and compelling it to do his will. The clouds advanced again, blotting out the sun, and the land was cast once more in darkness.

Thus was there a battle of night and day to mirror the battle of the forces of darkness and light below. The sky seemed forever divided, as if the very gods that dwelt there did not know which side they were on. Whatever animals that had not been scared off by the clashing of armies were undoubtedly confused by this seemingly sudden and swift passage of time. Some scurried to their burrows to rest for the night, only to emerge moments later in bewilderment as day dawned once more.

Then Lëolin, the current Alar Ardúnar, joined Oelinor at the front of their troops, and his presence gave day the advantage, so that it seemed that it would forever conquer night and chase away all and every shadow.

But his presence was as much a challenge as it

was a threat, and the Alar Molokrán was compelled to answer. He rose up tall until he was a thin pillar of blackness, and the Shadowspirits around him were drawn towards him, and then drawn into him, until he began to swirl. The motion forced dust into the air and knocked people from their feet, and those nearby were sucked towards the shadow, until it became a ravaging black tornado, moving slowly across the plains.

The Aelora fired beams of light towards it, but these seemed to only empower it, giving it new force and speed. The Magi of Boror tried their spells of encagement, but the swirling shadow broke through them effortlessly. Yavün watched on helplessly, just as he did when he watched his own hand end the life of Elilod.

And so the tornado bore down on the Aelora, and they began to panic as their magic failed to halt it. Every shadow was now part of the cyclone, adding their corrupting essence to its destructive force. Here and there an unlucky soldier was plucked from the battlefield and consumed by the windstorm. Everywhere the sound was deafening, and up above the sky was darkening again.

Ifferon charged in front of the swirling mass, clutching tightly the Scroll before him, which clattered in the wind, even striking him in the face as he tried to utter the words it bore. "*Dehilasü baeos!*" he cried, but the wind cried louder.

The darkness deepened, and the even darker work of weather drew close. Just as it seemed as though it was coming too close to Ifferon, and that he would surely die in its passage, Délin raced through and knocked Ifferon from its path. The two narrowly dodged the tornado's powerful pull as it was drawn by the power of the Alar Ardúnar, who could do little to stop it.

Yavün watched all of this unfold, and he felt as though his previous conviction, his prior drive, had been sucked up into the passing whirlwind, leaving him as helpless as any other who dared to fight the weather and its new ruler.

Then he felt the fire well inside his mind, and there once more he heard the voice of fire. "He is as much a portal as you are," it said. "Yes, a portal. An empty shell waiting to be filled."

But Yavün had been deceived by this before, and in letting his guard down, he had given up his own body so that it might be filled by shadow. Elilod had paid the price for Yavün's mistake, not him, and he wondered who else might die if he hearkened again to the voice of fire, which might instead be the voice of shadow.

In that moment of doubt, when he felt he understood more than ever Ifferon's reluctance, when he finally realised that he was as much battling with his own internal shadow as he was any external one, he began to wonder if being a Child of Telm was more than just a title, or more than just a list of names that had mostly been crossed out by Agon and his forces.

But he did not like this doubt, and he did not like the sight of Ifferon upon the ground, or the fact that this could be him in years to come, cowering in the face of fear, and letting uncertainty rule his life, or the fear of not making the right choice hold him back from making any decision at all.

And then he was given an extra push from the world outside, and the world beyond. One of the Felokar wolves that were guarding the Visage had slunk away from its duties and crept towards him, and he had not noticed it, for his eyes were fixed on the whirling darkness. It nudged him, and he started in fright, and he was suddenly reminded of his flight with Thalla from those beasts, and those tender moments spent with her before they were dragged apart in the rapids of Issarí's Chasm. The wolf nudged him again, pushing him slightly in the direction of the tornado. He instinctively resisted, but this only spurred the wolf to push harder, almost toppling him from his feet. It growled at him as he turned to it, baring its teeth, before nudging him again.

"Okay!" he cried. "I know."

And so he did what all others upon the battlefield must have thought was madness. He ran towards the tornado, even as others were running away from it. He raced towards it even as it pulled him and anyone and anything else closer to its destructive bosom. Amidst the howling wind he could hear other howls, the howls and cries of his friends and comrades, and the howls of the Felokar wolves, like the welcome song of the dead.

When it seemed that he was no longer running, but being dragged and sucked towards the shadow, he looked up to the twirling tower of blackness, like the weather's imitation of Tol-Úmari near the Peak of the Wolf and the Land of the Dead. It was daunting and oppressing, and the gods in Althar must have felt its violent force as much as the mortals down on Iraldas.

In that moment, when the wind lashed his face, and his hair swirled like a tornado of its own, time seemed to slow, and he felt a little of what it must be like in Halés, where Melgalés dwelt, and where he knew deep inside him that the Magus suffered because of him. The Beldarian was almost pulled from its chain as he approached the tornado, and he knew that soon it would all be over, that he would free another's soul just as he would free his own. His mind raced like a whirlwind, sending his thoughts in all directions, and he thought to say a prayer, but could only think of a poem instead.

The wind beats against my ears like the battle drums.
The air lashes me like the whips of slave-drivers.
The gust reels me in—on the wire my will succumbs;
As I'm caught, I see the ocean of survivors.
Who am I to covet their freedom from the net,
Or look at all I have, and dare to ask for more?
What more is given only adds upon the debt,
As I am taken up and shackled to the shore.
Though my eyes know envy, of it I have no need;
Though my heart knows yearning, of it I need no beat.
The wind is here enough to satiate my greed,
An avarice of love, so easy to defeat.
What will end my eyes' gluttony? What will suffice,
And fill the need like water fills the selfish sea?
What water for the land, a willing sacrifice?
If it won't come from heaven, it will come from me.

And then just as the tornado began to take him up, he leapt towards it, giving in to its embrace, like a little fish reeled in by life's eternal fisherman. And then he leapt again, this time out of his own body, and deep into the black wall of wind before him, in which the Lichelord dwelt. For a brief moment he saw only blackness, and then for an even briefer moment he saw what the tornado might have seen, if it had eyes. He saw people cower and run, and he saw the tower of darkness loom over Lëolin, even as Oelinor backed away.

He saw, even against his own will, for he tried to close his eyes, but could not, that Lëolin was sucked into the cyclone, and he was dragged and thrown, until the very light in him was sucked out and overcome by the darkness around.

Then Yavün saw the shell of the Alar Molokrán that was the centre of the cyclone, like an acorn from which a tree of darkness and death must grow. He saw that it was empty, and so he threw himself inside it, and suddenly he could see more clearly than ever with the eyes of the whirlwind. Just as easily as he might lift his arm or turn his head, he halted the tornado and slowed its spinning, until finally it no longer turned at all, and instead stood as a giant pillar from the earth to the heavens. He lowered this and condensed it, until at last it formed the figure of the Alar Molokrán, through whose eyes he could see, and with whose face he could feel the air, and with whose hands he could feel the ground.

And so he turned his attention to the opposing armies, which were already dwindling. He moved the pillar of darkness towards them, and they knew it was no longer a weapon on their side. Many cowered and many ran, but a few of the Nahamoni stood before the towering form and held up what looked to Yavün like scraps of a broken pot. He pushed the shadow towards them, knowing that they could not stand against it for long, but he began to feel a powerful and overwhelming resistance, which made the potency of the Molokrán feel tiny in comparison.

The strain of keeping the shadow on a leash was too much, and Yavün felt that he was losing control, and that the blackness that was now his body was beginning to seep into his mind. For a brief moment he thought that it would consume him, and then he thought no more, for everything turned to darkness and silence.

To those around, they saw the Lichelord's form shift violently, as if it was fighting with itself. One moment it was contorted and angular, and the next it was soft and flowing like a dark cloud. The Nahamoni unleashed the fragments of the Ferhassan that were confiscated from Délin, and they halted the dark pillar, as if it were turned to stone. Then the darkness suddenly dispersed, and those who had the clearsight could see, for the most fleeting of moments, that Yavün's spirit was cast out of the shadow.

The soldiers braced themselves for a renewed attack, but their swords and spears lowered involuntarily when they saw that the Lichelord fled from the field of battle, with the other Molokrán following in his train. A fear was upon them like that which they had cast upon all the peoples of Iraldas, and the soldiers watched their flight with a feeling that justice had been served.

Ifferon saw more than most, for he watched as Yavün was cast out of the Lichelord, like he had cast out the Shadowspirit from Yavün all those days before in the haunted hills of the Meadow-downs. The youth's spirit form turned here and there, as if lost, and it did not seem to see Ifferon, nor its own body laying still upon the battlefield. It wandered aimlessly for a time, and then just as Ifferon began to make for it, to guide Yavün back to his body, it shimmered briefly, and then began to fade. It turned one final time, and Ifferon thought it looked at him, and then it turned its gaze in the direction of the door of Halés, and Ifferon no longer saw the ghostly form.

XIII

THE BATTLE OF THE BEAST

The soldiers carried Yavün's body to the prison pavilion where the Visage was kept, and where the Felokar wolves kept guard, and where Affon marched back and forth as if she were keeping the night watch. Ifferon and the others who had journeyed with Yavün followed as he was lifted inside, and some kept their heads bowed, as if they were part of a funeral procession.

They brought him inside, and immediately the Felokar wolves reacted, but instead of pouncing on them, as they might have done with someone trying to free the Visage, they whimpered and paced about, and then they bowed their heads, as if they too were part of the requiem.

The youth's body was laid down upon a table, still clutching the ornate sword that had felled Elilod, and Affon ran up to see what was happening.

"Is he dead?" she asked.

It was the same question they were all wondering. He had not fallen by any mortal wound, like so many had that day, but no one knew enough about the spirit world, about the people they called Portals, or exactly how the transition to Halés worked. There was no acorn to use now, and it seemed to many that

171

he had already cheated death once, and that it might have finally claimed him.

"He could not find his body," Ifferon said, and he fought back his tears. He wondered if he could have done more, if he could have saved the youth.

"Some say the body is a prison," Délin remarked, "but I say that to wander between worlds, neither being fully of body or soul, is the real prison. It may not have bars, and it may not have a gate, but that endless wandering is its own lock and key."

"He looks like he's sleeping," Affon said.

Ifferon saw that Délin was holding back a tear. This moment was too like that seemingly endless time when Théos lay upon the plinth at the top of the Mountain Fortress, and where to some he looked like he was just sleeping, but to most he looked dead.

"Is there aught that can be done?" Délin asked.

What few Magi that had survived the last battle shook their heads. Thalla said nothing, but stared at Yavün, and her face was pale, as if she had seen the apparition that Ifferon saw. The scars of her meddling with magic in the White Mountains were still visible, however faintly, upon her face, but there were other scars too: the scars of one who has lost a beloved.

"There is only one thing we can do," Herr'Don said. "Bury the dead, and bury Agon with them."

"With them, no," Délin said. "But let us end this war."

"Are we to bury Yavün then?" Thalla asked. Ifferon thought that perhaps it would bring her some closure, when there had not been any for the youth before, nor for her mentor Melgalés, whose body still sat in the Rotwood, rotting away slowly.

"There is no time," Herr'Don said. "We have tarried long enough. It is one thing to be delayed by battle, but quite another to be delayed by battle's aftermath."

"There is always time to bury the dead," Délin said. "If we do not honour the fallen, then it is pointless to fight for those still standing, for a world without honour is not a world worth living in."

"Why waste time with the shell that remains?" Elithéa asked. "No wonder Man dwindles."

"Let the weak and wounded bury the dead," Geldirana said. "They are no good to us in battle, but perhaps may still be of some use."

So they agreed to this compromise, though to Délin it seemed more an affront. It was only the frequent reminder of Agon's vicinity, and his imminent release, that encouraged the knight to strive ahead with the others, leaving a bed of bodies in their wake.

They left the pavilion and turned their attention eastwards, to where they knew the Beast still tried to break free, and where they hoped Corrias was still alive to hold him down. Even as they stared in that direction, in the direction of death, the bodies of fallen comrades lay still around them. Ifferon knew that he was not alone in wondering just how many of those still standing would soon be joining the dead.

"And so we come at last to this battle," Délin said.

"A battle to bring the Beast to his last moments," Herr'Don said, and the soldiers cheered, cheered through their terror. There were none upon the plains who were not afraid, even those who pretended otherwise, for though the Molokrán sent fear into the hearts of all, nearby was the creature that consumed their master, and he sent fear past all hearts, into the very souls of all survivors.

Their rest was brief, for there was little time, and they knew they must march from battle to battle, as if each fight were one of their own footsteps. The time between was fleeting, and with each step forward there were fewer people to make the journey. Some abandoned the quest entirely, like Narylal, who led the Rebel Taarí back into the Telar Deeps. Some of those who stayed wished they could also flee, and all of those who stayed wished that they were marching home instead.

As the armies went, the tremors became stronger and came more often, toppling heroes of men and women as if they were but unsteady children not long out of the womb. To watch a great knight like Délin knocked from his feet, and helped up like he had helped Théos many times, was disheartening to Ifferon, much more so than his own falls and tumbles, which he expected, and for which he had little shame. The land moved around them even as they moved upon it, and it seemed to some that it was as much an enemy as Agon, as if even the very earth itself had given in and sworn allegiance to the Beast.

The sound of rattling chains preceded all others, and it grew so frequent and so loud that it dwarfed the wind, and it travelled to their ears as if it had shackled itself to every gale and gust. The sound was unnerving on many levels, for it spoke to them of the bonds of the Beast, but it also spoke to them of their own prisons, and that prison of death that Agon could send them to.

And then when the strange sound became like the everyday whistle of birds, and the terrible tremors became like the normal turning of the earth, the smell of sulphur charged upon them, invading their nostrils and attacking their senses. It burned their noses, singed their eyes, and left an ashy taste upon their tongues.

And when the sulphurous fume seemed somehow natural, like it must have done to Agon and whatever else lived in the darkness beneath Halés, and when the smoke and dust dispersed before them like a curtain pulled back by the hands of gods, they were greeted with a sight that singed their eyes more than any sulphur could, and this was something they could never grow accustomed to.

The sight was so horrifying that many were forced to immediately close their eyes, to block out the bleakness, but they found the evil had corrupted their imaginations, and their minds conjured new and terrible forms worse than their eyes had seen, and so they were forced to open their eyes once more, to free themselves from the tyranny of their own minds. What horrors they saw then made the false images of their minds pale in comparison, and it seemed that they were locked between the twin terrors of illusion and reality, and they felt a semblance of the torment of the Beast, where neither sleep nor the waking world brought any solace.

To some whose minds were weak, the sight of the

Beast was enough of a weapon to destroy them. Some fell instantly dead, and perhaps that would have been some relief, were it not for the fact that the horrors haunted them in the afterlife in Halés, and some of them became horrors of their own, to haunt the living that were yet blind to the Beast.

Others did not die in body, but they died in mind, with the walls of their sanity closing in and collapsing around them, and they wandered the battlefield aimlessly, and some wandered onto the sword edge of an enemy or ally, and some wandered straight into the Beast's jaws, and some others wandered far afield, even to distant lands, where after they were known as the Afflicted, and this torment of the mind was treated like any disease of body, and they were shunned, and they were feared. So did the terror of the Beast spread like a virus of its own, infecting minds, and building far and wide a civilisation built with bricks of fear upon a foundation of terror.

There were no records in any books of what the Beast looked like, bar brief and hurried mentions of his general anatomy, for how he appeared depended on who looked upon him, and what fears festered in their soul. Few who saw the Beast survived, and of those who did, none would dare unlock the images from the cage of their mind, and free Agon to torment them once again.

For Ifferon, he saw a mangled face like the combined deathly countenances of the remnants of a battlefield; Agon was, in all respects, the epitome of a mass grave. Had his agonised features been cemented in form, the mind may have grown accustomed to them, and so come to some sort of reckoning, no matter how harrowing. But his face shifted each time Ifferon looked upon him, and it was a new kind of death, a new kind of horror, and a new kind of memory that Ifferon desperately wanted to forget.

It was easier to not look upon his face, even though Ifferon could feel those dark eyes boring into him like the torture tools of the Visage. He looked instead upon the hulking form of Agon's body, and the lumbering limbs that stretched out from the cavernous hole like monstrous pillars.

One chain held the Beast in place, biting at the ankle of his left foot like a Felokar wolf might snap and snare a mortal soul and drag it down to Halés. A single chain, with a manacle crafted by the Céalari—of whom no Man or Ferian, or any other race, could imitate—was all that stood between the Beast and his freedom, and between the people of Iraldas and theirs.

Except Corrias.

For it was Corrias who held the Beast down as if he were a chain of his own, and the great weight of the god helped keep Agon in check, and keep him from tugging and pulling with all his strength on the chain, and keep it from snapping.

For a moment Ifferon thought of what they might have faced if they had not been victorious in returning Corrias to the world. Perhaps the Beast would then be free, and perhaps he, a Child of Telm, would have been the last protection, or the last small obstacle swept aside by Agon.

Then his eyes fell upon what looked little pebbles

lining the ground around Agon and Corrias. He was horrified to discover that these were not tiny rocks, but the remnants of those few Al-Ferian who had marched out with Athanda, and those fewer Garigút who had joined them on the orders of Geldirana. He looked to her now, and he saw that she too was just realising what had transpired.

But there was no time to mourn the dead—only time to avenge them.

Ifferon heard the wheels and cogs of the siege machines, a reassuring sound when they were allies. The catapults, trebuchets, and ballistae rolled into range, dozens in number and of all shapes and sizes, some plain and newly made, and some plated with metal, and some creaking heavily like old bastions of bygone wars. Ropes were slung, rocks were loaded, counterweights were pushed in place, and levers were cranked, and all these sounds combined to form the music of preparation, which was a prelude to the song of siege.

Then the sounds died down, and there was a moment of pause while Herr'Don argued with his commanders, many of whom had not slept since they set out from Boror several days before.

"We may hit Corrias," they warned, and some refused to act.

Ifferon was amused by how quickly the people of Boror had abandoned their faith in Olagh alone, when faced with the monstrosity of Agon, and the beauty of Corrias. Some still clung to their faith, seeing Corrias as Olagh, and Ifferon could not blame them for wanting the reassurance of Olagh's foretold victory against the Beast in the holy pages of the Olaghris. He could not tell them that Olagh was really Telm, and that Telm was dead, and they would not have believed it, even from the mouth of a Cleric of Olagh, or the mouth of a Child of Telm.

"We *will* hit the Beast," Herr'Don said, as if his own words were also promised in the Olaghris. "We have no choice, and Corrias will understand that."

"I cannot condone this," Délin said. "There is no honour in firing from range, and there is less honour when the firing is so chaotic that our own father god may become the target. We must engage the Beast in another way."

"We will," Herr'Don said, "but we will weaken him ere we approach."

And so he ordered his men to fire, and the siege weapons groaned and creaked, and great slabs and blocks of stone, and great trunks of trees, and great fiery balls, and great metal bolts, and great explosive kegs, flew across the battlefield and rained down upon Agon and Corrias. Some of these struck like tiny pinpricks, but others struck the faces of the gods, and there was apparent agony in their eyes. The Beast raged and roared, and Corrias struggled to contain him.

"Are you weakening or strengthening him?" Délin asked.

Herr'Don glowered at him, but did not respond. He directed his commanders to launch another volley, and this elicited a similar response from Agon, and a similar struggle from Corrias. Now, however, the father god seemed to be holding back his own cries of pain, for many of the bolts and bricks struck him as Agon dragged him this way and that.

Délin knelt down and closed his eyes. The other knights followed suit, and together they prayed to Corrias, as if he were still in Althar, and not trapped in Iraldas under fire from some of his own worshippers. Ifferon was amazed to see, however, that this prayer seemed to help the god, for he grew stronger and more resolute, and he held down Agon with greater power than before.

But Agon's rage was rising, and each falling rock seemed to fuel his anger, and each piece of shrapnel seemed to goad him into pulling harder on the last remaining manacle about his foot.

It seemed to Ifferon that Herr'Don was then talking to himself, for he turned to his side as if one of his commanders was there, but no one could be seen. This was not reassuring when the prince was in charge of the largest army upon the battlefield.

"So we will try a different approach," Herr'Don said.

Then the siege weapons rolled closer to Agon, and great hooks and ropes, and huge nets with weights attached, were loaded upon them, before they were fired upon the Beast. The hooks dug into his flesh, the nets landed upon him and weighed him down, and the ropes were pulled by men and women, and some of the siege weapons were cranked, for the ropes were still attached to them, and they grew tense as the people tried to tether and hold down the Beast.

But Agon had spent too long being chained and held down, and he had spent a thousand years tugging on those chains, hundreds of thousands of days trying to break them, and hundreds of thousands of nights banging his shackled fists upon the roof of his prison. All that anger, which had only grown and festered in this time, erupted now in Agon's violent flailing, even as he had erupted from the earth like a volcano.

The soldiers of Boror pulled on the ropes, but many were dragged into the air as their strength gave way to the terrible power of the Beast. Then some of the siege weapons were hauled skyward as Agon turned and thrashed, and the soldiers fled as their own engines of war came crashing down upon them. Others were crushed beneath the massive fists of Agon, and the ground shuddered beneath his terrifying thumps. All the while, Corrias tried to keep his grip—but it was slipping.

Archers fired their arrows, but they had little affect, and some brave, or perhaps foolish, soldiers charged up close to the hulking form and slashed and stabbed, only to be cast aside or crushed. One of these was Herr'Don, who worked himself into a frenzy, and began madly attacking one of the monstrous hands of the Beast, until finally he was flicked away. The breath was knocked from him, but he was lucky it was just his breath, and not his life.

And so the armies toiled, and Ifferon saw familiar faces join the fight, and he saw many more unfamiliar ones. Geldirana was there, swinging and cleaving, and Elithéa was there, striking and clashing. Thalla and the other Magi fired off bolts to match the ones shot from the siege weapons, and Délin and his knights moved in and out to strike here and there where one of Agon's arms came down like an avalanche. Yet none of this seemed to weaken the Beast, and as the armies grew tired, and their numbers dwindled, so did Agon grow more powerful, and his rage increased.

What then could be done, Ifferon began to wonder, if an entire army seemed powerless against this evil force, and if even Corrias himself could barely hold him down? And so he felt the armour of Telm come about him, as if he had inadvertently invoked it, and he felt the gentle thrum of the Scroll behind his shin-guard, echoing the violent thumping of the Beast.

Ifferon approached Agon and issued his challenge. "*Dehilasü baeos!*" he cried, revealing the Scroll as if it were a mirror that might show the Beast his ugly form. Those dark and disturbing eyes turned towards Ifferon, and he felt as though the lights of the sun and the moon were both upon him, singling him out in the darkness.

"Begone!" the Beast said, and his voice was like the rumble of an earthquake and the roar of a volcano. A gust blew from his mouth and knocked Ifferon from his feet, and the Beast mocked him with his probing eyes, even if he was too much in pain to deride him with laughter.

Ifferon clambered up and held the Scroll forth once more. "*Al-iav im-iavün im-samün im-samadas, dehilasü baeos!*"

Agon shifted in the chasm of his prison, and he shifted beneath the weight of Corrias, who held two of the Beast's monstrous arms in check. It was the kind of shifting any would do while mildly uncomfortable, not the casting into the Underworld that those same words had done when uttered by Telm with his dying breath so many centuries before.

"By fire," the Beast said, and a roaring fire erupted on his tongue. "And flame," he bellowed, and the fire spread around him. "And fume," he roared, and ears were rent, and his anger was palpable. "And fury!" he shouted, and the sky was full of a thousand thunders, and the ground was full of a thousand shaking troops.

Yet through all of this Ifferon stood resolute, with the armour of Telm around him, the shimmer of Telm's sword around the Scroll, and the glimmer of Telm's shield around the Shadowstone. Instead of trembling, like he thought he would, he stood firm. Instead of cowering, like he all but knew he would, he stood strong. The fears of what might be were replaced by the knowledge of what was, and Ifferon knew the threat of Agon, and he was afraid, but still he faced it, and still he challenged it.

"Begone!" the Beast bellowed once more, and this time he reached one of his great hands, if they could be called hands, towards Ifferon, and it came at him like a collapsing mountain. Délin raced in and pushed him aside, and the knight narrowly avoided being crushed beneath the hand, which splayed the ground and sent another tremor to all around.

Ifferon got up and began to trek back to Agon, crying aloud Telm's fateful dying words again, but Délin ran to him and held him back. "It is not working," he said. "The words are not enough."

"They have to be!" Ifferon said, and he shrugged

off the knight's gauntleted hand and continued on towards the Beast. Agon turned slowly to him, dragging Corrias along with him, who now tried to grasp at the Beast's throat, as if to silence whatever powerful words he might utter to counter those of Telm the Warrior-king.

Agon swiped at Ifferon again, but the cleric ducked and dodged the blow. For Agon's great size, he moved slowly, and his movement was hampered further by Corrias' restraining grasp. Were it not for this, Ifferon knew he would have perished swiftly beneath the awful weight of Agon's colossal fists.

Délin ran to Ifferon again and seized him by the shoulders, and they both ducked another of the Beast's swinging arms, before Délin dragged the cleric away from Agon's reach. "There is no victory to be won like this!" the knight cried. "There is nothing to be gained in your death."

But even as he spoke the words, Ifferon finally recognised what he had begun to realise since Agon broke through to Iraldas: that to return Agon to his prison, he would have to be more than just a Child of Telm, but Telm himself, and so give up his life just as that god had done. Surely, he realised now, the dying words were not strong enough without a dying breath.

This realisation must have been apparent in his eyes, for Délin looked at him with a sense of knowing, and he shook his head firmly. "No," he said. "There is always another way. We proved that with Théos."

"But this is different," Ifferon said. "This is bigger than all of us."

"Your life is more than just a key to lock Agon back in his prison," Délin said.

"Maybe it is not," Ifferon replied. "Maybe this is my purpose."

"And what of Affon?"

Ifferon did not know what to say. He had almost forgotten about her in the midst of the battle, as if he had never known about her, like he had not known for the past ten years.

"Is she not enough to live for?" the knight asked, and Ifferon saw in Délin's eyes the drive to defeat Agon, and to survive the onslaught, that he might see Théos again. Then the image of Affon came into his mind, and the image of Geldirana surfaced from where he had locked it inside the prison of his heart.

"Is she not enough?" Délin asked again.

Ifferon nodded and removed his helmet, revealing to the world the streams of tears he felt upon his face, revealing the sorrow he held for all that he had missed in life, all that he regretted, as if this indeed were his deathbed, and all he could think of was all he had wanted to do, and all he had not done.

"I barely know her," he said, "and yet she is everything to me, like Geldirana was."

"And may be again," the knight said.

"I think those days are over."

"Have faith, Ifferon," Délin said. "There is nothing permanent in this world, not even the gods themselves. Some things fade, and some things that seemed faded become clear again. The old may become the new, and the new may wither, and the old hurts may be the mortar that joins new loves.

Who knows what the future holds, only that we have a place in forging it."

And so the two walked away from Agon, and Ifferon felt as though he had failed in his quest, that he had not lived up to his purpose. The memory of Telm was not honoured in his blood, nor in his thoughts and actions. He knew not how this would end, only that his one and only weapon had little effect.

The features of Agon's face still haunted Ifferon's mind. He never knew what others saw, and they never spoke of it. The experience was enough, and their faces told him all he needed, and much more than he wanted, to know.

As he left behind the chaos of the battlefield, Ifferon heard an echo of Agon's words, which were themselves an echo of his own, and an echo of Telm's a thousand years before. "Begone," it said, and as Ifferon walked away, he felt, with a pang of deep regret, that he had obeyed that command, that it had more power over him than it did the Beast.

XIV

THE MONSTER WITHIN

❧

"We have failed," Ifferon said, and he sat down and unfurled the Scroll before him. It reminded him of how it looked when he saw it back in Larksong on that fateful day before his flight from there. It was old, ragged, torn, full of gaping holes and more damage than ever before, with pieces missing and pieces burnt, and when the edges were not wrinkled and worn, they were charred. If ever it reminded him of himself back then, it seemed an even greater reminder today. The promise it gave, that it could even make a moment of ending into something powerful, felt empty now, felt unfulfilled.

"Only in this attempt," Délin said. "He is not yet free, and that is our goal."

Herr'Don paced back and forth, his cloak swinging aggressively behind him. "If I had my other arm, I would take hold of the Beast and drag him down to Halés, even if it meant I could not return. I would hold him in place, and he would know my anger as more than he could ever muster, and he would call me *Beast*."

They returned to the prison pavilion, which had become a centre of operations for the battle, a refuge from the death and destruction outside.

As soon as they entered, Affon marched up to them and saluted by crossing her arms over her chest, like many of the older Garigút did. This act made Ifferon realise for the first time that Geldirana never gave this salute, but instead demanded it be given to her. Yet with the few remaining Garigút that were loyal to her now dead upon the field around Agon, there were none but Affon to give that salute.

"I hope your prisoner is not causing any hassle," Ifferon said.

"I've been keeping my eye on him," Affon responded, and she pointed to her right eye, and then pointed at the Visage, as if she thought this was somehow threatening. Both of the Visage's eyes stared back blankly, and he did not stir.

This stony reaction seemed to get to Herr'Don, for he gave a hateful glance to the masked man before sitting down with an angry sigh. Ifferon then realised that his reaction was perhaps partly due to the body of Yavün, which still lay upon the table in the corner of the pavilion, with his sword upon the chair beside him.

"We could not bury him," a guard whispered to Ifferon. "Those Felokar wolves kept coming and digging him up. We thought they were going to eat him."

The others were too distracted by the thought of Agon to give any thought to the young poet.

They joined Herr'Don at the central table, and they sat together like a war cabinet might, discussing their successes and failures, and what their next move should be.

"We go all in," Herr'Don said, and he pushed his cup to the centre of the table as if it were a stack of chips in one of the many gambling games played at Bardahan or Geldahan. "Throw everything we've got. Sooner or later we must succeed."

"There are no such guarantees," Geldirana said sternly. To the untrained eye she seemed unmoved by the death of her people, but Ifferon knew her better, and he could hear the distress in her voice, beneath the anger. "Tact is another weapon," she added.

"A slow one," the prince replied. "And we do not have the luxury of time."

"I held off my attack on Nahragor," the Waythane said. "And that patience paid off."

"It was paid off with the lives of your people."

She did not respond immediately, but her breathing deepened and her chest heaved, as if she were a volcano about to erupt. "And what do you want to do with the lives of yours?" she replied, keeping the lava down. "Throwing them at the Beast is a fool's errand."

"No more so than throwing them at the walls of Nahragor," Herr'Don said.

"We already tried the direct approach," Délin said, "and it has not worked."

"Agon is too strong," Elithéa said. "This is a fight of gods."

"So leave it to Corrias, you mean?" Délin asked.

"He's doing a better job than we are."

"I will not miss out on the battle," Herr'Don said agitatedly. He prodded the table aggressively, as if his fingers were knives. Edgaron placed his hand gently on the prince's shoulder, and this seemed to calm him.

"We have to act," Délin said. "Of that there is no doubt."

"I would suggest magic," Thalla remarked, "but he is quite a bit more powerful than any of the Magi."

They nodded and mumbled in agreement, reluctantly acknowledging that even the power of the Aelora was no match for that of the Céalari that Agon had consumed. Oelinor was silent, and Ifferon knew that he was just as disheartened as the rest of them, especially with the death of his close friend Lëolin.

"May the Visage make a suggestion?" the masked man said, his voice transmitting to them as if from another realm, and it was greatly disturbing, for it broke into their council like the news of a spy amidst their ranks. They had almost forgotten he was there, if that were truly possible, for his presence was strong, but they knew he could not help the Beast now from his own captivity.

"I have a suggestion," Herr'Don said gruffly. "Replace his mask with a gag."

"The Visage is silent when the Visage wants to be silent," the man said. "The Visage speaks when the Visage wants to speak."

"Can you speak when there's a sword in your throat?" Herr'Don asked.

There was silence from the Visage, and to the prince it seemed mocking, and to all others it was simply unsettling.

"What do you want?" Délin questioned.

"The Visage awaits an answer to an earlier question."

Délin sighed. "Yes, yes, make your suggestion then."

"Do not give him permission to speak," Herr'Don said. "Give him permission to die."

The Visage ignored him. "If this is a battle of gods, then surely only gods may win. Play, therefore, the only piece you have that remotely qualifies." He looked then to Ifferon, and the cleric shuddered, for he almost felt like he was back in the other tent awaiting torture.

Délin sighed again. "As much as I hate to say it, I think he is right."

"Aye," Edgaron said.

"Do not agree with him!" Herr'Don exclaimed, and Edgaron bowed his head and said no more.

"Our swords failed," Délin said.

"There is one sword," The Visage remarked.

They looked in the direction he was looking, and they saw Yavün's sword upon the chair. It looked even more unusual and ornate than it had done previously, and some of the company looked upon it now for the first time.

"What sword is that?" Délin asked.

"The one to silence this beast," Herr'Don growled.

"To silence *the* Beast, perhaps," the Visage said.

"Is that—?" Délin began.

"The Sword of Telm," Ifferon finished.

"*Daradag*," Oelinor said with wonder.

"Why would you tell us this?" Ifferon asked.

The Visage turned to him, and Ifferon immediately regretted drawing his attention, for the cold glare of that mask almost transfixed him.

"Consider this the Visage's interrogation," he said. "But unlike you, Ifferon, the Visage appreciates truth, and the Visage is more than willing to be forthcoming with any truths the Visage can give."

"Do not trust him," Herr'Don said.

"I don't," Délin replied, before turning back to the Visage, "but still I want to know what you know. Can this sword slay the Beast?"

"No," the Visage said.

"Then what good is it?"

"You are the one who studies the old tales, Trueblade."

Délin was clearly irritated by this, as if the Visage had broken through his armour. "Telm struck Agon with the Sword," Délin said, and he looked as though he was going through the tales in his head. "It weakened him, but the force of the blow sent it off into the wild, and it was lost. It did not kill Agon, but it weakened him."

"So then you have your answer," the Visage said.

"Still," Ifferon replied. "Why tell us this?"

"The Visage has lived a long life," the masked man said. "The end is nearing for us all."

Though it was hard to pick, this was perhaps the most unsettling thing the Visage said, not merely due to the words, but due to the tone of them, which made them seem that much more real and powerful—it was the tone of truth, and even the deaf could not avoid or evade it, for it spoke as much to the soul as it did the ear.

"Do you want us to defeat Agon?" Ifferon asked.

"The Visage has no desire."

Herr'Don leapt up again. "*I* have a desire," he said, "to end your petty little life."

"Calm down," Délin told him.

"If that … *thing* is the epitome of calm," Herr'Don said, pointing to the Visage as if his arm was the sword he wished to drive through the man, "then I would rather be in a frenzy, for at least then I would know that I'm on the side of good."

The Visage cocked his head, and his mask almost smiled. "Are you now?" he asked, and the words almost smiled in turn.

Herr'Don leapt up, and his sword leapt from its scabbard just as quickly. Both Délin and Ifferon grabbed him and stopped him from lashing out at the Visage. The Visage sat still and silent, and the stillness and silence were as much a derision as anything he had done or said before.

"Get him out of here!" Délin shouted, nodding towards the Visage. Brégest and three other knights seized the Visage and hauled him to his feet.

"I could kill him," Affon said.

Ifferon chuckled.

"No, really, I could."

Ifferon stayed his laughter, for he looked at Geldirana, and he knew that she had killed many at a younger age than Affon, and that she had no qualm with Affon killing many more.

"The Visage is willing to die," the masked man said. "Are you?" He looked in turn to each of them, or perhaps he only looked at a few, but everyone thought he was looking at them, and them alone. The question echoed in their minds like a curse.

"He mocks us," Herr'Don said. "Let my blade mock him back."

Délin and Ifferon struggled to hold him back, and Ifferon could almost imagine a grin upon the face of the Visage, behind those unmoving features on his mask.

"Get him out of here!" Délin repeated. The knights dragged the evil Magus outside, and the Felokar wolves followed. Affon began to follow also, but Ifferon grabbed her by the arm.

"No," he said. "Stay here."

"But I'm on guard," she said. "He could get away."

"We need you here," Ifferon said.

She sat back down, prouder than before, and it seemed that at any moment she might interrupt any one of them to give her own counsel. As Ifferon turned back around to the others, he noticed Geldirana's stare, a softer stare than he was used to since their reunion.

Herr'Don sat back down, banging his body against the chair as if it were his enemy. His breathing was heavy, and his eyes were almost rabid. Edgaron placed his hand upon the prince's shoulder, and he seemed to calm a little. Were it not for this, and for the Visage being hauled into another pavilion, Ifferon thought that Herr'Don might have worked himself into the kind of frenzy that even his own troops feared and backed away from.

"So there is the Sword then," Ifferon said, and he almost regretted saying it, for he knew that they would look to him to wield it. A part of him, however, felt an urge to grasp that hilt, to instil some greater sense of Telm within him that he felt was lacking now that the Last Words proved ineffective.

"Yes, yes," Délin said, "but a weakened Agon is not enough."

"It's a start," Thalla said.

"And I will finish him," Herr'Don boasted. He looked as though he might hop up at any minute and charge out to face the Beast, but Edgaron kept that calming hand upon his shoulder.

"Can we not fashion some new chains?" Elithéa asked.

"We could, but they would not work on Agon," Délin explained, and Ifferon could see the twinkle in his eyes as he recalled the tales from the ancient books. "The seven that held him down were crafted by the seven sons of Adag the Craft-king, the god of blacksmiths and artisans. When Telm went to battle with the Beast, he tried all manner of weapons, even some made by mortals here in Iraldas, but they all proved ineffective. So Adag made himself into his final sword, hammering and hewing, enduring the pain upon his own anvil, until finally he was no more, but the sword he crafted contained everything about him, and it was called Daradag, Adag's Hammer, for though it cut and sliced, it also came down like a thunderous hammer, and any who were struck by it were said to be on Adag's anvil, being recrafted from the shape of life into a shape of death.

"When Telm's dying breath banished Agon to the Underworld, the sons of Adag came forth and offered up their own lives, even as their father had, to shackle the Beast. So they used their own smithing skills to not only make the strongest manacles the world had ever seen, but to follow in Adag's footsteps and make themselves into those very chains, that they might use their own strength to cling to Agon and hold him down.

"Althar lost its best craftsmen then, and no weapons were ever the same again. And so if these chains have broken, there is little we can do to mend or replace them, even if we could forge ourselves into those bonds like Adag and his seven sons did."

Ifferon shivered at the thought of hammering his hand into his own creation, and continuing until there was nothing left of him, until he would only live on as what he crafted, like the Ferian and Al-Ferian live on as trees. At least there was something natural about that. Yet he could not fault Adag, for that god had made a terrible sacrifice, like so many of the Céalari had in their war with the Elad Éni, and their subsequent wars with Molok and Agon. It made Ifferon realise how selfish he was when he was not willing to make a similar sacrifice.

"Perhaps we are looking at this all wrong," Ifferon said, as if he were a cleric again back at Larksong, looking for a solution to life's great mysteries. The others turned to him like a congregation. "We keep thinking this war will be won by brute force. We marched here with many armies, and we killed many, and many of our own were killed. We laid siege to the Beast, and we battled him with everything we could muster, everything we could throw at him. But Telm did not win through force alone. Even the shackles used to hold Agon down were not just the strongest steel, but actual gods."

"But there are few gods left," Geldirana said.

"We are the new gods," Herr'Don said. "To whomever come after us, our deeds will seem great. Our names will live on like legends."

"I do not know if we can mimic them," Ifferon continued, "but I think we need to change how we approach these battles. Everything is alive in some way. The earth, the sky, even the shadows. If swords and chains can contain gods, there must be something we can do to give our weapons greater life."

It was an intriguing thought, but no one had any suggestions on how this might be achieved. Herr'Don was eager to return to using brute force, and insistent that it would eventually win the war, while others thought tactics might be employed to greater effect. But none could think of how they might emulate the gods, and though the Céalari had vanquished Agon once before, and this gave everyone present some encouragement, they had also failed in many ways, and this stayed much of the company's enthusiasm.

"The only thing I can think of," Ifferon said, "is to offer up my life."

"No," Délin said immediately, and a chorus followed.

"What good would that do?" Geldirana asked.

"That's a coward's way out," Affon said.

"How is it?" Ifferon asked, and he felt suddenly offended, and it showed in the frustration of his voice. "I have been a coward for so long, running and hiding. How can I still be a coward if I face Agon and do what I have always feared: die? I am not looking to escape my own prison, but to return Agon to his. If Telm could only do it with his dying breath, than surely the Last Words can only truly be effective if they are my last words too."

There was an intense and unsettling silence, where no one truly needed to speak, for their thoughts displayed upon their faces, and their emotions showed within their eyes. Some clearly racked their brains for alternatives, for some argument against what Ifferon knew was the only thing they had not tried, the only weapon they had not used.

At times it seemed like Délin would reiterate his refusal, like he had done so many times when faced with the stark reality of Théos' death. Though his defiance had eventually paid off, Ifferon could not think of any who would weep for him quite like the knight had for the boy. Though a part of him grew to know that Geldirana still felt some kind of love for him, he knew that she would not weep for him, that she would not weep for anyone, not even Affon.

"There must be an alternative," Délin said at last. "So many are willing to give up their lives to see Agon back in chains, and I know this willing sacrifice as much as any other, but what if you are wrong, Ifferon? What if instead of making yourself into the weapon that weakens Agon, as Adag did, you destroy the only real weapon we have against him: you?"

"I barely know you," Edgaron said, "but I agree with Trueblade on this matter. Do not die like this." He glanced at Herr'Don beside him, who sat in silence.

"And what if Ifferon speaks the truth?" Elithéa challenged. "What if that is our only real chance to defeat Agon? Do we pass it up because we do not want to see a comrade die? Do we all die to save him from that fate?"

"I will not accept that this is the only way," Délin said.

"You are so stubborn, Délin! You were like this with the boy. Why can you not accept death? Why can you not accept that something better can come of it?"

"Because I want to make that something better here and now, not delay it to the afterlife," the knight explained. "I want Iraldas to be a heaven to some, not just Althar. I have prayed to gods, and one of my patrons is out there now, fighting tooth and claw with evil, and yet I see how selfishness and greed win little wars of their own against us every day. And yet I do not lose hope, because I know that we do not need to pray for change, but make our prayers instead a list of actions we can make, that no one need face evil, and that if they do, they do not face it alone."

"Then let Ifferon face evil," Elithéa said. "If that is what it takes."

"And will you let him face it alone?" Délin asked.

"I will face it!" Herr'Don shouted, standing up, until Edgaron ushered him back into his seat.

"And I, if it comes to it," Délin said. "But I do not think you inherited death, Ifferon. That cannot be your heirloom. There must be some other way to shackle Agon."

"It begs the question," Elithéa said, "why have these chains broken? Have those gods weakened? Were there defects in their work? How is it that Agon can now break free?"

There was silence for a moment as they all pondered the question. Then a new voice broke the silence, and they turned suddenly to the body of Yavün, who was now sitting up.

"I know that answer," he said, his voice strained.

"Yavün!" Ifferon cried. "You are alive!"

"Cheating death again," Herr'Don remarked. "It seems you cheat a lot."

"I have been to Halés and back," the youth said.

"Bah!" Herr'Don said. "That explains the smell of sulphur. I need some fresh air." He got up and stormed off, leaving an angry breeze in his wake. Edgaron did not follow him this time, but gave him space.

Ifferon hurried over to Yavün and gave him his water cannister, which the youth eagerly drank from, as if his throat was filled with the burning dust of Halés. Délin fetched a blanket, while Thalla took a damp cloth to bathe Yavün's head. He gave a weak smile as he saw her, and a stronger smile as her hand touched his face. The others simply sat in silence, curious to hear the youth's tale.

"Speak already," Elithéa said.

"Drink a little more," Ifferon said.

"Who would think that water could be a dam?" the Ferian asked. "You clog his mouth with enough of it. We do not have time for rest when action is needed. Tell us more of these chains, boy."

Ifferon reluctantly backed away and sat back

down, but Thalla remained at Yavün's side, patting his head with the damp cloth. When he eventually spoke, his voice was still weak, and the colour was still lost in his face, as if he had come back as much a ghost as he was when he was drifting out of his body.

"The chains are alive," Yavün said in time.

"We know that," Elithéa replied. "The seven sons of Adag."

"No," the youth said. "Well, yes, but it's more than that. Agon has corrupted their spirits over the years. They clung to him, but he clung back. A thousand years they endured his anger and misery. In time they began to succumb to it, and they were as much chained to him as he was to them. They became demons, and Agon found a way to incarnate them in this world, to host their tainted and twisted forms inside the bodies and souls of others."

"That can't be good," Thalla said, and she looked as though she was going to say more, but she stopped, for her voice was distracting to Yavün. He looked up at her and smiled again, and he only continued his account when Elithéa's gruff voice seized his attention.

"Tell us of these demons," she said.

"I don't know much about them," Yavün said, "and what I know is in the form of verse."

"Ever the opportunistic poet," Elithéa remarked.

"These are not my words," the youth replied. "They are the Gatekeeper's."

And so he began, and perhaps it was the words themselves, or the mention that they came from the lips of the Gatekeeper, if he even had lips to speak them, but everyone shivered a little as he spoke, as if they felt Death had walked into the pavilion.

> *The first fears death, and, though devout,*
> *to an untrue god he prays;*
> *The second one is death itself,*
> *from the great and dark beyond;*
> *The third is the blackest stag*
> *with whitest horns and eyes ablaze;*
> *The fourth flies high, and covets relics,*
> *and from an egg it spawned;*
> *The fifth is pale, and tall enough*
> *to blot out the sun's fair rays;*
> *The sixth is dark, of equal strength,*
> *which he shares in brother's bond;*
> *The seventh is veiled, but powerful,*
> *a Magus of malaise;*
> *And together as they fall, the Beast*
> *can from his jail abscond.*

The group were stunned to hear these words, and Ifferon could posit what some of the lines referred to, and he knew from the looks of others that they could also.

"I know who the first of these is, or rather was," Yavün explained. "It was Teron, the head-cleric of the Order of Olagh, whom I never liked nor trusted."

"You are not alone," Ifferon said. "But how do you know it was him?"

"I met Melgalés in the Underworld," the youth answered. Thalla stopped bathing his head for a moment, but then started again. "He told me much of this, and he was able to decipher the initial piece of the Gatekeeper's riddle, for Teron had become a demon there, gifted a second lease of life by Agon, even if it was in a twisted form. They battled, and he was slain, and so this terrible series of events was put in motion, for the destruction of the demon was the destruction of the first chain."

"So then my decision to end Teron's life was a mistake," Ifferon said, and he felt as if he had let the Beast loose himself, as if he had given him the key to his own cage.

"No," Délin said. "Blame is another emissary of the Beast. We should not bow down to him."

"Trueblade is right," Oelinor said, breaking his lengthy silence. "There is only so much we can see ere it comes to pass. The Beast, Aelor save us, would have broken free in time, and if it were not some of us to break those chains, it would have been others, and we would be here at war just the same."

"They are the Vials of Wrath," Yavün said, continuing his account, "and they had been mentioned to me before, but I didn't know what they were then. They are the forces of constraint, empowered by Agon's anger, given life by his rage. Just as they contained him, they are also containers, and while they are whole, the bonds are whole. But should they break, as has been foredoomed—for glass vials almost yearn to be broken—then Agon will be freed."

"No," Délin said. "So much has been left to fate, and I will not have it that way, where we are powerless to do anything, as if we were mere characters in a tale. If it has been foredoomed that Agon shall be free, then let me foredoom that he shall perish in freedom, and that if he shall not perish, then he shall never be free."

Many nodded, and some applauded, and some said "aye!" and some cried "hear, hear!" Some said naught at all, for they were still pondering the poem about the Vials of Wrath.

"I know the third," Geldirana said. "We faced the black stags in Alimror, and we killed them all, including the white-horned one."

"And the fourth must be the monstrous crow at the Black Eyrie," Ifferon said.

"And I would think that we also met the second," Délin said. "For one of the dead Nahamoni attacked us."

"And the ground trembled afterwards," Elithéa said, shaking her head as if she did not know why she had not deciphered this before.

"The fifth and sixth must be the Nahamoni twin giants that caught us," Délin posited.

"And the final one," Thalla said, "the only chain left to break, is undoubtedly the one who stood in this room only moments ago."

They all paused as the realisation set in, as the ripples of this knowledge trickled over their minds, and as the aftershocks unsettled their souls, as if they were hearing again for the first time each of those six snapping chains, and the prospect of the seventh and final snap.

And as they looked around, especially to that empty space where the Visage stood not long ago, where he taunted them, as if he knew of his own true role, they realised that he was not the only one missing from the pavilion.

"Where is Herr'Don?" Délin asked.

They turned about, and did not see him.

Fear rose within them, and it seemed to all of them that they had a new type of clearsight, for they could see in their mind's eye Herr'Don leaving the pavilion.

Ifferon placed his hand upon the back of the now empty chair where Yavün's sword previously lay. The fear rose further, and their mind's eye showed the sword in Herr'Don's hand.

They raced after him, and in their minds they could see him stepping out to meet the Visage, could hear the ominous sound of each step, like the promise of the sound of snapping chains. They charged through the field towards the second pavilion, which seemed further away than it ever had before. They burst through the curtain doors, like Agon had burst through the earth, and they stopped suddenly as the bloodied body of the Visage fell to the ground before them, where the evil Magus' Beldarian lay crushed beneath Herr'Don's heavy boots, where Brégest and the other knights lay bruised and battered, and where the Felokar wolves sat like tamed dogs.

"Let the Gatekeeper mock him now," Herr'Don said, and the tip of his sword, of Yavün's sword, struck the ground, and it made a terrible sound. In answer came the echo of rending steel, and they knew it in the depths of their hearts, and in the depths of their souls, that the final manacle had snapped.

They were too late, and time seemed to taunt

them, even as their eyes beheld the horror, and their hearts feared what terror had been unleashed. The demon was dead. The chain was broken. Agon was free.

XV

DAWN

❦

In the depths of Halés, where the sleep of the dead was disturbed by the constant flailing and thrashing of the Beast's many limbs, the final chain that clung to Agon's left ankle strained and broke. The Beast reared up and pulled himself out of the chasm that he had made, the passage he had dug through to the world of Iraldas. He cast off Corrias from his back, as if that god were but a garment, and he placed his two monstrous feet upon the soil of the world above, upon the earth he had not walked for a thousand years.

He roared to the heavens in triumph, a sonic challenge to Althar, where he knew the Céalari were listening, but were powerless to stop him. The sound boomed and rumbled, and he stopped only when he was certain that all ears in the four corners of Iraldas had heard his answering call.

Ifferon might say "Begone!" and some might flee, but Agon's cry said the opposite. "Come!" it told them, even if it did not use words. "I am here. I am free."

Délin and Brégest seized Herr'Don and took the sword Daradag from his hand, but it was too late, and they almost toppled from the force of the quake and bellow that soon followed. It needed no explanation, for they all knew well enough what had been done, even if they dared not ponder what might follow.

"You fool!" Elithéa shouted at the prince.

"He was the last one," Ifferon said, shaking his head.

"Not the last to die," Herr'Don, struggling to free himself from the knights' grip.

"He was the last chain," Ifferon explained. "Agon did not break any of them. We did."

The words of Teron came back to haunt him, even if the ghost of the head-cleric could not. *You play the games that even the gods dare not play, and you played right into our very hands!*

Despite all the anger the company had for Herr'Don and his actions, they knew well that they could not afford too much blame, for they were just as guilty of this end. They had all felled the living chains of Agon, had all contributed in some way to his freedom.

"We've lost," Thalla said.

"No," Délin answered. "We cannot undo what has been done, but this is not over yet. We can still fight Agon."

"And die?" Elithéa asked.

"I guess it is time to try my suggestion," Ifferon said. "Ere long it might no longer be a willing sacrifice."

Some of them had clearly resigned to this fate, as Ifferon had, and they gave him the kind of mournful and pitying glances that they might give to someone dying. It did not help with Ifferon's resolve.

Then Yavün came into this second pavilion. They had almost forgotten him, and had left him behind in their attempt to stop Herr'Don. He limped and stumbled, and Thalla caught him by the arm before he fell. He looked deathly pale, and those same mournful and pitying glances turned to him now.

"Rest, boy," Délin said.

"Let me try a different weapon first," Yavün coughed, but it was clearly an effort just to speak.

"The Sword is not enough," Ifferon said.

"No, not the Sword," the youth replied. "The shadow."

There were some awkward and nervous glances, and some whispers back and forth, broken by Herr'Don's disgruntled remarks. "He is evil," he said. "The shadows speak through him."

"And I can speak through them," Yavün retorted.

"And what will you say, hmm?" Herr'Don asked. "Will you tell Agon to go back to Halés, and will he listen? No, I did not think so."

"We haven't set the Molokrán upon him," Yavün said. "It is worth a try,"

"You are too weak to try that," Ifferon said.

"It may be our only chance."

Oelinor nodded. "He is right. If light is not enough to banish darkness, perhaps darkness itself is the answer. It is time Agon, Aelor save us, faced one of our greatest foes. We have lost many good people to the Lichelord, Aelor save us, and if they can serve some new end, it will help atone for their great crime against this world."

"What makes you think they will have any effect?" Elithéa asked.

Oelinor looked to her with dim eyes. "They are not servants of Agon, Aelor save us, but Molok, Aelor save us all. They have been on the same side for many years, that is true, but perhaps we can change that now."

"But you are forgetting something," Délin said. "Agon consumed Molok. He is as much the master of the Molokrán now as Molok was, and if he did not fear Molok then, I see no reason why he should fear Molok's servants now."

"A worthy point," Oelinor said, "but we are running out of options in this war. We have thrown almost everything we have, but this is something we have not yet tried."

"I have to do this," Yavün said. "If I don't, I will always wonder if this might have changed things, if my curse could be used for some good before the end."

"You might not have much time to wonder," Elithéa said.

And so they agreed to Yavün's plan, mostly out of desperation, though Herr'Don would have no part of it.

"Let it be known that I resisted," he said, as if Yavün's curse might be the curse of all.

Corrias wrestled with the Beast, hand grappling hand, with their great feet digging deep into the earth. They leaned against each other like tilting towers, where force held back force, and where only equal strength kept one from tumbling down.

Who would wager against either of these great foes? Who would bet upon the lives of gods, would gamble against hope, or go all in with despair? Who could tell which of them would be the victor, and who could truly win, when all spectators were as much within the arena as those two contending forces?

They toiled, but the struggle was more in Corrias' face than it was in Agon's, for the Beast was happy to fight, if he were ever truly happy, so long as the fight was above ground, where the only chains were the ones people wore inside their minds.

Time was ticking by, grain by grain, and the father god's strength was giving way. It did not help to think that this was in some way Chránán's revenge, for upon the earth of Iraldas not even Corrias could escape the Lord of the Shadow of Time.

Thalla helped Yavün into a nearby seat, just moments before he felt his limbs give way. His legs shook like rattling bones, and he felt suddenly a kind of shame, for he was greeted by a group of worried eyes, which looked upon him as if he were an old man trapped inside a young man's body. Though he did not use magic, and though he wore a Beldarian, he thought that perhaps there was some other kind of magic, the conjuring of shadow, that had begun to age him before his time.

Those worried eyes turned to anxious ones, staring with expectation. None of them knew what to do, except Herr'Don, who knew that he should glare. Yavün might have been distracted by all these people were it not for his own fatigue, which helped him forget the world around him but for the chair he sat upon, and Thalla's hand upon his arm. He felt himself begin to root to the spot, as if he had become that rugged chair. He could not move his body, but he could move his mind.

He looked out at the world around, opening what he thought were his spirit eyes, though even now he was not altogether certain. In the world between worlds, where life and death tugged in either direction, there were few certainties.

Though the Molokrán had fled back to Tol-Úmari, Yavün hunted them out in his mind, which travelled more swiftly than his feet ever could. He climbed the walls of that tower, even as the Molokrán had climbed the walls of Nahragor, and he found the Lichelord hiding in his crypt.

The shadow was never so terrified as it was that day, for the Alar Molokrán did not go to his crypt to rest, but to cower. When good trembles at the thought of evil, there is little thought given to what evil trembles at, and how much more terrible it must be. That night it was Yavün, and he was a terror to behold.

Perhaps the Lichelord might have tried to fight, if his control of weather had any effect upon the shadow world, but it did not, and that powerful figure simply quivered. His shape changed constantly, and as Yavün approached, and as all other Shadowspirits backed away, the Lichelord seemed to grow smaller, dwarfed by the greater shadow of the menacing figure before him.

With a suddenness like the ending of the lives of many of the Ardúnari, Yavün dived at the Lichelord, and he entered inside that cage of shadow, where the door was left open. There was no resistance now, and though Yavün was very tired, he felt completely in control.

Now he looked out at the world around, opening his shadow eyes, and he looked upon the great claws of shadow that were his hands, and the great mass of shadow that was his body, and though he had no weapons, he felt almost that he bore a whip called Fear and a scourge called Terror.

He left Tol-Úmari with an unearthly speed, like the swiftness of shadow as it flees the hunting rays of the sun. Though there was a distance of days between him and where the Beast now walked the earth, the mix of spirit and shadow, and his grim determination, spurred him on like the lash of another whip.

In time he passed the pavilions, where he could almost sense the worried eyes grow more worried, and the anxious eyes grow more anxious. Perhaps some of them felt a mighty gust of wind as he passed, and perhaps they all felt a coolness in the air, and perhaps the clearsighted saw the fleeting shadow. All he knew for certain was that ahead of him he could feel a different kind of air, and instead of cold he felt heat, and in place of the clearsight he would see with shadow eyes what the Beast looked like.

And so that moment came at last, for the dust gave way, and he saw before him two giant forms, wrestling hand in hand. For the briefest of moments they looked like colossal statues, sculptures crafted by the Elad Éni, when even the smallest creations were monstrous in size. But then they moved, and they became suddenly more frightening, like statues brought to life.

Corrias seemed to struggle more than Agon, for Agon had gained strength through his constant struggle with the chains of Halés, while Corrias had been weakened when he incarnated in Iraldas, where the passage of days was the passing of life. Yet both of them held each other in check, like two great mountains leaning against one another, stopping each other from falling over.

Yavün did not take long to watch this tussle, but sprang immediately into action.

He dodged between the gigantic legs of both deities, a shadow within their own enormous sha-dows, and when they moved, and those colossal limbs came down around him, he felt that he might at any moment be crushed in his shadow form and knock back into his body, or knocked straight into the Halls of Halés.

It was hard to find the right position from which to launch his attack, for it was like trying to assail a mountain that kept moving, and though it was by its great size impossible to miss, he knew that he had only one real chance at this, and that he had to make it work.

He passed through Corrias' legs once more, and then he crawled up one of Agon's legs, his shadow fingers seeping into the very pores of the Beast's flesh, and Agon clearly felt it, for he turned his evil gaze to his own body, just as Yavün climbed further, until finally he stood upon the shoulder of the Beast and began to claw and strike at Agon's face.

Agon roared, and the force of that roar almost knocked Yavün from him, and it would have done so were he in his human form, but the shadow clung to him like it clung to earth when the Molokrán were first formed by the malignant Molok. Agon swiped at him, like he might swat a fly, but Yavün crawled behind his head and then around to his other shoulder.

Agon was so distracted by this gnat of a being that he used two of his great arms to try to crush it, holding Corrias back with his other two arms. This gave Corrias new strength, and though the father god was clearly tired beyond measure, and rued that he should feel such exhaustion in this weakened form away from the healing air of Althar, he pushed with all his might and knocked Agon onto his back.

The fall was like a collapsing mountain, and though the shadow could cling to anything, Yavün struggled to keep his grip as Agon came crashing down. His eyes started to glaze and grow dim, and he knew he was losing his own grip on the shadow, even if it would not let go of Agon. The strain was becoming too much, and so he knew he had to let go of the Beast if he was to retain control of the Lichelord. And so he tumbled from Agon's shoulder, even as Agon was toppled, and he fell into the dirt before the Beast's terrifying face.

There was a moment where Yavün could see deep into Agon's anguished eyes, where for a time he felt almost consumed by them, and perhaps he would have been if he were not in this other form. Then he felt Agon's penetrating gaze through the veil of shadow, spying for him, looking through him as much as he had looked into the eyes of the Beast, and lived.

Then that face—which Yavün would never forget, which would haunt him forever when he closed his eyes, would stalk his sleep, would even follow him into the sleepless realm of Halés when the time for death would come—began to change. It morphed slowly, and yet it seemed that in no time at all Yavün was looking upon the demented visage of Molok, who gazed at him through this cage he called Agon.

"Begone!" the Beast spoke, and it was with the voice of Molok, and so it held a sway over the Molokrán like no other could, like not even Telm's similar dying words could cast aside the shadow. Yavün felt himself thrown backwards inside the shadow form, as if he were falling once again, and there was nothing to grip hold of, nothing to keep his footing. The shadow dispersed around him, and for a brief moment, a fraction of a second, he fell in ghostly form before the face of Agon.

The shock of this fall was only surpassed by the shock of what happened next, for though he expected to baulk before the Beast without the shield of shadow, the Beast flinched instead, as if he had seen the power of his own destruction.

"And flame," Agon said, and that was the last Yavün recalled from there, for he awoke suddenly back in his own body, with an intense fever as if his very flesh were in flames.

"Did it work?" Ifferon asked, a question echoed in all those apprehensive eyes around him.

"No," Yavün said, "but I know how to stop him now."

XVI

MESTALARIN

They looked to Yavün with expectation, and none of them spoke, though their eyes pleaded for the answer to the riddle of Agon's defeat.

"We are the words," Yavün told them, much to their confusion.

"We are?" Délin quizzed.

"Well, some of us."

"What do you mean?" Délin asked, and he seemed less patient now.

"What is my name?" the youth asked in turn, and this only wore down the knight's patience a little more.

"Dear Olagh, he's forgotten his name now," Herr'Don remarked. He never had any patience to begin with.

"No. What is my name?"

Suddenly Ifferon was brought back to that moment in the monastery when he first met the youth, when he said: *Yavün Arri. My name.* So much had changed since then. He wondered if all of their names should be changed too, for perhaps they no longer fitted.

"Yavün Arri," Ifferon said.

"Ignore my family name for now."

"Ignore him altogether and save us some sanity," Herr'Don quipped. He looked to the emptiness beside him, as if for approval. Perhaps it granted it.

"I do not understand where this is going," Délin admitted.

"What does my name mean?" Yavün asked, and the fever flooded his face with crimson, as if that colour was the meaning of his name.

Elithéa struck her staff upon her thigh. "Are we going to sit here playing riddles all day, or can you tell us the answer ere Agon destroys us all?"

"I think I understand," Ifferon said, and he felt the realisation like the sudden break of day, which chased away all the shadows of ignorance in his mind. The realisation was so simple, and yet so profound, that he found he had to clutch the side of a nearby chair to stop himself from falling.

"Little fire," Oelinor said, and he lit up like Ifferon thought his own face must have. "You have an Aelora name."

"Yavün," Ifferon added. "Derived from *iav*, fire, and *ün*, little. Little fire. Flame."

"And does this mean something?" Elithéa wondered.

Suddenly Délin's eyes lit up, and Ifferon knew that he had made the connection also. "By fire and flame," he said, as if it were an exclamation of surprise, "and fume and fury."

"He is one of the Last Words," Ifferon said.

"He is Flame," the knight added, and nodded emphatically as though he realised that they had discovered the way to end Agon's reign.

"So the words are living powers," Geldirana said, and she almost smiled, the kind of smile an Ardúnar makes when casting light against the shadow.

"I knew we needed more than just the Scroll," Ifferon said, and he was not sure if he was relieved or disappointed that his own plan, to die like Telm did, was no longer needed. That part of his mind, which he now locked away, whispered that they might still need it.

"But what of the other words?" Délin asked. "*Iavün* is an obvious one, but we don't have someone called *Iav*, or *Samün*, or *Samadas*."

"We have someone called Fume," Geldirana said. "Though I named her in the Bororian tongue."

Ifferon's eyes lit up once more. "Affon," he said.

The girl perked her ears and clambered over. She sat before them and beamed, and for a moment it seemed that her name meant Proud instead.

"And how do we know this is not just mere coincidence?" Elithéa asked. "What if I had been called one of those names instead? Surely the gods do not control us like that."

"He *recoiled* from me," Yavün said, and he patted his forehead, where the sweat recoiled from his brow. "The Beast was scared, and he said the word that gave him fear. *And flame*."

"But how do we know that this girl will have the same effect?"

"I'll scare him," Affon said, and she furrowed her brow and clenched her fists, and perhaps she thought she was frightening to them all. Ifferon smiled a little, and he saw his smile mirrored on Geldirana's face.

"In the Garigút, we pray for the nine months we are with child to find their perfect name," Geldirana explained. "To some, Affon is a boy's name. To me, it was the only name for her."

"I'm stronger than a boy," Affon said.

"So we have two," Délin said. "What of the other two?"

"I don't know," Yavün answered, and the previous elation on many of their faces turned to sudden disappointment, as if their hope had been murdered on the doorstep of safety.

"This is a good start," Ifferon said, taking out the Scroll of Mestalarin and unfurling it upon the table. Oelinor and Délin grabbed nearby objects to hold down the curling sides. They all gathered around it like the lost around a map.

"I see no clues within the Scroll," Délin said.

"Nor I," Oelinor said, with a hint of sadness. "There is nothing unusual about the runes of the Aerbateros used here. In other texts, the letters might be changed in form, if ever so slightly, to signify a special meaning beyond the literal words, but I see none of that here."

"How then do we find the other Living Words?" Thalla asked.

"Maybe we should just march up to Agon one by one and hope he cowers from us," Elithéa said derisively.

The company looked at one another. "That's not a bad idea," Thalla said.

"Not if you have a death wish," Elithéa replied.

"It might be worth a try," Délin said.

"And what if none of us are the other words?"

"Then we will rule each of us out," Délin said, "but I think the gods have ushered us to one another, that we might fulfil a greater end together."

"Perhaps so, but maybe it is the evil gods that goad us so," Elithéa suggested.

Ifferon did not like the thought. They had already done much in evil's favour, as if they were the unwitting pawns of the opposing side. As they stood upon the board with their backs turned, they could not tell who were their masters, could not see what king or queen they served. For some it was always a game of black and white, but for him it seemed like a game of grey. He felt so close to the end, but he could not tell if it would be a happy ending.

"Come then!" Herr'Don cried. "There is no doubt that I must be Fury, and though we did not know it ere this day, Agon shall know it more truly."

He charged out, despite Edgaron's attempts to hold him back, and he paused only to glance to one side and mumble something to himself, perhaps another invocation of his anger to prove to him and all around that he must be one of the living Last Words.

The last they heard of him, he was shouting to the sky, roaring in all directions, and the last they caught of his bitter voice was: "His last words shall be: *I have fallen to the Great.*"

"I guess he's first then," Elithéa said.

They left the pavilion and followed Herr'Don to where Corrias held Agon down upon the ground, where Yavün had seen him last. The Beast twisted and turned, and he toiled endlessly, thrashing against his captor, who looked as though he might at any moment give in and let Agon free.

Herr'Don raced up to the Beast, shouting "Fury! Fury!" and brandishing his blade wildly and with a fury of his own. He approached the ever-shifting face and sliced at it, but his sword struck weakly, and Agon's resulting roar sent the prince tumbling into the distance, where he landed on his back only feet away from the others.

"I guess you're not Fury then," Elithéa remarked.

"Let me try next," Affon said, and she began to march towards the Beast, but Ifferon held her back.

"No, Affon. We already know you are one."

"But I want to prove it," she said.

"You will prove it soon enough, child."

"Corrias is straining," Délin said.

"We don't have much time," Thalla added. "I will go next." And so she set out, and as she walked she formed many protective shields around herself, white orbs, blue watery vapours, and cubical grids. She approached the Beast cautiously, but he did not cower from her.

"I do not think we can afford to go one by one," Délin said. "Let us approach in small numbers, and if he baulks, then we know it is one of our small group."

"Many of us already fought him," Geldirana said.

"Yes, but there was little way to tell his reaction when we set everything we had upon him. We must do this in smaller numbers."

"Let the knights go together then," Elithéa said. "And rule them out."

And so Délin, Brégest, and the other surviving knights, who numbered only four, approached Agon in a similarly cautious manner to Thalla. They had armour of a different kind, but they knew it offered little protection against the Beast. Yet as they approached, Thalla, Oelinor, and the handful of Magi left standing cast their own shields around them.

And nothing came of it, for Agon barely reacted to the knights, instead continuing his great struggle with Corrias. While there, the knights knelt for a moment and gave a silent prayer to Corrias, and this helped him a little in his bitter wrestle.

"Let's go next," Elithéa said, gesturing to Geldirana. The Garigút Way-thane accompanied the Ferian as she approached the Beast, and again the Magi shielded them as they went. And then the Beast reacted. As he bashed and struggled, his eyes turned darkest black, and he turned his head away from the approaching women. "And fury!" the Beast roared, turning to them with renewed anger. They were knocked back several metres, but they knew that one of them was Fury. Both looked to each other with fiery eyes, and anyone watching would have had a hard time telling which was the better candidate for the role.

"Mother and daughter," Geldirana said. "Fume and fury." She approached the Beast once more, and he baulked before her, like the Shadowspirits had so many times before. So many of the other Ardúnari had fallen, and she kept going, for she was Death-strong, and now even Agon knew to fear her.

The women returned, and the company rejoiced.

Few were surprised to find that Geldirana of the Garigút was the living Last Word called Fury.

"And what of Fire?" Délin asked.

The remaining people, numbering several dozen, approached the Beast in groups of three or four, and they all returned, some running, without success. A few thought Oelinor might be the one, but there was little reaction from the Beast.

"I don't suppose you are Fire," Délin suggested to Ifferon.

"No," the cleric said. "I do not think I am much of anything now. I might be the Scroll-cleric, but there are some here who are the contents of that Scroll."

"I am sure you are more than that," Délin said.

"There must be hundreds of thousands of people here in Iraldas," Elithéa said. "We cannot march them all up to the Beast."

"Will three of the Last Words be enough then?" Délin wondered.

"I do not think so," Ifferon said.

"Then all of this is pointless," Elithéa said.

As they talked and argued, Yavün's fever began to grow more intense, and it dulled his senses. He faded in and out of consciousness, and Thalla sat by his side like a mother. She removed his shirt to expose his sizzling skin to the cool air, and she paused for a moment as she uncovered the Beldarian he wore. Then she continued on as if it did not matter, but Ifferon noticed that her hand instinctively reached for her own Beldarian, which she hid deeper in her robes, as if Yavün's secret had exposed her own.

The company continued their debate, with new

voices joining as old voices waned. The conversation turned time and time again to Yavün, whether he could truly be trusted, and whether or not they should rush his weakened body to the Beast or let him fight his fever. Some of the Magi suggested it was a curse, the work of evil sorcerers intent on hindering their mission, but Oelinor cautioned them against paranoia, which he said was a fever of its own.

Yet regardless of the source, Yavün's sickness was growing worse, and his strength was failing. He was no longer lucid, and he began to mutter and mumble to himself. No amount of Thalla bathing his head made any difference, and the company began to wonder if he might die, and if the hopes of vanquishing Agon might die with him.

Time passed, and no healing salve nor magical trinket helped to cool him down. Even Oelinor tried the laying on of hands, but the Aelora were not as adept at this as the Taarí were, and they all rued that the Rebel Taarí had abandoned the battle under the leadership of Narylal, for she might have been able to save him. In time Oelinor was forced to give up, for even his own hands began to burn, as if he had caught the plague of fire.

"I can do no more," Oelinor said, but then he saw a flicker of fire in the Beldarian about Yavün's neck. "Is that gem hot?" he asked.

They looked to the pendant now as if it were an oracle, but like many oracles it showed them little they could understand. The fire inside the *beldar* gem grew more intense, swirling about as if it were a living creature. Perhaps it spoke to them, but if it did, it spoke with a tongue of flame, and perhaps only Yavün could understand it.

Suddenly Yavün awoke, and his fever began to quickly abate. "The fire," he said.

"I know," Thalla said, bathing his head. "We are trying to cool it."

"No," he said, though the heat choked his words. "I spoke with the voice of fire."

She paused, and her hand trembled.

"It's Melgalés," he said.

"But he is no longer with us," Délin pointed out.

"So our quest is doomed," Elithéa said. "How can we say *By fire and flame*, if only the flame yet lives, and perhaps does not live for long."

"We have to find a way," Délin said.

Elithéa stamped her staff upon the ground, and the sound had a certain finality about it. "I do not think there is a way ... if he is now a ghost."

Herr'Don tapped her on the shoulder. "I think I know a way," he said, and he turned to his side, where he held out his arm, as if to show them something. "Let me introduce you to Belnavar."

XVII

MEETING GHOSTS

꒰ꕤ꒱

The company stared where Herr'Don gestured, and though some of them like Ifferon and Geldirana had the clearsight, their puzzled expressions made it clear they could see nothing there.

"He has finally cracked," Elithéa sneered.

"This ordeal has been a strain upon us all," Délin said, and that was more irritating to the prince than Elithéa's outright accusation of madness. Others looked awkwardly to one another, and some gave sympathetic glances to the prince.

Herr'Don became flustered by their reaction. "Doubt me all you will, but I know what my eyes see, and what my ears hear!"

Edgaron looked around. "Can you show us you are here?" he said, and Herr'Don shook his head, for his old friend was looking not at Belnavar, but to where a real emptiness was.

"I would shout," Belnavar said, "but I would only deafen Herr'Don, and still prove nothing of my existence."

"There's little point saying that to me," Herr'Don replied, and he hoped the others knew it was a reply, and not just a random comment to himself.

"Did he lose his brain as well as his arm?" Elithéa

asked, and this inflamed Herr'Don so much that he felt like charging at her and proving that he only needed one arm to end her life.

"Come now," Délin said. "There is nothing to be gained in discourtesy, nor anything to be won through violence."

Elithéa scoffed. "If you can talk to ghosts, tell Aralus I said *hello*."

"She has quite the mouth," Belnavar remarked.

"I wish she could hear that," Herr'Don said.

"Hear what?" she asked.

"Much mouth, no ears," Belnavar replied. "Not that what I say matters."

"Maybe it matters more than I previously thought," Herr'Don said.

"Let us take a moment," Délin said, "lest we confuse ourselves beyond repair. Herr'Don, please tell us how you think we might bring back the ghost of Melgalés."

"I'm not sure how I did it," Herr'Don said.

Elithéa cocked her head. "Well, that's useful."

"I went to the place where Belnavar was buried, and I gave a song of remembrance."

"And nothing else?" Délin quizzed. "I was there when we buried him, and I recall you giving a hymn then, and nothing came of it."

"I do not think it really struck me until later," Herr'Don said, "until I felt a loss of my own."

"Many of us have felt losses," Délin said. "But why did he return for you?"

"Perhaps it is because he meant something to me."

Belnavar smiled. "Why, that's very sweet of you."

"This takes a lot of faith," Elithéa said, and the look on many faces suggested quite a few others agreed with her.

"Everything we have done so far does," Délin said. "Perhaps we should trust that there is a greater purpose here, that we have a chance to make things better."

"So then we need someone close to Melgalés to go back to his final resting place," Ifferon said.

"Then I will go," Thalla replied. "He was my mentor, my master, my friend. He was a father to me, even a mother to me, when my own parents could not be that. I don't know what I was to him, only what he was to me, and that I would give anything to see him again, even if it is just his ghost."

Her testimony proved to them that she was the best candidate for the heartfelt eulogy that might act as an invocation to the dead. None knew if it would be successful, but they knew that she was their best chance, and perhaps their only chance.

"We cannot let her go alone," Délin said.

"I will go with her," Yavün proposed.

"No," Herr'Don barked, and he almost snapped his teeth at the poet. "*I* will go."

"I'm the better rider," the youth said feebly.

"You can barely stand or walk," Elithéa noted.

Yavün gave a weak smile. "I don't need to do either on horseback."

"And just how are *you* the better rider, boy?" Herr'Don asked. "I've ridden dozens of horses, to war and back. What have you done in your small allotment of years?"

Yavün glared at the prince. "I've helped horses give birth. I've fed them and cleaned them. I've talked to them and trained them. I've ridden horses, not to war, no, but in all kinds of weather, for no reason at all beyond the enjoyment of it, and of their company."

"Let him come with me," Thalla said.

Elithéa smirked. "I wonder why."

"Perhaps it is best that Yavün goes," Ifferon said. "Apart from Thalla, he is the best connection to Melgalés we have. If her requiem does not work, then we may depend on Yavün more than anyone or anything to make that link."

Most of them acknowledged the truth of this, but Herr'Don stormed off, clutching the hilt of his sword as though it were Yavün's neck.

The others ignored him and made immediate preparations for Thalla and Yavün's departure. A small amount of rations were packed, weapons were stowed, and Brégest went in search of the few horses that had survived the battle.

Délin pulled Ifferon aside to talk about Herr'Don. "What if he is just crazy?" he asked. "He has always been a queer sort, and some thought he was mad ere he lost his arm. What if he really is crazy?"

"What if he's not?" Ifferon asked in turn. "We have exhausted all options."

But Yavün brought them new conviction, for he faded in and out of consciousness, and on one of these occasions he found himself in that twilight place between Iraldas and Halés, where the living are not quite living and the dead are not quite dead. Then he saw Belnavar standing beside Herr'Don, and he knew that the prince was neither lying nor insane.

When the news of this was conveyed to the others, it brought some relief, and it quelled doubt and quietened despair. But there was still concern among them all, even Thalla, who was fearful, and Yavün, who was feeble.

Brégest found the horses tethered to several large posts. There were only two left. The others had clearly bucked and ran when the tremors came from Agon's location. No one present could blame them, and some wished that they could also flee.

"Two horses, two riders," Délin said. "May this prove a boon to us."

"Would that there were three," Herr'Don said, "but I am needed on the battlefield." He held his cloak tight and tilted his head to the sky, as if it were the gods who ordained him a captain of war.

The horses were soon made ready, but before they rode off, Herr'Don approached Yavün and pulled him close, so close that he could feel the poet's breath upon his face, and could feel his fear through the tremble of his skin.

"You won her," Herr'Don told the youth, and he growled to hold back his tears. "Well done, boy! Enjoy your stolen prize."

"I'm not a prize, Herr'Don," Thalla said. "There are no winners or losers."

"Then how come I am the only one who lost?"

"You're not," she said, and she looked up with

sorrow in her eyes, with an echo of that look she had when Melgalés first fell.

But Herr'Don looked back with a different sorrow in his eyes, and he might have spoken were it not for the anger that clogged his throat, even as the tears dammed his eyes.

"Goodbye," she said. "I hope we will return, and return successful."

He watched as the two rode off together, and knew in his heart that they had ridden off together in their hearts a long time before. All that was left was the dust that was kicked up by the feet of the horses, and amidst those tiny specks of dust stood Herr'Don, and though he was surrounded by many people, he stood alone.

"It will take them days to get there, and days to get back," Délin said. "Even if Yavün can ride as swift as he claims."

"What then do we do?" Ifferon asked.

"Everything we can to delay and weaken Agon."

"Éala weakens," Elithéa said.

"So this is Chránán's triumph," Délin said. "The Lord of the Shadow of Time gets his retribution by depriving us of time."

"We still have the Sword," Ifferon said.

"And I hope you know how to use it," the knight said sternly, like he might have done to any young knight just learning what it meant to live in a world at war.

The survivors of the previous battles returned to the battlefield, where Corrias was barely surviving in his struggle with Agon. So few gods remained, and yet it was up to him, the father god, to keep Agon from crushing the world. So few warriors remained, and yet it was up to them, mere mortals, to delay Agon for long enough that he might be crushed instead.

"Corrias cannot hold him for long," Délin said.

"Neither can we," Elithéa replied.

"What can we do?" Ifferon asked.

"We need to distract him," Herr'Don said, and he pondered long and hard. "Whack him a few times."

"I think we tried that," Délin said, "and it was not very successful."

"We need to whack him with something bigger," Herr'Don suggested.

Ifferon held up Daradag. "If this is the Sword of Telm, and Telm matched Agon in size, then maybe this is as big as we can get."

"Go on then," Herr'Don said. "Hit him a few times."

Ifferon looked up at the towering figures. "Eh ..."

"Give it to me then and I'll have a go," the prince boasted.

"It will hit harder if it comes from a Child of Telm," Délin said. "Of that I have no doubt."

And so Ifferon held aloft the Sword of Telm, and he read aloud the Last Words, and the shimmering armour of Telm formed around him, and to all eyes he seemed to grow in size. Yet still he was dwarfed by the gods before him, and he looked even smaller when he marched out to meet them in battle.

The ground trembled as he walked, and yet he did not tremble with it. Those around him were clearly afraid, and yet he did not feel fear like he had done before. Weeks ago he might have fled, but now he marched. Weeks ago Agon had sought him out, but now it was he who sought out the Beast.

He swung the Sword of Telm at Agon's ankle, and it sliced through, and Agon gave a cry. He did the same to the other foot, but this time Agon's lashing tail struck him and sent him back. Were it not for Corrias holding him in place, Agon might have turned to Ifferon and crushed him.

The other survivors joined the fray, racing beneath the giant bodies of the two warring gods, lashing and slashing, and throwing spear and javelin. They ran to and fro, for the legs of those same gods came down around them, and they turned about as they tussled, and the people below had to duck and dodge, and run and roll, to avoid being crushed beneath those monstrous limbs. Some of the soldiers were not so lucky, and as the battle raged, and the gods rumbled, there were fewer beneath to fight a different kind of war.

Ifferon charged in again, and he struck once more at the ankles of Agon, replacing the bite of iron chains with the bite of a steel sword. The Beast screamed to the sky, bellowed to the ground, and cried to the four winds. He seemed to weaken just a little, and the strain in Corrias' face lessened in turn, but they both continued their struggle, and Ifferon continued his own in the battleground below the gods.

Thalla and Yavün rode side by side for what seemed like hours. Initially the necessity of their mission made the time disappear beneath the stampeding hooves, but now it seemed that each gallop was just another tick upon an endless clock.

Their horses sped for many miles, but they soon grew tired and needed rest and water, and between gallops they could only trot along. During these moments Thalla and Yavün talked, sharing what had transpired since their parting in the tumble at the Chasm of Issarí.

"What happened to your face?" Yavün asked, gesturing to the faint scars.

Thalla turned away, embarrassed.

"I didn't mean to offend you," Yavün said. "I was just curious."

Thalla took a moment to respond. "I played with fire, and I got burnt."

"Does it hurt?"

"Not now," she replied. "It hurt when it happened."

Yavün paused. "When you say you played with fire, do you mean magic?"

"Yes," she said.

There was another long and awkward pause. "I see you have a Beldarian," Yavün noted.

"I see you have one too," Thalla replied, and the look in her eyes unsettled him.

"I meant to tell you," he said. "I wanted to, but … I didn't think you'd understand."

Thalla did not respond, which made him wonder if she still did not understand.

"I didn't steal it," he said, when the silence accused him.

"I'm not angry," Thalla said. "I would have been, had you revealed it to me earlier. But I guess if you are a thief, then I am one also."

"But I didn't steal it," he insisted. "I wasn't in control."

"But you are now?"

"I guess," he said. "But I can't give it back."

"I know. Neither can I."

"How did you get yours?" Yavün asked.

"From another Magus. He fell in battle, and I needed to fight. I needed to use magic, and I needed a Beldarian to protect me from the flames." She turned away again, hiding another shame.

"I guess we're both locked up in other people's lives now," Yavün said.

"Yes, I think you're right."

There was another long pause before Yavün felt he had to slay the silence. "You're still beautiful, you know."

She turned to him with questioning eyes.

"I mean, the scars don't make a difference, to me at least."

She gave a faint smile, and she might have given a bigger and more distinct one were it not for those scars.

The horses began to speed up, and when the galloping wind joined them, the conversation ended, though it still continued long in their minds, where there were other scars that a Beldarian could not prevent.

*　　*　　*

The battle between Corrias and Agon waged on, and there was little that Ifferon and his companions could do to help. They clung to hope, even as it seemed to be slipping away.

Then something happened that destroyed their faith almost entirely. Agon mustered all his strength, goaded by his pain, and seized the Sword of Telm from Ifferon. It grew in size until it fit Agon's monstrous hand, and until it fit Corrias' colossal heart, wherein it plunged.

"Begone!" the Beast bellowed, and Corrias faltered.

Délin gave a shout, and if he could have caught Corrias as he fell, he would have. But the father god collapsed upon the ground, and the world shook, and many souls shuddered.

Then Agon rose up and cast aside the Sword of Telm, which shrunk again in size as Ifferon ran to grab it. The Beast strode north, his monstrous feet crushing the earth beneath him, his monstrous arms reaching out to feel the air that he had not felt for so long. He marched off with his long and angry strides, and the company saw where he was marching to: the land of Boror.

In time Thalla and Yavün reached Ardún-Fé, and they were reminded of that time when they first met, and when Melgalés was taken from the world. The horses would not go into that damned land, and though they were exhausted, they fled as soon as Thalla and Yavün dismounted.

"Well, that's not a good sign," Yavün said.

Thalla did not respond. Her eyes were fixed on the bristle-like trees of the forest in the distance. Once the Harwood, now the Rotwood—it was a place of pestilence and death, and it was where Melgalés died, and where his body joined whatever else rotted away slowly there.

Yavün urged caution, and he was weak and tired, even more so now from their long journey. Thalla might have heeded his advice were it not for the mounting anger she felt as the memories of Melgalés' passing came back to her, as if the floodgates had finally opened, and instead of a river of water bursting forth, there came a river of fire.

"I want to find and kill those monsters," Thalla said, and she spoke this through her gritted teeth, as if they were another dam, holding back another fiery deluge.

And so she charged forth, racing over rock and leaping over log, and not even slowing as she passed into the spindly cage of the Rotwood. Yavün found it difficult to keep up with her, for she crashed through the trees like a monster of her own.

As they went deeper into the forest, they felt the familiar crunch of the undergrowth, and of the things that did not grow. The needle-like trees prodded through the crust of the earth, and they were barren of branches and empty of leaves. They offered little protection from the heavens, but the crispness of the soil below, and whatever lived beneath it, showed clearly that the rain rarely fell here, that even the weather did not like this place.

Yavün walked as Thalla stormed, and fear was

a new companion, though only Yavün knew it, for Thalla was preoccupied with reaching the body of Melgalés, and destroying anything in her way.

Then Yavün yelped as something grabbed his foot. Thalla turned, with flames already forming at her fingertips. The youth was embarrassed to admit that it was just a piece of fallen bark that had rubbed up against his ankle.

Then something really seized him, and he saw the world turn upside down, until finally his eyes settled on a hulking mass of branch and twig, made bigger by the bones of countless victims. He cried out, and he struggled, but he had little energy to fight off the Karisgor that held him, that dangled him before its open maw.

Suddenly the wood set ablaze, and a great and terrible moan came from the creature as parts of it fell off, still burning. Yavün fell to the ground as the Karisgor fell apart, and a mountain of bones came tumbling over him. He cried again as he knocked some of the bones aside and backed away quickly to where Thalla stood, dripping embers.

Yavün sat down, panting for a moment. "You know, I wish I could do that. I've got the Beldarian for it."

"I could teach you," Thalla suggested. "So could Melgalés."

"Not sure I have the stomach for it," he replied, and he grimaced as he looked at the molten mess of what used to be a Karisgor.

"Let's go," Thalla said, and she turned to leave.

"A moment, please," the youth begged. "I just

need to catch my breath."

Suddenly they heard the crashing of trees and cracking of wood from all around them, followed by a chorus of low-pitched moans.

"Breath caught," Yavün said, as fear helped him to his feet.

They trudged onwards, and when the crashing sounds grew louder they then began to trot, and when the moaning grew closer they then began to run. The sounds mounted, until finally Thalla and Yavün halted suddenly as a wall of Karisgors greeted them. They turned, but another wall of beasts stood there, until finally they were caged, and all that was left were the sounds, and nowhere to run from them.

The groaning noises became quickly unbearable, and Yavün covered his ears. Thalla erected an orb-shaped shield around them, and this drowned out much of the terrible noise. Then, as the Karisgors trudged in, she let loose so much fire from the heavens and from her hands that her Beldarian began to strain, and Yavün wondered if perhaps she instead was really Fire, and his own Flame was nothing in comparison.

Blazing columns crashed down upon the Karisgors, and those that were not crushed were set alight, and those that were not burned were torn apart by many hands of flame. In a matter of moments the Karisgors were laid to waste, and all that was left was the rubble of their bodies, and a steady stream of smoke, like the ethereal substance of the dead. And so the forest was an even greater waste. Once the Rotwood, now the Ruinwood.

"I guess we didn't need to run then," Yavün said, but he caught Thalla as she suddenly began to fall.

"I'm fine," she said, but clearly she was not. Yavün could see the dull complexion of her face, and the dull complexion in the *beldar* gem. The magic was taking its toll, and the Beldarian could only do so much.

They stumbled onwards, each hanging out of the other, for they were both tired beyond anything they had ever known before, as if they had in these past few weeks lived the entirety of their lives. They did not admit it, but they were glad to spend some of this fleeting time with each other.

They wandered for a time, and then they came upon the clearing where their earlier battle with the Karisgors did not go so well, where Melgalés had called the creatures to him, that the others might escape. They could not help but wonder: if he had known that he was just as important as Ifferon, would he have so easily given up his life?

Yavün was surprised to see that the Magus' raven still stood there, pacing back and forth, stretching its legs and flapping its wings from time to time. It turned to them suddenly and cawed, and its eyes brightened as it saw Thalla. It flew over and landed before her, where it flapped its wings again, though less aggressively. It said something in its tongue, but neither understood what it meant. Then the bird trotted back to Melgalés, and they followed.

The Magus' body was half decomposed, and it was a grim sight to behold. His face had shrunken and darkened, and the skeleton showed through, revealing the frailty inherent in them all. His clothes were tattered, but mostly intact, and the only thing that took away a little from the sombre sight was the colourful beads plaited into his hair. They were the only colour in this ashen place.

Did he look peaceful? was what Thalla had asked Yavün so many weeks before. He had lied then, but he could not lie now. Melgalés was there to tell the truth.

Thalla collapsed before his body, partly from exhaustion, partly from sorrow, the exhaustion of the soul.

"You were supposed to be there for me," she said, and she looked up and then down, as if she did not know where to address her words. She did not look at the remains.

Yavün stayed silent. Even though he had come to know Melgalés in death, and first did not even know it was him, he did not feel he had any right to comment. This was about remembering the man as he was while alive, not as he was while dead.

Thalla was not a poet or a bard, so her tribute came in the form of prose. "You saved me from the House of Hataramon," she said. "You saved my life, and I could not save yours. You taught me magic, even though you did not want to. You took me as your apprentice, even though all the rules said you couldn't. You were an Ardúnar, a Warden of Light, and you were a Magus, but you were a father and a friend to me, a teacher and tutor. You saved my life, and I could not save yours."

As they sat there, Thalla releasing all her long-held pain and anguish, and Yavün feeling that per-haps he was unable to release his own, he began to ponder the meaning of Melgalés' name. Perhaps it did not have the same kind of significance Yavün's did, but it meant *Memory Passage*, and Yavün could not help but notice how, in some way, he only lived on in the passage of memory.

They buried the body, and the raven seemed confused, as if its master had just disappeared before its eyes, a new kind of magic for which it was not prepared. It looked around and began to peck at the dirt where Melgalés sat before, and then it looked at Thalla and Yavün and gave a sad shriek. So it was that the bird gave an elegy of its own.

Thalla wept, and though she seemed that she was all fire, she cried tears of water, and they were perhaps the first drops the starved soil of that place had seen in a long time. Every tear she had held back came flooding forth, and Yavün was also moved to tears, for he could not bear the sight of Thalla in so much pain.

"Come, child," a voice came quick and sudden. "I've had plenty of time to count all the stars in my eyes, and though new ones won't grow for me, no, they certainly will grow for you!"

They turned, and there stood Melgalés, shimmering in a halo of fire.

XVIII

THE BATTLE OF THE LAST WORDS

Back in Telarym, where Corrias died and Agon lived, there was no time for horror, no time to lose hope or linger in despair. The horror lay before them. The despair walked ahead of them. It was called the Beast.

"He is heading for Boror," Délin said, and Ifferon could not help but think that the worry in his voice was less for the Bororians and more for Théos in Arlin. With Telarym now desolate and broken, Boror was the last true barrier to the knight's Motherland.

"If he keeps this path, he will walk straight into Fort Onar," Ifferon said.

"Fort Watchful," Herr'Don mused.

"It's less watchful now that it is abandoned," Ifferon remarked.

"And thank Olagh that this is so!" Herr'Don cried.

"At least there are no people there to kill," Ifferon said. "He will destroy a ruin."

"And perhaps he will find a surprise," Herr'Don said, and his eyes glinted, as if the Beast might open the box called Fort Onar and find Herr'Don inside.

"What do you mean?" Délin quizzed.

"All of the abandoned forts along our southern border have been lined with explosive kegs. They were designed to stop the forts falling into enemy hands when we retreated from them. Periodically they are checked and replaced, and so perhaps Fort Onar shall be watchful once again."

"Can we lure Agon into the explosives?" Ifferon asked.

"Perhaps," Herr'Don said, "though I am not sure it will stop him."

Ifferon knew for certain that it would not. "But it may slow him. And that is our real weapon at this time until Thalla and Yavün return."

"Let us rest assure," Délin said, and his voice was grim, "time is the weapon of Chránán, the master of Agon's master, and so it can never be our ally."

"Yet Agon serves no master, and so let us hope that time is not his ally either!" Herr'Don said.

Though luck was not an ally, and time was more an enemy, the company found that there were new partners in their battle against the Beast. As Agon strode forth, crushing the ground beneath him and lashing it with his tail, the ground itself began to strike back, for here and there the rocks erupted, and out from the various chasms came the Moln. Some clung to his legs and slowed him, and some began to pound upon him like he pounded the earth, and like he pounded the ceiling of Halés for a thousand years. Others cast themselves at him as if they were flung from a catapult, and some began to erect themselves into walls ahead of Agon's path, which he broke through with ease. None of this stopped Agon's advance, but it slowed him, and though the company followed through a graveyard of rock, where the very gravestones were the heads of cloven Moln, it was clear that Agon's strides were now slower than they had ever been.

In time they came once more to the Issar Chammas, the River Barrier, but it proved no barrier to Agon, who had broken through the greater barrier of his own bonds. He strode across it as if it were not there at all.

Though the river prophesied, it was not large enough to tell Agon of his doom, and so even as he crossed over it, it shrunk in size, as if it saw within itself its own end, and the end of all rivers at the vanquishing fires of the Beast.

To those that followed, the river spoke little of their fate, but some saw within its shallow waters what might await them in the coming battle, and what might await the world if it was not won.

Soon they came upon the border of Boror, another barrier that Agon passed through with little effort, and so the Beast passed into the kingdom without a king. Ifferon saw from the rage in Herr'Don's face that he took this entry somewhat personally, as if indeed Agon had broken through the doors of Ilokmaden Keep. And so, it seemed, he might still do.

Fort Onar came into view, despite the dust of Agon's heavy footfalls, which could not hide the great size of Boror's largest fortress town. It was lucky for the company, and for all Bororians, that Agon made for this settlement, for it was the most sprawling and the most heavily fortified, and though it was now the most ruined, it also had the largest stockpile of explosive barrels, and so perhaps was the largest trap for the Beast. It was likely its sheer size that attracted Agon to Fort Onar, for he knew not that it was empty, or that it had been settled instead by a supply of booby-traps. He yearned for destruction, there was little doubt, for even the ground below him cracked in agony beneath his heavy strides, and in Fort Onar he would find destruction by the barrel load.

The company followed, hiding in Agon's monstrous shadow, which made upon the ground a moving mockery of the Molokrán, whom the company never knew they would no longer fear. The sun was periodically blocked by the Beast's height and width, and though it threatened to break through the numerous clouds, as if to threaten Agon with its pinpointing rays, the sky was mostly bleak, as if it watched with cool depression as the Beast approached the great stone archway that led into Fort Onar.

And so the destruction began, for Agon crashed through the arch, and the bricks and rocks were thrown apart as if Agon himself was an explosion. The company were glad that they held back far in Agon's train, for they would have been crushed by the falling debris.

When the rocks no longer rained and when the dust no longer blinded, the company clambered across the ruins of the archway and into the greater ruins of the fortified city. As soon as they entered, they scattered in all directions, looking for hiding places amidst the debris. They raced through the crumbled streets of Fort Onar, every now and then peeping their heads over wrecked walls and jagged pillars.

Ifferon felt his heart race ahead of him, as if to pre-empt each of his steps. For a brief moment he thought that perhaps as he forged ahead in one direction, his heart was trying to flee in the other, and though at one point he might have went with it, it now went with him—into the winding streets where Agon crashed through.

Ifferon turned a corner and pulled himself back sharply, for there a massive foot came crashing down, and he felt his body shudder from the force, and shudder from the presence of the Beast. He hoped Agon had not seen him, and yet knew that he must somehow attract the Beast's attention, to lure him deeper into Fort Onar, where no granite walls could cage him.

From this vantage point he could see a few of his comrades racing further up the streets, and when he peeped his head around the corner he could see a beam of light that Oelinor shot into the air to lure the Beast towards him. Then Ifferon saw why Oelinor was so desperate to distract Agon, for the Beast had spotted Affon, who could not run as fast as Geldirana.

And so Ifferon did what madness would do, if it could act: he leapt out in front of the Beast and shouted at the monster. "Begone!" he cried, and Agon came to a slow halt, sending up a plume of dust before him, like tiny spectators to this paltry cleric's challenge. The Beast settled his intense and glaring eyes upon Ifferon, and though Ifferon did not look up to them, he could feel their stare, breaking through his bones and his body as Agon broke through the walls and columns of Fort Onar.

It was perhaps only a second before Ifferon began to flee, and it was less than a second before Agon began to pursue him. Though the streets of Fort Onar were empty, Ifferon was a kill that would bring a pleasure and relief to Agon that a hundred other slaughters could not do.

So Ifferon ran. There was something in Agon's stare that gave speed to his legs. There was something in the Beast's presence that made it vital to do everything to get out of it. He raced down a thin alleyway, where he knew Agon could not tread, and yet the collapsing buildings behind and around him showed that there was nowhere that Agon could not go. To Ifferon there were passages and pathways, designed by the architects of Boror many centuries ago, but to Agon the entirety of Iraldas was his walkway, and though his bonds had held him in check in Halés, there were no longer any barriers to him now.

And so Ifferon raced. His heart pulled him on, and fear pushed him. He turned a corner sharply, knowing that Agon's size was the only thing that slowed him. Then he turned another, even as the previous corner became a pile of rubble. The sound almost distracted him from the three barrels ahead of him, which were painted with a red star. He tried to slow, but he realised he had no time, and so he closed his eyes as he leapt over the barrels, and only opened them again when he was sure he did not feel his limbs exploding. He turned again, and this time he was thrown forward by a great gust of air, and he heard the Beast roar.

Good, he thought, even though only seconds before he was thinking the very opposite. He felt Agon's presence dim a little, and he knew it was not the explosion, but Agon slowing in his pursuit. Ifferon kept running, but this time he looked for a way to get to some higher ground, and soon he spotted a stone staircase that led into one of the armouries. He jumped up two or three steps at a time, and he came out onto a rampart that circled a cloistered area, where many straw dummies had been laced with explosives.

So far the cat and mouse game was working, but Ifferon could not help but think that it was a poor game to play when he was the mouse. Fort Onar might have stopped a thousand armies in Boror's heyday, but it was not built to hold back the Beast. Those streets could not restrict him, nor those walls hold him. Delay was their only weapon. Only time could cage Agon.

But the cat is a hunter, and Ifferon was prey. The Beast crashed through the armoury, hauling up the largest bricks and casting them aside like pebbles, until finally he saw Ifferon there, miniscule like a mouse. Perhaps Agon smiled, though his mouth was so twisted that it was hard to tell, and perhaps Agon's eyes glimmered, but they were so mangled that it was hard to see.

There was no moment of gloating, no last words from Agon before he ensured that Ifferon could never speak again. He raised his massive fists, until one of them blotted out the sun, and Ifferon took a deep breath. He thought that he would cower and close his eyes before that fateful final moment, but he did not. He accepted his imminent end, and he felt a kind of peace, even though he knew that death and life were deep in an eternal war.

Then a barrel hurtled through the air and exploded in Agon's face, and the Beast burst into rage, casting his eyes around as if they might leap out of his head and explode upon the bodies of his attackers. He saw Herr'Don and Délin almost immediately, loading barrels onto a catapult at one of the fort's arsenals, and he saw Elithéa and Edgaron helping them, but he did not make for them yet, but turned instead to crush Ifferon beneath his angry fists. Yet Ifferon was not there, for he had crept away into the shadows that crept away from Agon. He felt Agon's rage rise even further, and if it was not palpable from his eerie aura, it was felt through his thrashing of the ground around him, where he hoped to strike the fleeing cleric.

Then another barrel stole Agon's sight once more, and with it went his body and his rage, and with it fell another row of buildings as the Beast clambered towards his attackers.

Herr'Don waved the flag that stood on a pole beside his arsenal, as if the barrel blasts were not enough announcement to Agon. He cheered and taunted, and to any watchful eyes, even the angry eyes of Agon, he seemed right at home.

"Well, we have his attention," Délin said. "What now?"

"Fire another volley!" Herr'Don shouted, and he struggled to roll a barrel up onto his foot and then hoist it to the catapult's cradle. The way he kicked it and bashed it made Délin nervous in a way that only the approaching Agon could surpass. "Away!" the prince cried as he launched the weapon. It flew towards the Beast, but this time he bashed it aside with one of his monstrous arms. It exploded on impact, but it did not elicit a cry of pain from Agon like the others had.

"*Away* is the right word," Délin said, and he made for the stone stairway leading towards the west. "Come!" he cried as he turned and saw that Herr'Don was not joining him, and that Edgaron stood by his side. "Herr'Don!" he called, but it was like speaking to the granite walls of Fort Onar, which was now Herr'Don's dangerous playground.

"Let Agon come!" Herr'Don replied, and yet he gave his words to the wind, that they might be a further taunt to Agon's ears.

"It's madness to stay here," Elithéa said. "We need to delay Agon, not kill him."

"Death is the best delay," Herr'Don said, and he looked to Edgaron with a manic glee.

"Edgaron!" Délin called, but the man shook his head, as if he had resigned himself to his fate. Délin rolled his eyes and left with Elithéa, while Edgaron stayed and set his eyes upon the approaching Beast.

Herr'Don moved about at a frenzied speed, and he felt so full of life, so in his element. He turned and grinned at Belnavar, who stood beside the banner as if he greatly yearned to wave it.

"I'd help with the kegs," Belnavar said, "but you have more useful arms than I."

"You can help with the taunts," Herr'Don suggested. "Surely ghosts can haunt the Beast."

"Death still haunts the dead," Belnavar remarked, "threatening its reprise."

"Let's deal the first and second deaths to Agon!" Herr'Don cried. "In one fell blow if we can, and yet," he paused, "perhaps make it two, that we might have twice the glory!"

But the glory of battle comes at a price, and Herr'Don successfully attracted Agon's attention. The Beast charged towards him, hastened by the anger that each new exploding keg tore from him. In time his four arms came crashing down upon the arsenal where Herr'Don and Edgaron worked, and the building was quickly turned to rubble.

Délin and Elithéa charged back up the stairs, but they were too late, and they could not see either of the men beneath the slabs of rock in the haze of dust. The Beast loomed tall above them, and he began to tear down nearby buildings that still were standing.

"Pull them out," Elithéa said, and she charged off before the knight could stop her. He glanced to where her nimble legs raced and leapt and jumped, and the final thing he saw was her unleashing her staves and swinging them to and fro, like a mating call to some wild beast. And so Agon caught sight of her, and he bounded after her as she disappeared into the serpentine streets.

Délin immersed himself in the rubble of the arsenal, clearing away stone and wood, which seemed heavier than sword with the weight of worry upon them. He looked for his buried comrades, but brick revealed boulder, and slab revealed stone, and all the while his sight was buried beneath the dust. In time he found a hand, and he cleared away more debris to find that it was Herr'Don, who clambered up as soon as the largest of the rocks were removed from him. He was doused in dirt, yet he looked almost ready to race back out to battle, but Délin directed his energy towards digging instead. Minutes passed like hours, until finally they unearthed Edgaron, who was bathed in blood as much as dust and dirt.

"Edgaron!" Herr'Don cried, and his frenzy weakened, replaced by the frenzy of concern. He clasped the man's hand, and Edgaron barely clasped it back.

"Herr'Don," Edgaron said weakly. He tried to smile, but the pain was stronger than his muscles were.

"No, don't die," Herr'Don whimpered. "I already have a ghost. I need a friend who lives."

"I held your hand in Ilokmaden," Edgaron struggled, the words spluttering up with blood.

Herr'Don clasped Edgaron's hand tighter. "I have your hand," he said.

"I have to let go," Edgaron whispered, and Délin could tell it was intended to be spoken aloud. He looked down to the reddened rubble.

"Do not die like this," Herr'Don said. "Fight death. Fight with me. Please. You said you'd fight with me."

"I fought."

"Keep fighting."

"I'm trying."

"Take my strength," the prince said, and it seemed that he would almost slit his own hand to replace the lost blood of his friend with his own.

"I never got to tell you," Edgaron said, struggling with the words. Then his face grew pale, his hand grew limp, and he said no more.

"No," Herr'Don said, shaking his head in disbelief. Délin placed his hand upon the prince's shoulder, but it was shrugged aside. Herr'Don's hand began to shake as she still clutched the hand of Edgaron.

"He was a good man," Délin said. It had been said of so many soldiers before. Even all the slabs of stone they sat upon were not enough for every tombstone.

"What god lets Telm speak the Last Words, but does not let us Men do the same," Herr'Don said, and he looked to the sky and ground, and all around him, as if for answers, but all that was there was the uncaring dust and the silent stone.

His frenzy died like his friend. Yet it could do what Edgaron could not; it could feed upon his rage, and so bring itself back to life, into a more powerful life than ever before. Délin saw it first in his eyes, and then in the redness of his cheeks, which contrasted with the paleness of Edgaron. Then it seemed almost like something snapped, as if the very building of Herr'Don's mind also turned to rubble.

Before Délin could do anything, the prince leapt up and threw himself down the pile of rubble, unleashing his sword as he slid and stumbled. He screamed and shouted, and the words made no sense, for they were in the language of the grieving. Délin could make out only one word, and it was "Agon," and the prince cried it aloud like it was the only name on his list.

He raced down the narrow passages, made narrower by debris, and though the dust still hindered his sight, he saw the silhouette of Agon through the haze. He charged at the Beast, who stood with his back to the prince, flailing madly at the few stone towers left standing. Herr'Don dodged the rain of rubble, cleaving at the feet of Agon as he bobbed and weaved between boulder and wood. Though his anger was mighty, his strikes were minuscule against the monstrous frame of the Beast, which dwarfed even the Sentinels he had fought in the Old Temple in the White Mountains.

Then the prince realised that Elithéa stood before Agon, ducking and dodging, swinging and striking. Buildings came down around her, and they would have been upon her were it not for her quick evasion. Yet her attacks were also ineffective, serving only to raise the ire of a creature for whom ire was like blood.

Yet as Agon's anger mounted, his attacks grew fiercer and quicker, until it seemed that he was like Henishanad the Hundred-handed, fists flying in all directions, bashing and pummelling, seizing and crushing. Herr'Don was knocked aside, where a new mound of rubble pinned him down, but Elithéa was seized by Agon, who held up her tiny body, kicking and flailing.

Herr'Don struggled with his stony prison. He shouted to the Beast, but it was too late. Agon tightened his grip upon Elithéa. She cried out, and she was crushed. Her body tumbled from his hand, slamming into the ground below, where the rolling rocks became her tomb.

Agon turned about, gloating above the wreckage he had wrought. He roared to the south, which he had conquered; he roared to the north, which he was conquering; he roared to the west, which knew to fear him; he roared to the east, which would soon learn of that fear; he roared to the heavens, where the gods trembled; he roared to the depths below, where the dead cowered from him like they cowered from the second death. In every part of every world, all heard his roar.

Just as all looked lost, and the ruin of Fort Onar echoed the ruin in the company's hearts and minds, Thalla and Yavün returned. It seemed to many eyes that they had returned alone, but their accomplished expressions and the presence of a familiar raven suggested otherwise.

"Gather together to arrange your attack," Délin said. "We will do what we can to hold Agon's attention. But hurry! I do not think we will hold it for long." He charged off, making for the arsenal directly opposite the one that Agon had destroyed.

Ifferon reunited with Geldirana and Affon, and they ran to Thalla and Yavün, who ran to them in turn. When they met and ducked behind one of the taller buildings, where Agon's probing eyes could not spot them, they began to talk over each other in their anxious need to formulate a plan. They were in such a hurry that they barely had time to acknowledge Melgalés' presence, nor to appreciate their success in bringing his ghost back from Halés.

"Let us go in turn," Ifferon said, "as the Scroll dictates. Fire, Melgalés. Flame, Yavün. Fume, Affon. Fury, Geldirana. I trust you know the Aelora for those words by now."

"And what about you?" Yavün asked, and he flinched as he heard an explosion, and he looked to the second arsenal, now manned by Délin.

"I guess I just bear the Scroll," Ifferon said, a little despondently. "I am not one of the words within it."

"That can't be so," Yavün said.

"We do not have time to wonder," Geldirana said. "Let's go!"

And so they ran back into the fray, where barrels exploded and buildings toppled, and where Agon thrashed and trounced, and where Brégest and Oel-inor, and a handful of other survivors, raced about, dodging their deaths.

When Ifferon and his companions reached Agon, the Beast turned to them sharply, and he puffed his chest and flexed his many arms. Even his eyes burned more fiercely, as if he were flexing the fire within them. He was as daunting as ever, if not more so, for the presence of the Last Words brought back the anger of ages past, and with that anger came the strength that he had used to topple Telm, to knock the crown from the head of the Warrior-king. As Agon posed before them, like a statue from an ancient era when everything that walked the earth was monstrous in size and monstrous in heart, it seemed to those who looked upon him that it was impossible to topple him.

Yet they tried.

Melgalés stood before Agon like he had stood before the Karisgor in Ardún-Fé, and though he had been felled by those beasts, and by Teron's evil curse, he seemed stronger than ever in his halo of fire. In this ghostly form, which only Thalla and Yavün could see, there was no doubt that he was Fire. He proved it when he spoke the word. "*Iav*," he said, and he burst into a fireball, which spat at Agon and exploded around him like a thousand kegs.

But the fire dissipated, and through the embers Agon's eyes burned more fiercely.

Yavün stepped forth next, and though he did not have a halo of fire like Melgalés had, the presence of the Magus gave him courage, and brought from within him the flaming lion that lived beneath the guise of a stable-boy, beneath the vesture of a poet. "*Iavün*," he cried, and he knew then that this was far more than his name, for a rain of tiny flames came down upon Agon.

But the rain cleared up, and Agon's fists carried flames of their own.

Affon marched forth, placing her hands upon her hips as if to strike a pose to counter Agon's. She seemed even smaller now before the monstrous size of the Beast, and yet she did not show her fear, even though Ifferon was certain she felt it just as he did. "*Samün*," she shouted, and a wind bashed at Agon's form like a sudden hurricane, blowing out his flaming fists.

But the wind weakened, and Agon's fire returned.

Geldirana came next, and she did not tarry, and she did not need any time to muster the fury that was her title and her mission. "*Samadas!*" she bellowed, as if speaking to every enemy she every killed, and to every enemy she had yet to lay her hands upon. The earth shuddered beneath them, centring on Agon, and he stepped back as his balance was rocked.

But the quake subsided, and Agon still stood strong, with his burning eyes and his flaming fists. He had not toppled. He had not been cast back into Halés. It seemed to the company that these would indeed be their last words, for they stood face to face with Agon, and none, not even Telm, had done this and lived.

This time he had an answering word for them. "Begone!" he said, and they were knocked back from the force of his voice, and they felt in it the mockery of their actions, that they thought that they could fight the Beast and win.

But Ifferon realised in Agon's word what they had missed. *Dehilasü baeos! Al-iav im-iavün im-samün im-samadas, dehilasü baeos!* They had used the forceful words, but they had not used the words that opened and closed them, the words that actually told Agon to leave.

So Ifferon stepped forth, and even as his foot graced the ground, the armour of Telm came down from the clouds, and he seemed to grow in height, and he was a cleric no more. "*Dehilasü baeos!*" he cried, and all who heard it heard Telm's voice, and they knew it was Telm, even though they had never heard him before.

Agon halted, and his form weakened. His arms drooped a little, and the fire in his eyes dimmed. He did not look so powerful now.

Melgalés pressed forth again. "*Al-iav*," he said, adding in the full words, giving them every strength, feeding them with all the fire he could muster.

Agon toppled backwards as the fire engulfed him, and before he had regained his footing, Yavün sprang forward and shouted "*Im-iavün!*" The fire grew fiercer than ever around him, and the Beast cried out as a new pain joined the thousand other pains he felt. He stumbled further.

Affon and Geldirana came next, and their cries of "*Im-samün!*" and "*Im-samadas!*" brought back the avenging air and the angry earth. The ground rocked and the sky rumbled. All the while, Agon gave out a series of forceful cries, each in a different tongue, each louder and more painful than the last. It was as if he was trying to counter the Last Words with ones of his own, and though Ifferon began to feel a force stirring as if from the depths of the Void, he crushed that call with some final words of his own.

"*Dehilasü baeos!*" he cried once more, and more than ever the company were certain that they heard Telm and saw Telm, and if there was any doubt, it was removed when Ifferon held up the sword Daradag and lunged it forth into Agon's flesh.

And Agon fell. The Beast fell. He toppled like a tower built upon a weak foundation, and as he struck the ground his body began to crumble, as if it truly were made of stone. His many shifting countenances combined into a single one, a mass of features that faded into a blended form, which acted as a canvas for all minds, where the horrific images would not so easily fade away. The force of Agon's fall knocked everyone from their feet, and many stumbled even in far distant lands. The world shook, and it was the final quake caused by the Beast.

It took a moment for what had happened to fully sink in. Délin pulled Herr'Don from the rubble, and they both searched for Elithéa, but could not find her body. In time they all regrouped, though some came out slowly, as if they were not altogether sure that it was over. They sat with each other upon the ruin of Fort Onar for their first rest of the day, and their final rest together.

"So evil is dead," Yavün said, and he beamed.

"You are still naïve," Herr'Don responded. "Agon is dead. Evil always survives."

"Because good survives," Délin said. "With one comes the other."

"Evil takes on new forms," Herr'Don said. "In the time of the Elad Éni, it was Chránán. In the time of the Céalari, it was Molok. In our time, it was Agon. Maybe in our children's time, it will be us."

"That is an evil thought," Délin said.

"And no less true because of it," Herr'Don replied. "Agon is no longer in chains, and so the greatest evil of our world is no longer a god. What I have seen in the streets of Madenahan is a different kind of evil.

It is smaller in form, but no less in its ability. For the Age of Gods, a god shall be evil. For the Age of Man, the evil shall be Man."

"There is always a price that is paid," Délin said, casting his eyes about, as if he still searched for Elithéa.

"Too high a price," Herr'Don replied, and he looked to the wreckage of the eastern arsenal, where the body of Edgaron still lay.

Yavün glanced once at the remains of the Beast, and it only took that single look to shock his soul and yet stir some inspiration within him to express his joy and relief that Agon's evil reign had been ended. Yet even as he thought about it, and as words began to rouse within his heart and form upon his lips, he realised that Agon had left behind a scarred world, a world in need of mending.

He did not need to interrupt anyone for his sombre hymn, for they were all silent with solemn litanies of their own. He began:

The Beast is dead, and with him dies his deeds,
Though none will forget what evil he wrought,
Nor what foul things he made to meet his needs,
Nor what wicked wars we against him fought.
A dark tree will leave behind some dark seeds,
And so the soil remains forever fraught.
Thus we must trim the vines and tame the weeds,
Until the land no longer is distraught,
Until when asked of Agon's painful pleads,
The land will say of that: "'twas all for naught."

Though the day was evening out, and this vespers song spoke of some darkness yet to come, it seemed to few that the night could truly fall again, for they had all seen a darker night before, a dark night that had now ended. And so in the hope that sprung anew, this was as much a morning song, and though they would sleep again before the sun came out, they knew it would shine more brightly than it had shone for a long time.

"So we have come to the end of our journey together," Délin said.

"Would that it were not the end," Herr'Don replied.

"All things must end. Even Corrias. Even us."

"Some shall live on," Herr'Don said. "In tales and songs."

"That is true," Délin acknowledged. "And perhaps young Yavün will write them."

They looked to the youth now, who seemed a little older from the tiresome journey and wearisome war that had undoubtedly aged them all. He simpered, but then he looked down to the ground, as if he knew that he would not be the bard for their tales, that he would not be the minstrel of their accomplishments.

"It is sad to part," Ifferon said. "We were united by necessity."

"I think more than that," Délin said. "We were united by a common goal, and the commonality between us all, all races and creeds, all types and ages. Everything that Agon hated, and everything that Agon could never be."

"Let this be a new beginning for us all," Herr'Don

said. "More battles await!"

Délin smiled and looked north to Arlin. "I think my days of battle are over. I think it is time that I retire from the battlefield and lay down my sword."

Herr'Don shook his head violently. "No!" he cried. "What is Trueblade without his blade?"

"Quite a few things," the knight replied. "Some day we must all retire."

"Death shall be my retirement," Herr'Don remarked. "I will take no day of rest ere the Gatekeeper comes knocking."

"Let us hope he does not knock for a long time," Ifferon said, "for any of us."

"And so we part," Délin said, and he bowed his head to them. "May we meet again, and if we do not, let us forever have fond memories."

And thus they exchanged their partings, and some hugged and shook hands, and some saluted, and some gave well wishes, and some gave words of wisdom. There was pain in their parting, but there was also peace. When war is over, even the most unpleasant partings are made that little bit easier.

XIX

THE BONDS OF LOVE

Thalla and Yavün said their goodbyes to their friends and companions. Ifferon hugged them in turn, Délin wished them well, and many others gave their blessings. Herr'Don alone was silent, and in that silence his anger could be heard.

Melgalés waved to them all, though they did not see it, and he said his own goodbyes, though they did not hear them. Belnavar alone saluted the Magus, and the others gave their parting words to the wind, which blew in all places of the world, even Halés.

The two Magi and the poet did not go northeast to Madenahan, as many of the others did, but travelled west until they came upon Lake Loft on the outskirts of Madenloft Forest, which they reached by nightfall. It reminded them of the Shallow Lake in Telarym, where Thalla and Yavün had last parted ways.

"I think our journey is over," Melgalés said, and they all halted together. "Yes, over now at last."

Thalla said nothing, though her eyes spoke into his soul.

"What will happen to you?" Yavün asked of Melgalés.

"I do not know," he replied. "Perhaps I will wander as a ghost, or perhaps I will return to Halés to sit upon the doorstep."

"I can ask neither of you," Yavün said.

The Magus shook his head, and the beads in his hair shook in sympathy. "You are not the one doing the asking."

"Yet I am the one that can provide the answer," the young poet replied, and he looked as though he had come to a decision that would greatly affect them all. "I cannot truly be free until you are. I must break the Beldarian."

"Though I yearn for my eternal rest," Melgalés said, "I cannot ask that you give up your life, and all that this world has to offer, that I may be at peace."

Yavün sunk his head. He felt a terrible guilt inside him, one that had grown and festered since that fateful day when he was led to the body of the Magus, and the Beldarian that would become as much a prison to himself as it was the key to Melgalés' freedom.

"If I were to take this extra lease of life, it would be time borrowed—no, stolen—from you," Yavün said. "That would not be living, and I think neither of us would be at peace. You may think you cannot ask it of me, but I cannot let is go unasked. I must die this day."

Thalla was in tears, and Yavün might have joined her, were it not for his guilt, which was heavier than his sorrow.

"You must realise, Yavün, that there have been no records of this ever having been done in the past," Melgalés explained. "We do not know for certain what the outcome might be. You will die, there is no doubt, but what will happen to you then is beyond my ken, and I have knowledge of death that many will never know. Perhaps you will enter the Halls and be at peace—*perhaps*—but you might also become one of the Waiting, or the Endless Lost, or you might even become nothing at all, for the Void is the Underworld to Halés."

"I know the risk," Yavün said, "and I will have to face it some time, whether it is tonight or fifty years from now."

"Then why not wait? A mortal life passes swiftly compared to the eternity of the afterlife. Yes, *quite swift indeed.*"

Yavün shook his head. "Because then you would have to wait, and you have waited long enough. My final fate is outside my hands, but there is still something I can do now to help the passing of another. I have to do this. You made your sacrifice. Now it is time to make mine."

Thalla looked to both of them in silence, and though perhaps she meant to say something to stop Yavün from this final act, it was clear that she was torn between them, that she could not wish for life for one, when it would come at the expense of the other.

"Though this affects me greatly, and I cannot deny that I feel a certain selfish desire," Melgalés said, "this is your decision to make, no matter what may come of it."

He nodded to them both with a knowing look, as if indeed he knew exactly what they would both decide. Yet he respected that they might not be so conscious of the decision that seemed apparent on their faces, and so he left them for a time and gave them space to talk.

"He will not tell you, so as not to sway you, but Thúalim awaits his rest also," Yavün said to Thalla.

"I know," she replied. "I can feel him through the Pendant. It is not just a matter of waiting; it's a type of torture, to be so close to rest, yet denied it—to be unable to do anything but sit and watch as others pass through the Gate, and to endure the mocking of the Gatekeeper."

Yavün sighed, as if to expel the guilt from his lungs; it could not be expelled from his mind. "So you have seen and felt what I have seen and felt."

"Yes," she said. "And that is why I have made the same decision. My time here is over."

Yavün was silent. Though part of him wanted her to live out her life and find joy and happiness wherever possible, another part of him wanted her to go with him, that they might face death together, and so live forever in what awaited them, even if it was only in memories.

They returned to Melgalés and shared their decision, and he nodded and wished them well. Had he a corporeal form, he might have hugged them, and, if the gods were kind, Thalla and Yavün might one day embrace him in the Halls of Halés.

"I feel now that Halés calls me back," Melgalés said, "and perhaps I will see you there again." Before he could say more, his form faded, though Yavün still felt it strongly through his Beldarian.

The two young lovers looked to one another and smiled. It was a sad smile, filled with nostalgia. Their eyes embraced, and glisten spoke to glisten, and tear whispered to tear.

They felt the Beldarians around their necks, like manacles around their throats, chaining them to life, and chaining them to the dead. They took them off, and they were heavy, weighed down with two souls each, and the guilt and shame that went with them. They placed them on the ground, and yet felt no relief, for the burden still weighed upon their hearts.

They took large stones from the nearby lake and brought them to the place that might become their grave, and so those rocks might become the first part of their own tombstones. The thought was unsettling, but the alternative was unbearable.

"Perhaps we can make some good of this evil act," Yavün suggested. "In place of a pendant, we might wear a different jewel. Perchance, a ring?" He took out the twined ring he had been gifted by Elilod previously, and it did not seem now like a tool of bondage, but a means to show to all the bonds of love.

Thalla said nothing, but her emphatic nod said it all. She stretched out her hand, and on it he placed the ring. It was crude, with no diamond set into its frame, and the rust of ages was upon it, as if to remind them of the endless onslaught of time. Yet it seemed to glimmer more now under the pale moonlight than it had when Elilod gave it to him, and Yavün saw a glitter in Thalla's eyes, which no diamond could ever imitate.

She raised her palm to him, and he placed his own against it, and slid it up until he wore the second loop around his finger. So then they clasped their hands, so that their final grip might keep the ring in place, and seal their love.

"We do not have a cleric," Yavün said. "Perhaps Ifferon could have been that to us now."

"I do not need a priest," she said, and the tears rolled down her face like the fabric of a wedding veil. "This is enough for me. My constant yearning. I am now complete."

Yavün mustered his muse, and he quickly composed his final poem, and wrote the words with the ink of his heart. When he spoke, his voice trembled, like the gentle tremor of a violin, like the music to a last love song:

The world shall minister to us our end,
And join us now in death when life could not;
What union was not had, may marriage mend
These aching hearts, and end this deadly plot.
This ground shall be to us our nuptial bed,
And in matrimony we shall cherish
Each time we have as one, alive and dead.
Parted once, as bride and groom we perish.
These last moments shall symbolise the heart,
Wherein we were betrothed before this time.
While some speak the words "till death do us part,"
May death instead unite us in our prime.
And thus I speak, and if you will allow,
My final words shall be my wedding vow.

And so they lay together, staring into each other's tear-clogged eyes, hand in hand, and rocks raised high in the others, above the two Beldarians that lay between them, the only barrier to their eternal union. They held their arms up for long, so that final moment seemed to last a lifetime, and thus make some worth of what little time they had spent upon Iraldas, and what less time they had spent together.

Soon their arms grew tired, and they began to falter, and they both knew it, for as their rock-laden hands grew weak, their ring-bound grip grew stronger. The fateful moment came, and the rocks smashed through the *beldar* gems.

There was relief. For the briefest of moments, they felt what seemed like an ocean washing over them, and in that ocean there was only them, buoyed by their love. Then everything faded, until the only thing that remained was their union, which even in the blackness could never fade.

When they awoke again, they found that they were in Halés, standing before the steps to the Halls, the very steps upon which sat Melgalés and Rúathar, who looked more real now that they sat in a place where nothing was corporeal.

"So all are free," the Gatekeeper said, and his voice was menacing, and it startled them.

The presence and voice of Melgalés brought cool reassurance. "All are free," he said. "Though Agon gained his freedom, he lost the ultimate freedom of his life."

"And what have you lost?" the Gatekeeper jeered.

"I have gained my reward," the Magus said. "A final rest, in the company of those I love."

"It is wonderful to see you again," Thalla said, and though her tears were no longer real, they stung her spectral eyes all the same.

"And it will be a long time seeing, yes," Melgalés replied, and they hugged. "Let us make up for lost time with eternity in the Halls."

Though it looked liked Thalla had a thousand things to say, she captured all of them with a single smile. The two people she loved most, her mentor and her partner, had been returned to her. All that was lost had been found again. Death, it seemed, was a very small price to pay.

"And you," Melgalés said, turning to Yavün, his voice initially severe. "Thank you for my freedom."

"I was wrongly the jailer," the poet replied. "Thank you for letting me correct my error."

"The long wait was worth seeing the end of Agon."

"Perhaps you desire a longer wait," the Gatekeeper said, "since you dally on the doorstep."

"Just long enough to toy with you in turn," the Magus said. "Perhaps eternity has an end for Chránán, but for you it must be endless. It must be a different kind of pain to that which Agon felt to usher the dead unto their final rest, and yet find no rest of your own."

This must have angered the Gatekeeper greatly, for his presence vanished and the doors to the Halls swung open.

"Our life in the world is over," Melgalés said. "Our life in the Underworld is just beginning."

They walked in together, and the doors shut firmly behind them, watched by the envious eyes of the Waiting, yearned for by the jealous hearts of the Endless Lost.

XX

JUDGEMENT OF ALL

When morning came, it was as if the entire world awoke from a restless slumber, from a place of dark and disturbing dreams, of a place where shadows reigned beneath the greater shadow of the night. The sun shone intensely, and even the tired and the sleepy welcomed it, for in its warm rays were the many promises of a bright and hopeful future, and it seemed to all who looked with dazzled eyes upon it that one of those rays reached out to each of them, as if to illuminate the many new paths that each would take.

Délin did not immediately return to Arlin, even though he yearned to do so. Honour demanded that he pay his final respects to those that had fallen, and so many had fallen. His prayers, though long and fervent, were not enough for the myriad souls that were now ushered into the Halls.

When the survivors began to bury the bodies, he stopped them from burying Elithéa in Boror, a land of kings, or Telarym, a land so devoid of trees that it seemed like it would be an insult to her memory, even if she had so little regard for the body after death. He told his fellow knights that he would bury her in Féthal, her homeland, and Brégest agreed to help him with this.

Yet before they departed, they also paid their final respects to their god Corrias, whose body was nowhere to be seen. Though they were certain that he was dead, they were unsure of exactly what happened to the Céalari when they passed on. Perhaps they went to Halés, or perhaps they went to the Void. Délin thought that it would be a cruel irony for Corrias to join the Elad Éni in the prison he had locked them in. The thought gave him no comfort, and he pined for Corrias, and he pined for a world where Corrias was no longer the father god.

"To whom do I pray?" he asked the heavens. He thought also of that moment when Théos was taken from the world, when he had abandoned his faith in Corrias, had cast his prized pendant into a grave of snow. He felt a certain guilt, even though he hoped he had in some way made amends for his failings.

His eyes looked to Althar above, and it seemed that few eyes looked back. There were few to watch, and perhaps fewer to hear. Though he heard no words in answer to his plea, in time strange thoughts came into his head: *Pray to the living. Pray through living. All life is prayer.*

When Délin and Brégest reached Féthal, they were halted at the border by a contingent of the Éalgarth, all in similar attire to what Elithéa wore.

"What is your business here?" they asked, and they mumbled what might have been Ferian insults among one another.

"We come to honour one of your own," Délin said.

"You are a Man," the main guard said, as if that were the greatest sin. "Your race does not honour ours."

"We are here to do just that," Brégest said. He showed the body of Elithéa.

"Why do you bring the body?" the Éalgarth asked. "Where is her acorn?"

"It was buried in Alimror."

The guard grew incensed, and the others drew their staves as if they had been greatly insulted. "An acorn is sullied when it is planted in Alimror soil."

"I said buried, not planted," Délin said. "This is Elithéa, one of your finest."

The guard scoffed. "Ah, so she has returned, dead in the arms of a Man. Telarym has tainted her. Yet our spies in Alimror say that her acorn was tainted also. Perhaps then the soil of Alimror can do no more."

"Will you let us bury her in Féthal?"

"No," the guard said. "We do not bury the body."

"What do you do with it?"

"Let nature take her course, and return the body to the earth in time."

"Then will you take her body to be honoured in your land as your people will?"

"No," the guard replied. "If her acorn is in Alimror, then her body can go there also, where the taint of the soil may be her most appropriate bed."

"Whatever might have become of her acorn, she was the best of you," Délin said, holding back his anger. "She came as a scout, but she stayed as a soldier. She fought and died with many, while none of you came to fight Agon. History will remember that you never came to the aid of those in the east."

"We fought evils of our own," the guard said, and he glowered. "You know nothing of the wars in the west."

Délin prepared to speak, to challenge the guard, but Brégest pulled him aside, before an ill choice of words might be their doom. He suggested they bury Elithéa in Alimror, where she had placed her acorn, and so they returned to that location and dug a new grave, and spoke new prayers, and hummed new solemn songs.

On the return journey to Arlin, Délin confessed to Brégest that this would be his last war, that he would retire from the knights and live out the remainder of his life away from the battlefield. Brégest was saddened by this, but he understood Trueblade's decision, and he was honoured to be chosen as Délin's successor as both Knight Commander and Lord of Ciligarad.

When Délin returned to Ciligarad, the city erupted in celebration. Word had already reached them of Agon's demise, but they were one of the few settlements to hold off their rejoicing until their lord and leader returned.

Among those waiting for him was Théos, who stood under the watchful eye of the knight Talaramit. The boy stood out against the backdrop of tall knights around him, all of whom wore their finest ceremonial armour. None of them were fighters any more, for many of them were old, some were sick, and others had skills that were better suited to a settled life. Yet as they stood in regiment behind Théos, they looked as strong and intimidating as any of the younger and battle-ready knights that had travelled to Arlin, of whom so few returned.

The sun glinted off the silver and steel, until all eyes squinted. Théos' golden hair seemed more golden than ever, and his smile was broader than Délin had ever remembered it. He held the stuffed toy tree in his hands, hugging it close to him. He seemed ready at any moment to race towards Délin, and from time to time he looked up to Talaramit, as if for permission to leave his place. In time the knight nodded, just as Délin descended his horse, and the boy charged up to him, and they hugged, and Délin lifted him up into the air, even as a Standard-bearer might lift the flag of victory after a hard-won war.

"*Thraslith hassúl,*" Théos whispered to Délin. He did not know what it meant, and it reminded him of the gap of language, and of the one who bridged that gap, who was now no longer with them.

Then he was surprised to hear what followed. "Welcome home," the boy told him. He accented the words oddly, so much so that it was obvious he was from a distant land, but they were words that he could recognise, and though they always had meaning for him, it seemed then that they had more meaning than they ever had before.

Délin was so taken aback that he could not find a response. Talaramit seemed to notice this, for he came to them and placed his hand upon the boy's shoulder.

"I taught him some of the Common Tongue and Old Arlinaic," Talaramit said. "He is a studious child, and a faster learner than many—even you."

"For you," Théos said, and he handed Délin a pendant. It was a perfect replica of the one he had cast aside on the White Mountains, when his whole world turned to darkness. Had it not been for the lack of scratches and tarnishing on this new pendant, he would have thought he was holding the old one. Yet this one seemed more significant than the other ever did, even though Corrias was now dead, and even though it was as much the symbol of his faithlessness as it was his faith.

"I pray," the boy told him, "you come back."

Délin smiled in his heart and soul, to match the smile upon his face. "I prayed that you would be safe, that you would be happy, that Iraldas would be saved for you."

Perhaps the child did not fully understand all of those words, but his smile and the look in his eyes showed that he understood enough.

"Thank you for this gift," Délin said, holding up the pendant again.

He held the pendant in one hand, and in his other arm he held Théos, and he never felt so glad to not be holding a sword, to hold instead what meant much more to him than all he had dedicated his life to.

Then Théos took the pendant and placed it around Délin's neck, just as Délin had taken off the pendant Théos wore, which symbolised so many evil things. For the child there was freedom in not wearing that chain, and yet for Délin there was a new kind of freedom in donning once again the symbol of his faith.

After Délin exchanged greetings with his fellow knights, Théos was eager to show him his room. Trueblade was heartened to see that upon the small table by the window, which served as an altar in the sparse rooms of the knights, sat his old, battered helmet, almost like an idol in a place of worship.

"Metal head," Théos said, and he tapped his knuckles gently against Délin's forehead. The knight smiled and returned the gesture.

"Délin," the boy said; it was the first time he had used his real name. "Can I be knight?"

Délin smiled again. "Yes," he said. "Of course you can."

They looked once more towards the old, battle-weathered helmet, which might one day be worn by Théos into battle.

There were mixed emotions for the victors of this war, for Délin learned from his fellow knights that Issarí had passed away only a few days before, that her body had risen to the top of Lake Nirigán, before disappearing entirely the following night. No prayers to her were answered, nor were the prayers to the other gods in Althar that she be restored to life. It was speculated that she died when Elyr Issaron, the River Man, her spouse and lover, passed on, and so she lived up to her final promise that she would not speak with the Knights again, even though Iraldas had been saved.

The celebration of Agon's defeat was short-lived, and it was followed by a week of mourning. Candles were lit upon little wooden boats, which were pushed out into the lake. They numbered in their hundreds, and were not enough for the tears that Issarí had shed, and were not enough for those who had died in this war.

Délin and Théos crafted a little boat together, and though neither spoke of who it was for, it was clear to them both that it was for Corrias. It was more elaborate than many of the others, but the candle that sat upon it was the same, and when the wax burnt low, it erupted in flame like all the other barges of the dead.

When the week had passed, Délin brought Théos to Alimror, to where Elithéa buried her sullied acorn. The boy remembered the location better than he, and he placed his hands over the spot and said, "A tree." Délin smiled, but shook his head. He prayed for a moment, and he thanked Elithéa, wherever her soul now wandered, that she had spared Théos, even if the world had not spared her.

Thus ended his honouring of the dead, at least for the time at hand, and so he began to honour the living. He returned with Théos to Arlin, and he taught the child many things, and they both knew joy as if it were another knight that lived with them.

After a year had passed, they returned to the sacred spot in Alimror, which was less sacred to Elithéa in those sorrowful moments when she buried that sullied seed. They saw a wonderful sight: in the soil that was once empty there was a sapling, and though it was small, it hinted to their hearts that it would one day grow into a great tree.

Each year they returned to that place to honour Elithéa, and each year as Théos grew a little, so too did the tree. It even seemed that upon the tree there were some natural notches here and there to mark the boy's advancing height.

Délin sometimes thought of what might have been, that he might instead be visiting the tree that grew from Théos' acorn. Though these trees were everything to the Ferian, to Délin they were not enough. To him a person was so much more, and yet he knew that it was folly for him to worry about a clash of culture, which was its own kind of war.

Yet it was a war in which he hoped both sides were giving up their arms and coming to some kind of understanding of one another, meeting out in the no man's land to share words instead of swords. To him, Théos did much to bridge that gap, and as the boy learned new things, the knight found that he learned just as much, that in the child there was wisdom that sometimes the old were lacking.

"Why do the trees grow, and the young grow, but the old do not?" Théos asked him on one of their many outings.

"The old grow in a different way," Délin told him. "There is height in the body, but there is also height in the soul. Some shoulders grow broad, and some stay at a certain size, but there is always room for the heart to grow broader."

"So we are always growing?" the boy asked.

"Yes," the knight replied. "The seeds of the mind are nurtured by knowledge and watered by questions. The seeds of the heart grow by loving and being loved. The seeds of the soul are planted by our actions, and they sprout from our words, and they grow from our deeds."

And so Théos grew in body, and Délin grew in heart and soul, and Elithéa's tree continued to grow, and from it fell the seeds that began the saplings of other trees, and so in her own way she had a family in the forest.

Herr'Don spent some time at Fort Onar, building a tomb for Edgaron out of the many bricks and slabs that lined the place. Others offered to help him, but he refused, and Belnavar would have helped if he could, though he helped in his own by offering his company.

It was a small tomb, nothing like the splendour of those made by the Tibin in the north-westernmost parts of Iraldas, nor even like the opulent cube of Ilokmaden Keep, which, though it housed hundreds of the living, was its own kind of tomb. It was not truly fitting for Edgaron, Herr'Don thought, just as the mound that became the Amrenan Adelis was not truly fitting for Belnavar. He hoped that when he eventually parted from the world, there would be a monument so massive that all in Iraldas would know of his greatness and glory.

Though Herr'Don prayed and told tales of Edgaron's contribution to the world, just as he had done for Belnavar, no ghost appeared to comfort him, nor to wander with him. The comfort and the wandering resided only in his heart, and in those fond memories that would never leave his mind.

From Fort Onar, even as he placed the last slab upon Edgaron's tomb, he heard Boror begin what would be a month of celebration, less for the defeat of Agon and more for the coronation of Aranon, the chosen successor of King Herr'Gal. As one age of opulence gave way, there was another to take its place. Herr'Don was not only not invited to the crowning ceremony, but was actively prohibited from attending. In addition to several messengers being sent out to issue the prince, or former prince, the notice, a second guard was put in place at all four entrances into Madenahan. Herr'Don was not hurt by this, however, for he had no intention of witnessing the beginning of Aranon's reign, and though he could not deny that he resented the short, thin man that replaced the tall, fat one that came before, he had no desire to cause any havoc on the royal day.

"You should be king," Belnavar told him.

"You should be alive," Herr'Don replied with a smile. "Some things do not go our way. But come! I am king of battle, and my kingdom stretches far."

"And what of your crown?" Belnavar asked.

"My helm," Herr'Don said, "though I do not wear it."

"And your sceptre?" the ghost inquired.

"My sword, though I do not need it."

"And what will they call you?"

Herr'Don grinned. "I think you know."

Belnavar smiled in turn. "Herr'Don the Great."

And so began their new journey, back where they had last met each other while both were still alive, on the outskirts of Larksong, where their last quest was set in motion. They cast off in a small boat, and Herr'Don paddled, and Belnavar paddled with a spectral oar. They sailed off into the mist, and they were not seen again for a time. Yet here and there tales began to appear of sightings of a man talking to himself in a boat, and further tales spread of a wandering warrior who went here and there, quelling quarrels, avenging innocents, and freeing slaves. Some said he lost his arm to a monster of the air, and some others said it was a creature of the sea. Some said it disappeared a little day by day from a witch's curse, and others said it never existed in the first place, and that this is why the old king banished him. Some said he walked alone, but others whispered of another great warrior who walked with him. And so the tales travelled on a journey of their own, and in time they became the most awe-inspiring legends.

Ifferon also did not attend the coronation, for Geldirana would not enter Madenahan, where she knew that the new king might be different in many ways, but would be no different when it came to treating the Garigút.

"He is not my king," Geldirana said.

"I guess he is not mine either," Ifferon replied.

They held each other's gaze for a moment, as if swearing fielty to one another.

"It is an odd feeling," Ifferon commented, "to finally come to terms with my bloodline, and now there is no longer any need for it. With Agon dead, what good is the blood of Telm?"

"There are always other evils," Geldirana said.

"That may be so, but I am not a young man any more."

"No," she acknowledged, and he saw in her eyes the memories of their time together ten years ago.

"So then the bloodline comes to an end," Ifferon said.

"It continues on," Geldirana replied, and they looked to Affon, parading about the land as if the war was still ongoing. In some parts of Iraldas, it was.

Ifferon cast his gaze back towards the smoulder of Fort Onar. "Who knew that such a place, so glorious in years long spent, would be the resting place of the Beast? Perhaps it is fitting that he has a ruin for a grave."

"Fort Onar is not the only ruin," Geldirana said. "Boror is but a shadow of what it was."

"Perhaps we can make it better ... together."

Geldirana took her time to reply. "Perhaps."

Ifferon looked to the east. "I need to see one last ruin, to put it all behind me."

He sailed out with Geldirana and Affon to Larksong, which was now an island not far from the coast of Boror. Though it was once overrun by the Nahamoni, Ifferon found traces of a certain warrior prince who had passed through and cleared out the island. Now it was home to larks once more.

Yet though it was now a place of beauty, there were still signs of its former life. Some of the ruins of the monastery still stood, and though it was deathly quiet, it was the kind of deathly quiet that hinted at the voices of the dead.

There were too many memories there, too many reminders of who he was, of his hiding place, and of the people who died because of his cowardice. Though he had done much to atone for this since his flight from Larksong, he felt that there was no true redemption for his actions, or his lack of action.

"*Bêtalajal,*" Geldirana said with a smile.

"Less-of-home," Ifferon translated. He mirrored her smile. "I guess that's true," he said. "I no longer have a home."

Geldirana looked away for a moment, to the sea in the east, where no doubt there were many other lands which were the home to many other peoples. "You do," she said softly, and she turned to him and looked him in the eyes. "All of Boror is our home."

He smiled, and they kissed. A thousand fears crumbled in that kiss. A million worries faded. What was and what might have been was replaced by what is and what might be. Though guilt still lived with Ifferon, there was absolution in Geldirana's lips.

As the two sat hand in hand, Affon marched up and planted a branch into the ground. "I claim this land for the Garigút!" she cried, and she saluted. "Blood for the Garigút!"

"I guess we have more land to claim," Ifferon said.

They left Larksong Island behind, and with it their hurts and sorrows, and though the future would bring new hurts and sorrows, it would also bring new comforts and joys. As they headed back to the mainland to rebuild the Garigút, and to rebuild Boror, they heard the larks begin their melodic song. It seemed to them like an anthem for this new age, a lay for the living, a canticle for all the Children of Telm throughout Iraldas, for all the sons and daughters of the gods everywhere in the world.

About the Author

୬ଵ

Dean F. Wilson was born in Dublin, Ireland in 1987. He started writing at age 11, when he began his first (unpublished) novel, entitled *The Power Source*. He won a TAP Educational Award from Trinity College Dublin for an early draft of *The Call of Agon* (then called *Protos Mythos*) in 2001.

He has published a number of poems and short stories over the years, while working on and reworking some of his novels.

Dean also works as a journalist, primarily in the field of technology. He has written for *TechEye*, *Thinq*, *V3*, *VR-Zone*, *ITProortal*, and *The Inquirer*.

www.deanfwilson.com

Lightning Source UK Ltd.
Milton Keynes UK
UKOW03f0519220814

237326UK00001B/2/P